CHRISTMAS
— *on* —
MIMOSA LANE

CHRISTMAS
—on—
MIMOSA LANE

—A SEASONS OF THE HEART NOVEL—

Anna DeStefano

 Montlake
Romance

Text copyright © 2012 Anna DeStefano
All rights reserved.
Printed in the United States of America.

Published by Montlake Romance
P.O. Box 400818
Las Vegas, NV 89140

ISBN-13: 9781612185873
ISBN-10: 1612185878

To Michelle Grajkowski and Lindsay Guzzardo, for saying, "Yes. Do more, reach for more, write the series of your heart wherever it takes you. We're in!"

Author's Note

The opening poem in *Christmas on Mimosa Lane* and the snippets at the beginning of each of its chapters come from the collective works of Emily Dickinson.

Her poems enchanted me as a little girl. The feelings, the honest emotion, and the internal journeys you take as you explore her world continue to change me as an adult. The richness of her language and philosophy speaks to healing and hope through even the toughest journey—an endearing message from the past to guide us through our now.

I've left mere glimpses of Emily Dickinson's imagination and the beauty that explodes from her words. If you enjoy these quotes, I encourage you to dive into the rest. Simple, challenging, surprising, may her poems inspire you to dream, as they always have me.

Hope is the thing with feathers
That perches in the soul,
And sings the tune without the words,
And never stops at all,

And sweetest in the gale is heard;
And sore must be the storm
That could abash the little bird
That kept so many warm.

I heard it in the chillest land,
And on the strangest sea;
Yet, never, in extremity,
It asked a crumb of me.

—Emily Dickinson

PART ONE

Floating

Chapter One

Not knowing when the dawn will come
I open every door...

M allory Phillips woke slowly, floating, with long-ago Christmases racing through her mind. Images jumbled together in a flurry of sound and motion that warned of something ominous, something unwanted, lurking too close.

She jackknifed until she was sitting in her bed. Her eyes opened to silence and serene shadows and the lingering echo of who she'd once been. There was no threat. There was nothing to fear except for the dreams that consumed too many of her nights.

She hugged her crimson comforter against the chilly darkness, then pushed it away in frustration. Fully awake, she scrubbed at her eyes and breathed deeply, focusing on how far she'd come and her determination to stay right where she was until she could feel every bit of the picturesque world surrounding her. This was her fresh start. This Christmas on Mimosa Lane was her reboot. She was finally, completely, moving on.

Yet it still swirled within her, that shadowy connection to another time, another Mallory, while moonlight dazzled her, dancing through bay windows that overlooked the backyard of her cozy ranch-style house. Snuggling into her pillows she stared at the property that she'd made hers free and clear three months ago. She hadn't hung curtains in the house. She'd wanted nothing to obscure her view from this peaceful place. The back of the home was almost entirely glass, allowing streams of sparkling light to wash over her as she tried to relax enough to sleep.

It was the abundance of windows that had first excited her, then the privacy of the twelve-foot fence secluding her backyard from the others on her cul-de-sac. After searching forever for just the right place, she now owned a piece of the everyday charm that was Chandlerville, Georgia—a historic town northeast of Atlanta that she'd moved to before the start of the school year.

Mimosa Lane was a twisty-turny, horseshoe-shaped road. Over the years a sprawling community of more than fifty homes had sprouted along its wooded splendor. At its center dangled a cul-de-sac where one side of the lane curled in sharply, around, and then returned to its twin. The cul-de-sac's secluded curves and the houses at its heart seemed to exist on a totally separate road. And within that bubble of isolated perfection, Mallory had found her dream house.

Surrounding her property were sedately aging homes and large lots bursting with trees and manicured landscaping. Only cul-de-sac residents or their visitors came this far down the lane. It was easier to reach the other houses from Scenic Highway, the main street running through Chandlerville that both ends of the lane eventually rambled into.

A paradise for young families, Mimosa Lane was the idealistic solid ground Mallory had craved as a little girl when her idea of heaven had been a yard she could call her own, a happy family and friends to play with, and doors and windows she'd never have to lock. She'd just spent Thanksgiving weekend feeling soul-deep gratitude for this chance—especially to her grandmother, who even after her death had been adamant that one day Mallory would have her fantasy come true.

So why couldn't she banish the past for good and embrace this world she'd wanted so desperately?

A rustle reached her from the direction of the living room. Her eyes flew open.

That wasn't a restless memory, set free by her mind's nocturnal wandering. The next odd sound sent her scrambling from bed, her ears ringing.

She couldn't feel her legs except for their shaking. After two tries she crammed her feet into fluffy slippers and wrapped herself in terry cloth. She pressed her back to the wall beside her open bedroom door, willed her panic into submission, and ticked off her options. If someone had broken in, her choices were to confront them in her ancient Tinker Bell robe or to hide and wait for whomever it was to either leave or find her.

Instinct, unwise and unstoppable, propelled her into the hallway. The hell with hiding. She'd be damned if she'd let anything make her afraid in her own home.

The rattle came again, almost too faint to hear, drawing her the short distance to her living room where more windows waited, and more shadows. Plus the floor-to-ceiling artificial Christmas tree she'd assembled weeks ago, lit, and loaded with sparkling ornaments and lights, to the amusement no doubt of every conservative neighbor up and down the lane. The tree's flickering illumination revealed nothing to her except the room's sparse furnishings.

Her heart eased down her throat as she told herself to remain calm. But there was someone there. A childhood of self-preservation had armed her with a second sense she'd never shaken, and her intuition was screaming that she was no longer alone.

She heard a sniffle and stepped closer to the tree. A shadow in the corner moved, and only then did Mallory see her. A tiny, forlorn ghost lurked amid the sheer panels that would have been curtains in another house, only Mallory kept them tied back. She sighed at the child who kept wandering over to stare through Mallory's windows. The seven-year-old had ventured inside this time and was hiding behind Mallory's tree.

"Polly?" She checked the mantel clock. "It's after midnight, sweetie. What are you doing here?"

What did it say about Mallory that this child was the first person who'd stepped inside her home since she'd moved here? No matter how badly she wanted to take part in the community thriving around her, three months of trying had proven an experiment gone sometimes comically awry. And while she attempted to figure things out, she'd managed to keep the locals at a comfortable distance. All of them except this wandering child.

Most afternoons since Mallory put up her tree, Polly had appeared out back. She would just stand there gazing through the glass Mallory kept sparkling clean—the sun setting on fire the red highlights in her dark hair. It was like catching a glimpse of a terrified woodland creature that was too paralyzed to flee yet too fascinated to look away. For weeks Polly hadn't ventured closer or said a word.

Then one evening just before Thanksgiving Mallory could have sworn she'd seen the little girl outside after dark. But when Mallory had stepped onto her patio to check, she'd found nothing but closely cut grass and the breeze that never completely abandoned north Georgia. One moment Polly had been there. The next she'd vanished.

There was a door in the gate that separated Mallory's property from the Lombard house. Maybe, just for a while, locking it would be the gentlest way to break the little girl of her escalating obsession with seeking Mallory out, first in school and then at home. Except where would the kid go the next time her single father didn't realize she'd wandered away?

Polly looked poised even now to escape through the sliding glass door she'd left open behind her. She was an ethereal, barely there illusion of light and shadow. A mystery hovering amid holiday fancy, crying and alone.

"I couldn't sleep," Polly said, still sniffling.

The defiant tilt of her chin dared Mallory to offer a hug or say something empty, something adult that would make what Polly was going through worse. Instead Mallory inched closer without speaking, her heart aching.

Before spending a decade pursuing the rocky path that had brought her to Chandlerville as the local elementary school's clinic nurse, a day hadn't gone by that Mallory hadn't wanted to run just like Polly. Even though this child lived in a perfect house, complete with an enormous backyard play set that would be a happy kid's heaven on earth, she clearly longed to be somewhere else. It was as if she didn't fit on the lane any more than Mallory did.

"I can't sleep sometimes myself," Mallory said. "But I keep trying. Especially when I have a busy day ahead of me like tomorrow. It's Monday. We both have school."

"I don't want to go to school."

"Where do you want to go?" The bulk of Mallory's love seat stood between them, but she was close enough now to stop

Polly from dashing away. "What's outside, what's in here, that you need to see more than the pretty bedroom I'm sure you left behind at your place?"

The little girl stared down at her princess slippers—embroidered on each pink-swaddled foot was a cartoon blonde wearing a bejeweled tiara. A screen print of the same character sparkled on her gauzy nightshirt. She was covered head to toe in pretend.

Mallory glanced from the child's probably just-bought ensemble to her own faded cartoon mainstay. When she looked back Polly was wadding the hem of her thin gown in both fists. It was supposed to drop below forty outside tonight, unseasonably cold for the southeast. The kid must be freezing.

"I don't want to go home," Polly said.

"Okay." Mallory sat on the edge of the love seat, never more certain that something was terribly wrong.

She didn't want this tie. This knowing. This connection. This wasn't the peace she'd come to Mimosa Lane to claim. But as a pediatric nurse and a former mixed-up kid herself, Mallory couldn't stop herself from trying to help.

"What do you want?" she asked.

Her scared little rabbit scowled, sensing a trap.

"You keep coming over here and to my office at school," Mallory said. "But you never tell me what I can do for you, sweetie."

From day one Polly had looked so defeated. From their first encounter Mallory had wanted to take away just a little of the weight pressing on those tiny shoulders. In each quiet moment like this one, when a little girl who'd lost her mother half a year ago couldn't put into words the cry for help she kept acting out, Mallory had needed to see this sad princess smile.

"Franken Berry?" Mallory blurted out, not above bribery. "When I was your age, it felt like Christmas morning every time I ate it. Strawberry flavoring and refined sugar and bleached corn flour...Crunch and sweetness that will make your back teeth smile." And it could only be special-ordered from the manufacturer's website a few months out of the year, since most stores no longer carried it. But for Polly, Mallory would break into her secret stash. "Ever had any?"

Polly shook her head. "My dad says healthy food only. I need to eat healthy to stay healthy."

She stepped closer, and Mallory considered grabbing her. Except grabbing at kids who were hell-bent on running only made them more certain that they'd never be safe.

"Well there's not a redeeming, healthy thing about Franken Berry," she said, "no matter what the packaging says. In my book that makes it heaven in a bowl."

The child was underweight. Eating anything sounded healthy enough to Mallory. As Polly's nurse she knew there were no food allergies or preexisting medical conditions to be concerned about. And in the moon's reflection Polly's eyes were glittering at Mallory's description of the decadent treat.

"Let's live dangerously." Mallory shrugged off her robe and draped it over the little girl's shoulders. Then, catching a chill in only her matching flannel PJs, she led the way to the kitchen, turning on lights as she went. She checked once to make certain she was being followed.

Polly's slippered feet skidded to a halt inside the door. She blinked at Mallory's retro-looking, circa 1950s, pink and blue and green appliances. They were one of the few splurges, besides her Christmas tree, that Mallory had indulged in when she'd furnished the place. An early Christmas present, she'd rationalized. Actually, Christmas and Valentine's Day and her birthday and maybe Christmas again. But the hit to her budget had been worth it. This room made her heart sing.

Her dreams came to her in black and white and gray, stark visions that refused to bloom into the colors she'd always craved. But in this house, the first world that was totally, completely her creation, she was surrounded by a rainbow of life-affirming hues each morning and at the end of every day while she cooked and ate and cleaned up after herself.

She stopped first at the thermostat beside the door, easing the heat toward supernova so she'd stop shivering. Then she plucked the box of cereal from the pantry where her guilty pleasure nested amid other breakfast options. Her cinnamon-flavored hot cereal would be healthier and would take only a minute to microwave. It might warm Polly's tummy if Mallory could get the kid to eat some of it. But for a little girl Polly's age *magical* trumped *healthy* every time.

"Have a seat." Mallory rummaged through the glass-front cabinet above her sink. "You're in for a surprise."

Her fingers closed around the plastic bowl and plate she'd snapped up at a local tag sale. She placed them on the table in front of Polly, the bowl on top. A cartoon princess, scratched and well used, smiled serenely from dishes someone had bought for another little girl, then discarded.

"Sit," Mallory repeated.

Polly hung back until Mallory poured the cereal, then added the milk she'd taken from the fridge. Her guest slid into the chair, trancelike, watching creamy white liquid transform to fantasy pink.

"Eat," Mallory urged, "while I call your father."

Polly's first spoonful of sugary goodness paused halfway to her mouth. Some of it slopped back to the bowl.

"It's okay." Mallory already had the kitchen phone in her hand. She could have gone into the other room to make the call. But she didn't lie to kids. Ever. They deserved to be treated like they understood and could handle what was happening in their lives. She knew better than anyone just how resilient a child Polly's age could be. "Eat. You don't want your daddy taking you home before you've drunk the strawberry milk from the bottom."

She winked and dialed the number she'd jotted on the pad on the counter. Pete Lombard had coughed it up yesterday morning, grudgingly, when he'd called. His child had spent yet another hour in Mallory's yard, watching without saying anything, scared when she realized she'd been spotted, but not leaving until her father showed up to take her home. Fifteen minutes later his call had been the man's first acknowledgment that he and Mallory had a problem.

Their conversation had lasted all of thirty seconds, which sadly had been longer than she'd managed with anyone else on the lane. She'd agreed to let him know if Polly came back. He'd promised to keep a closer watch on his daughter. Like that had solved anything.

Polly filled her mouth with cereal. Her eyes widened. Her spoon swooped in for a bigger bite. Mallory smiled, then frowned at the husky "hello" that rumbled through the phone connection.

"Are you missing something again, Prince Charming?" she asked, her words catching then stumbling out in a rush. She regularly became tongue-tied talking with her neighbors and the parents she encountered at school. But dealing with this man was worse. His child's situation ignited a flash fire of unwanted confusion inside Mallory. It was a daily battle to keep her frustration and anger from spewing all over Polly's father.

This had to stop. Her neighbor's inability to keep track of his daughter, let alone help the child properly grieve for her mother so Polly could heal and move on…It had to stop.

Mallory wasn't going to be sucked any deeper into these strangers' lives. She was nothing like them. They knew nothing about her. And, besides, what possible good could she do? She was having a hard enough time in Chandlerville trying to patch together her own version of happiness.

"Excuse me?" Pete mumbled. "It's nearly one in the morning. Who is this?"

There was rustling on his end of the call, and Mallory imagined him sitting up, all sleepy and sprawling and mussed. Brown, unruly hair the same shade of mink as his daughter's. Brown, emotional eyes. Dark stubble that he let grow along his chin and jaw each weekend. Did he sleep in the nude?

"This is your conscience speaking," she said, irritated with her wayward thoughts. The man had made no secret of his dislike for Polly's involving Mallory in their family problems. And he was right. Mallory's interjecting herself into their situation could only make things worse. Except his child seemed to have her own agenda. "I've once again stumbled across something very precious to you."

"What are you…?" His voice thinned from groggy to suspicious. "Polly?" Mallory actually heard him stumble out of bed and across the floor, presumably toward his daughter's room. "Who is this?"

"It's your next-door neighbor," she said. "Your daughter let herself inside my place this time. She's in my kitchen eating what you'll no doubt consider offensive cold cereal. The patio door's open. We'll see you when you get here."

Chapter Two

Forever is composed of Nows...

W hat kind of man couldn't keep his child tucked safely
in bed at night?

Pete Lombard shoved his feet into the beaten-up sneakers that had stood sentinel outside his patio door since late
September, the last time he'd mowed the lawn. Without tying
them, taking only a moment to pull on a sweatshirt over his
pajamas, he sprinted through the chilly November night. A
fenced backyard ran catty-corner to his own, the curve where
Mimosa Lane twisted into their cul-de-sac transforming the
house next to his into his backyard neighbor as well. He let
himself through the partially open wooden door he'd helped
old Mr. Lancer cut out because Polly had loved to play with his
basset hound, Charlie Brown.

What a difference two years could make.

The Lancers and Charlie had retired to sunny Florida. He
couldn't remember the last time he'd seen Polly play. And now
he was making a midnight visit to his new neighbor who at best
thought he was an idiot, more likely an unfit father.

Light blared from inside Mallory Phillips's place. Her Christmas tree had been up and decorated like a gaudy holiday farce since two weeks before Thanksgiving, twinkling through the thermal-paned windows the Lancers had installed to make the twenty-year-old ranch more salable. Was the tree what kept drawing Polly over? Pete had caught her staring at the monstrosity from her second-story bedroom window.

What the hell was she doing out of bed in the middle of the night? And how, *how*, couldn't he have known she was gone? He saved lives for a living, but he hadn't been able to save his wife. Now he was failing his child.

Thank God they lived on quiet, insulated Mimosa Lane. Still, as an EMT for the fire department he saw enough each week to reinforce the tragic things that could happen to a kid who slipped away from the safety of home. Especially an emotionally fragile little girl his Polly's age. Too bad the house she'd shared with her mother was now the last place on earth Polly felt safe.

Emma, what am I going to do? How many times had he asked that of the soul mate he'd lost forever? He kept trying to figure things out, to reason them through, to get something of his falling-apart world back under control. But nothing made sense anymore, for him or Polly. *I'm screwing this up. Help me, darlin'. Somehow, you've got to help me.*

The sliding glass door leading into his neighbor's house was open. He knocked anyway. There was no answer.

"Hello…"

He stepped into a room overwhelmed by an artificial, ornament-filled tree. It was like Christmas had swooped in and attacked the poor plastic thing, inflicting forced cheer on anyone who caught a glimpse of it. Standing there he felt himself drowning in the festive holiday season he'd been trying to fake for Polly's sake.

*Fake…*That's what the monstrosity was screaming—every mass-produced inch of it. Looking around the room he realized there wasn't another decoration in sight. Just Mallory Phillips's *christmas, Christmas, CHRISTMAS* tree.

The small home's family room stretched the entire width of the house, and sparse would be too generous a word to describe its decor. There was a soft-looking oversize cream couch, a brass lamp with a beige shade, and a sad-looking recliner covered in a tweedy kind of plaid that for some reason made him think it was secondhand. Probably because there'd been something like it tossed into the corner of his fraternity's front room. They'd needed furniture because visitors had to sit somewhere, but his college buddies hadn't really cared what any of it looked like. Clearly, neither did the elusive Mallory Phillips. Even her floor was covered in a nondescript oatmeal Berber.

I-give-up carpet, Emma had called it when he'd hastily picked something similar for their place in the hope of skirting her out of the store and home to work on making the baby they'd been so desperate to have.

"Hello?" he called, louder this time.

"Hey—" Across the empty dining area to his right a butler's door pushed outward, flashing a glimpse beyond of a kitchen filled with crazy colors. A tousled-haired blonde burst into the room in plaid Disney pajamas that made her look ridiculously young, tempting him to smile for the first time since spring.

For a moment he didn't recognize her. At school, Mallory kept her hair pulled back. She dressed in boxy scrubs covered in outlandish cartoon animals. So far no one in the community had gotten much of a look at her in anything else.

She didn't tend to her own yard like the rest of their neighbors—she had a guy come over once a week to do the bare minimum. The entire time she'd lived in Chandlerville she'd only attended a single Mimosa Lane get-together, a Sunday-night barbecue at the beginning of the school year that she'd arrived at late and had left after less than ten minutes, hardly speaking to anyone. She'd made herself scarce each evening and weekend and most recently during the Thanksgiving holiday, though no one had seen her pack her car for a trip.

It was as if Mallory Phillips were living among them, only she wasn't.

Her silky hair was down now, bouncing about her shoulders. The softness of her purple-plaid nightclothes accentuated generous curves that weren't the least bit childlike. Basic politeness said Pete shouldn't be staring at the swooping neckline of her pajama top, but he couldn't help himself. She clearly didn't realize or didn't care how she looked just rolled out of bed, or how a man could find himself reaching for something that warm and inviting and never want to find his way out of it.

"Good," she said, all business. "You're here. I was about to resort to another blast of sugary bribery." Still moving toward him, she held out her hand.

"Ms. Phillips." He shook briefly and let go.

His gaze made a discreet pass over the cartoon fairy embroidered on her top. The perky thing danced above the kind of firm, athletic breasts he'd preferred since falling in love with the high school track star who'd become his bride.

"I'm sorry about all this." He decided to look at his neighbor's summer-blue eyes for the rest of their conversation. And only her eyes. "I'm not sure why my daughter keeps seeking you out."

"I think it's pretty clear Polly's looking for something, Mr. Lombard." Her directness each time they spoke was unsettling, given her skittishness whenever she'd interacted with others on the lane. "I can only assume her behavior has something to do with missing her mother."

"Call me Pete," he said, the offer not coming out entirely friendly.

He'd asked her to use his first name when he'd phoned yesterday. She'd ignored him then. Just as he'd sidestepped her daily attempts when he picked up his little girl from the clinic at school to talk about Emma and how losing her was affecting Polly.

Everyone else in his life, his family and friends and his colleagues at work, got that he couldn't talk about it yet, losing the love of his life. This stranger to his turned-upside-down world couldn't be expected to understand. But the least she could do was stop asking questions that chipped away at what was left of his heart.

"Mr. Lombard?"

She'd repeated his name a couple of times, he realized. How long had he been standing there staring?

"Does Polly leave your place a lot after dark?" she asked.

"Of course she doesn't wander around the neighborhood at night." He was doing the best he could, damn it. He loved his daughter, and he'd do anything to keep her safe. "I have an alarm that sounds off in my bedroom if any of the doors or windows open."

His neighbor raised an eyebrow.

"I checked the system before I came over." The pulse at his temple thudded like muted cymbals crashing against his skull. "Polly must have disengaged it."

"She's a smart little girl." A smile transformed her features the way sunshine set morning mist to sparkling. Then all that glitter disappeared behind a frown. "And a desperate one."

He rocked back on his heels. "Desperate for what?"

She shrugged. "Freedom?"

The breath rushed out of him.

He could see his wife, propped up on pillows in their bed, home from the hospital for the last time, looking beautiful and serene and frail. *I can feel it,* Emma had said, the words breaking him while he clung to every syllable. *The freedom. It's going to be okay. I'm finally going to be free of it.*

Free of the cancer that wouldn't turn her loose, and the world that couldn't keep her without causing more pain. Emma had needed to hear him say it was okay to let go. She'd held on until he found a way to give her that last gift. But he refused to do the same for his child. He couldn't lose Polly, too. Thanksgiving had been a disaster, and she seemed to be preparing to hate Christmas just as much, but somehow he'd make things right for her again. Failure had never been an option for him, and he'd already lost too much of his family. He refused to watch Polly slip away, too.

"I'd like to see my daughter." The bite in each word was impolite, but he didn't care. It was late. He was at his wits' end. This woman needed to get out of his way.

"Of course." Mallory turned.

A view of Tinker Bell's backside twitched between her shoulder blades. She marched off, a leggy, flannel-draped queen leading him through the swinging door into the next room.

Her tree wasn't the only garish thing she'd blown her money on. Her refrigerator was blue. The oven, a sage green. The dishwasher's front was powdery red. The counters and tabletop were a blinding-white Formica, with the kind of chrome edges that belonged in a fifties-era sitcom.

Polly sat amid it all wrapped in a vintage-looking bathrobe covered in more frolicking fairies, shoveling food into her mouth like a normal seven-year-old. A box of cereal was open at her elbow. She stared first at Mallory, panic creeping into her sprite green eyes. Her face lost its animation when her attention shifted to Pete. Every trace of the happy child she'd been until six months ago faded away. She dropped her spoon into the bowl and wiped at her milky mustache with the bathrobe's sleeve. Her gaze fell to her lap.

She never looked Pete in the eye anymore. He'd felt her pulling away for months. Then she'd run from the Thanksgiving table at Emma's parents' house, screaming to go home. She hadn't stopped crying until he'd tucked her into her own bed. She'd barely slept or spoken to him since. She couldn't stand to be around anyone anymore.

And the hell of it was, he understood completely. He was going through the motions of staying positive for his daughter's sake, but he didn't want to be around anyone, either. Not friends, not family, sometimes not even his own child. He'd never admit it, but sometimes he wished they'd all go away. It hurt too much, feeling close to the things and people he'd shared with Emma.

Fear had been Pete's constant companion since his wife's death. In his job he was a pro at pushing through the uncertainty of not knowing what would happen next. A rescue worker had to act regardless of the desperation of the moment. But with his little girl, after months of trying and failing to comfort her and be the father she deserved, fear had become a paralyzing mainstay. Fear and the crushing loss of the happy life they'd taken for granted.

Out of answers, he felt his neighbor's gaze boring into him as he knelt beside Polly's chair.

"You scared me, darlin'." He stroked the dark curls that were even softer than her mother's had been. "You can't keep wandering away from me. And you absolutely can't leave the house at night."

"Ms. Phillips doesn't mind if I visit her at school," Polly said to her lap.

"You're in her house now." The home of a woman who clearly wasn't the *Won't you be my neighbor?* type. "We talked about this last night. You haven't been invited. It's a no-no to just walk into someone's yard and their home when they don't know you're coming."

"I wanted to see her tree. It's the best tree ever, but I can't see all of it from my window."

Why the hell did Mallory insist on never closing her curtains? What was her back door doing unlocked in the middle of the night, so Polly could let herself inside?

The community rumor mill kept buzzing with each new quirk they discovered about this woman. Beginning all the way back when she'd arrived after closing on the Lancer place with a single U-Haul trailer hitched to an ancient Beetle. After which she'd greeted the steady stream of good-natured neighbors who'd brought over baked goodies and housewarming gifts with stuttering attempts to welcome them that had morphed into a strained thank-you and less-than-subtle excuses for saying good-bye before anyone was invited inside.

No one had gotten the impression that she was being intentionally rude. It seemed more likely that she didn't have the first clue what to do with any of them. She was a puzzle no one in Chandlerville could solve. Which evidently made her the only person his child could bear spending time with.

"I couldn't sleep," Polly said. She looked to Mallory. "I just wanted to see what your Christmas looked like up close."

Mallory patted her on the back and closed up the cereal box. She handed Polly her spoon. And damn if the kid didn't dive back in for her without complaint.

"We'll go buy our tree this week," Pete promised, forcing himself to sound positive while their broken holiday shattered into even more pieces. Polly had refused every attempt he'd made to get her excited about decorating the house—something she and Emma had always done together. "We'll make our own Christmas great, just as soon as you're ready. And if you can't sleep, you need to come get me up—not bother Ms. Phillips. I'll read you a story. I know it's hard at night, but I'm always going to be here, Polly. You can come get me no matter how late it is. We'll put you back to bed and make whatever's bothering you better."

His child shook her head, her bangs falling into her eyes. Pete reached to smooth them back, and she jerked away—the same as she had when he'd tried to comfort her at Emma's parents'. A tear rolled down her cheek.

He wanted to take her into his arms and hug away her loneliness and his, but that would mean another tantrum like the ones she had each night at bedtime. Her doctors said not to push closeness on Polly, but not to let her pull too far inward, either. Give her time. Give her space. But give her love, whether she accepted it or not.

How was he supposed to do that when each time he reached for his child he found a stranger in his grasp instead of the daughter who'd once worshiped his every move? How were they supposed to survive Christmas, Emma's favorite holiday, when not having her there was unbearable for them both?

"Did your wife read her bedtime stories?" Mallory asked.

"What?" He'd forgotten where he was. His neighbor's question froze time, then accelerated it. He stood, his scattered thoughts free-falling yet again.

The memory was so clear. Him coming off a day shift at the station, driving home to find dinner left warming on the stove and the house smelling like Polly's bubble bath. Emma was cuddled up with their sleepy little girl reading one last story before bed. Pete settled in to watch like he always did, loving them both so much and content with being exactly where he planned to be every night he wasn't working, until Polly was too old to think of their nightly ritual as heaven on earth.

It had been warm there where the three of them were happy, where he could no longer return. Warm and real and already forgotten by a child who cried now whenever he tried to read to her the way her mommy had.

"If Polly's having difficulty with you at night," Mallory said, looking perversely curious as she stared him down, "I was wondering if it used to be a time when she was especially close to her mom."

"Of course it was a special time," he snapped.

"Then maybe she—"

"Can I speak with you privately?" He was already halfway through the swinging door. She was likely a damn fine nurse, and she clearly cared about his daughter's well-being. But his neighbor's meddling in private matters she couldn't possibly understand was officially over.

He stepped into her excuse for a dining room and waited for Tinker Bell to join him. Once Mallory had, he swung the door closed and turned on her, losing his stranglehold on his temper.

"Exactly who the hell do you think you are, lady, questioning how I parent my own child?"

"I seem to be the only one of the two of us your daughter will talk to." Blue eyes sparked with frustration that rivaled his own. "And whether I like the situation any more than you do, it's something we'd both better deal with. Or the next time Polly slips away from your oblivious ass, she might just be gone for good."

***

Mallory sucked in air so fast she hiccupped. Her lapse of professionalism was appalling. Not to mention her breach of basic courtesy.

Long ago she'd accepted that ruthless honesty was how she'd become who and what she wanted to be. *You're strong enough to make anything happen*, her grams had always said, no matter how difficult Mallory made their last years together. *Even learning to trust people again. You just keep on bein' strong, and you'll figure the rest out eventually.*

Mallory never meant to be cruel to others, even while helping them face their own harsh truths. But one of her many flaws was that she didn't know how to back down when she was challenged. And on the rare occasions when someone who made her feel as off balance as Pete Lombard pushed too hard, she came out swinging.

She was an unflappable ace at what she did best. Personal relationships, unfortunately, fell far short of that top spot.

It had been forever since she'd allowed anyone but her grams close enough to see her lose control. There'd been a few going-nowhere dates in high school and college, one long-term relationship since that had fizzled painfully, and some less-than-successful attempts along the way at meaningful friendships with women. Preserving emotional distance at all costs was another survival instinct she'd mastered too early and too well. Which made allowing someone beneath the surface a losing proposition from the get-go.

So how had this man already tunneled deep enough to bring out the worst in her?

She knew nothing beyond the obvious about his problems, regardless of how much Polly reminded Mallory of another little girl who'd been trapped in a totally different set of circumstances, who'd longed for security and a new life and a world light-years from the one holding her hostage. In Polly's silence and acting out, Mallory saw the runaway still lurking within herself. But that didn't make Pete the irresponsible parent Mallory's mother had been. She had no right to berate him or suggest that she could better parent anyone's child.

"I'm a good father," he bit out evenly. "I'll do whatever it takes to help my daughter survive what's going to be the worst Christmas of her life. I don't need any damn help. Certainly not from you."

The absolute certainty of the statement lost its impact when he closed his eyes. He jammed his fists into the front pockets of his sweatshirt. *UGA*, it read, above the image of the university's mascot, a bulldog. Fitting. His reserve, even when he was angry, hinted at a steely will that would push tenaciously through any obstacle until he'd reached his goal.

He tilted his head back. He whispered an expletive so softly it became a prayer.

"I'm sorry," he said. "I know you're only trying to help. But you have no idea what Polly's dealing with."

"You're right." She should leave it at that. She should retire to a neutral corner and silently watch these people slip back out of her life. Yet, for Polly's sake, how could she? "But I do know a lost soul when I find one standing beneath my Christmas tree."

She'd bet money that this capable, controlled man had never before the death of his wife had even a cursory experience with the kind of emotional turmoil ripping at his child.

His stormy gaze took her measure and found her lacking. "You shouldn't be insinuating yourself into our problems."

"Right again." Mallory stared down both him and the cowardly impulse to excuse herself to her bedroom while he collected his daughter and left. "Someone like me shouldn't be butting into a family matter. But I'm Polly's health care provider at school, and she's in my office several times a day. Every day since August. She seems almost desperate to get away from her class and friends and teacher. And short of locking her in her room when she's at home, you can't keep her away from me here either."

"You heard her. It's that damn tree of yours. She's obsessed with it. It's all she talks about when she bothers to say anything to me at all."

"Then why haven't you put up one of your own?"

"Because she said she didn't want one. That's the one thing she's adamant about. No Christmas this year. Not at our house."

Mallory absorbed the pain in his words, finding hope in his reluctant honesty. Her heart melted even more.

"I've tried to discourage her from visiting me," she said, "as gently and as firmly as I could. But she needs something, Mr. Lombard. And she seems to think she'll find whatever that is—"

"*Here?*" His bewilderment came as no surprise.

She followed his gaze around her nearly empty house, picturing how it must appear to someone who knew only this part of her. Still, she was proud of what she'd created, a reality where she felt safe, if not included. She was once more a social misfit. But in Chandlerville she could revel in watching the beautiful world beyond her windows without resorting to the dead bolts and blackout curtains she'd once needed to feel safe. Add that to the sounds of laughing children and happy families filtering through her solitary evenings like sweet music on continuous replay—plus the Christmas she was going to celebrate like a lunatic this year—and she was in heaven.

So what if her failed attempts to be neighborly had ended in odd looks and awkward moments? So what if she never figured out how to blend into this kind of normal? She could handle that if she had to. She'd handled far worse for most of her childhood.

And as far as her decor was concerned, she was rarely there and had more important things to spend her money on than furniture and decorations she'd never use. There was no one to impress with how she did or didn't indulge herself, so what did it matter what the inside of her house looked like? Except Pete and Polly had barreled headlong into her privacy, and they likely couldn't fathom a world where white fences and clusters of picture-perfect homes didn't dot the landscape to the cotton candy horizon.

Pete was a fireman, a local EMT hero. *ALS* was the term someone at school had used to describe his job, because he was certified in "advanced life support." He was one of the good guys. Like she'd snarked when she'd called him, he was Prince Charming. He kept the world safe for everyone, especially the magical princesses in his life.

Her colleagues at school had filled in the blanks about the Lombard family when it became clear that Polly would be a daily part of Mallory's clinic work. How Pete had lost his wife to a fast-growing brain tumor no one could do anything about. His happily ever after had crashed and burned, leaving him and Polly grasping for the enchanted life their tragedy had ripped away. He was fast becoming as much of a misfit as Mallory, and he had no idea how to deal with it.

Which must make cataloging her faults a welcome distraction. Something she supposed she could deal with for one night, as long as it meant moving him and his daughter along and back out her door.

"Were you at least awake when Polly came in?" he finally asked. "Did she maybe see you and then come inside to talk?"

"I was asleep." Mallory got why he needed to believe that tonight was somehow her doing. "On a school night I'm in bed before eleven."

He inhaled slowly. "She walked into a house she'd never been in before and woke you up while you were in bed?"

"I heard her rustling around in here."

"I thought you weren't awake."

"I'm a light sleeper. But if I weren't, yes, she might have made her way into my bedroom, in the dark, before I knew she was there. I don't think she would have, though. I found her hiding in the corner by the tree."

He rubbed his forehead. His hand was shaking. "Lord, what if she'd gotten farther away or stumbled into someone else's home? Someone I don't know?"

"You're missing the point. Polly coming to me wasn't about my house being next to yours. Like I said, I think your daughter's looking for something."

"And you're that something?"

Mallory's professional training wavered beneath a rising flood of compassion. Desperation was rolling off this man at the thought of not being able to fix his child. The empathetic part of her longed to give him the blanket reassurances he wanted. After years of experience working with families in crisis, she knew better.

"I'm not responsible for Polly getting better," she said. "I don't know her, but I care about her. So whatever her *something* is, it's okay with me, even in the middle of the night."

"And I'm not okay with what my daughter needs? It's all I think about."

"I understand. Really, I do. You're her father, and your job is to make things better for her. At night that means making sure she sleeps. But you just told her that if she came to you, you'd put her back to bed and read some more. Because it's not okay for a child her age to be up this late."

"It's not."

"I agree." It was sad and unhealthy how Polly's issues were escalating. "But since I'm not her parent, I don't have to fix that problem—at least not in Polly's mind. No problem, no conflict. No conflict, and it starts to seem like an escape to hang at my place instead of yours when the shadows feel too close and she needs to get away from them. And maybe it's easier to enjoy my Christmas when her holiday feels terrible this year."

"Or maybe you never bother to turn your garish tree off, and little girls like sparkly things. You indulge her at school, so why wouldn't she assume you're a ready-made excuse at home to keep pulling away from everyone who loves her? Me, her grandparents, her friends and neighbors, and her teachers at Chandler. You need to stop encouraging this attachment she's built to you. She can't keep avoiding me and everything else that used to make her happy, just because I'm the one who has to set limits. I don't have the luxury of filling Polly with sugary cereal or ignoring the way food like that and staying up this late exacerbate how fragile she's become since losing her mother." He crossed his arms, muscles bulging beneath age-worn cotton, reminding her that EMTs had to remain physically certified to work just like the rest of the fire department's rescue professionals. "Please consider how much harm you're doing the next time you're tempted to indulge her."

"As soon as I discovered she was here, I walked her to the kitchen and made her a snack she couldn't refuse. I watched her relax into a happy kid for a few minutes while we waited for you. The conflict sleeping has become between you two went away for a while. No permanent harm done, even if I violated her pediatrician's dietary guidelines. Polly might even sleep better with something pasty and soothing in her system. Is that what you consider indulging her? Limits are important, but so is listening to what she's trying to tell you she needs."

His belligerence crumbled beneath exhaustion and resignation. It was an ugly personal moment, and they both hated that she was there to see it. *Lost.* In that moment, the guy looked positively lost.

"I can't get her to eat anything," he said. "She cries whenever I try to make holiday plans. Thanksgiving was a nightmare. She spent most of it in her room here, when we were supposed to be away with family all weekend. She doesn't want to be anywhere else but our place, but she hates being anywhere that reminds her of my wife, too."

Mallory nodded. "Her teacher says she's agitated with things that used to make her happy. That it's getting worse the closer we get to Christmas. Polly comes to see me halfway through lunch every day with a stomachache. Ms. Caldwell invariably tells me she hasn't eaten a bite in the cafeteria, so she doesn't understand what could be causing it. Then I call you, and she's upset when you take her home."

"She's hungry. That's what's causing it." He raked a hand through sleep-rumpled hair. "She's losing more weight. She's starving, and she won't eat."

"I've started bringing her a cheese sandwich each day," Mallory confessed, another of her secrets revealed. "She eats it in my office just fine."

"You what?" The man was simmering again, edging toward full boil. "Lady, you have no right to do something like that without my permission."

"You signed a medical release her first day of school, to allow the staff to stay informed about how she's doing physically. I cleared her school diet with her doctor, and I follow up regularly in case something's changed. I'm not giving Polly anything that would make her sick."

"That's not the point. She's not eating when she gets home."

"Exactly."

"Because you're feeding her crap at school."

"You don't really believe that." Her respect was growing for the frazzled but deeply caring parent she was beginning to believe he was. She suddenly wanted very much for that confidence not to be misplaced. "Whole-milk cheese and five-grain bread isn't crap, Mr. Lombard. Not when I suspect it's the only real meal she's getting that day. And once she starts eating she practically swallows her food whole. As you say, she's starving."

He had trouble swallowing himself, as if something awful were wadded in his mouth, clogging his throat. She could almost hear what she now suspected was a highly analytical mind processing everything she'd said and reevaluating his options.

"Why...you?" he asked, the question husky and halting. "Why does she feel safe enough to eat with you, talk with you, enjoy your Christmas...?"

Why her? Why would any child turn to a stranger to make things better when her family would give anything to be that healing place for her?

"It's not me, Mr. Lombard. I'm not a rival for your daughter's affection."

"Don't you think it's about time you called me Pete?"

The animosity behind his repeated request to do just that was gone. Something between them was shifting. Slowly. Resentfully. Like the revolving seasons that took a ridiculously long time to come to this part of the country, but eventually found their way. He didn't seem to appreciate the inevitability of this moment any more than she did, but they were clearly united over their concern for Polly.

She nodded her head in agreement and said, "Call me Mallory."

"If it's not about you, Mallory, then what? She won't eat for anyone else. She's firmly refused to have Christmas this year, except she's been obsessed with your tree since you put it up. Don't think I enjoy asking you for insight into my daughter's psyche, but...nothing else seems to be working."

"I think I'm not a part of the life the two of you lost when your wife died," she said. "I suspect my ridiculous tree might be a safe alternative for Polly this year because it's not part of your family's holiday memories. I'm Switzerland in your daughter's world, and as a nurse I think I represent healing and someone who can make something inside her feel better. All in all it's good that she's reaching out, even if it's to me. It's taken six months, but she wants to get better, Pete. I truly believe that, no matter how hard she's making this for you."

Mallory heard herself rambling and stopped. And waited. Could he trust someone to help him, the way Polly was starting to? She braced for his continued resistance. She accepted how badly she wanted him to walk away, because clearly she couldn't.

"What else do you recommend?" he asked, the question reasonable and controlled, impressing the hell out of her. Most parents would do just about anything to avoid admitting they didn't have all the answers where their kids were concerned. "Beyond feeding her food I don't approve of and letting her flit in and out of your life whenever she pleases while you put no demands on her whatsoever to snap out of this."

"*This* is depression." Mallory wanted to reach for him. His arm. His hand. She wanted badly to comfort and soothe, and she couldn't. She absolutely couldn't. Not this man. Not this close, dark, unpredictable night. "Polly is grieving and losing herself in it and fighting depression she might very well have to deal with the rest of her life. Childhood trauma can do that, and there's no amount of snapping out of it that will permanently repair the place in her heart where one moment she had a mother and the next she didn't."

Tears were in Mallory's eyes, her words hitting too close to home. All while her neighbor was leaning away the way she longed to, his open expression closing down, becoming brittle, emotionless.

"You talk like a shrink." The rigid set of his jaw spoke volumes about his opinion of formal therapy.

"A credentialed social worker," she clarified. At least she had been. "My degree and certification are in a box around here somewhere if you'd like to look at them. My concentration's in early childhood development, with an emphasis on grief recovery and crisis care."

"All that so you could be a school nurse in Pleasantville?"

His pop culture description of their community was so unexpected and dead-on she laughed. She slapped her hand over her mouth, grinning behind it and charmed by his crooked half smile in response.

"No," she admitted. "Nursing school was always in the cards, but it came after."

"After what?"

She paused, then made herself give him the truth, as much of it as he needed to trust her with Polly.

"After I realized that while I want to help every child who has nowhere else to turn, it's not something I can do successfully day in and day out. Not without it damaging me too deeply to be useful to anyone."

A thoughtful, vertical wrinkle formed between his eyebrows. "So you've settled for becoming a fairy godmother for kids like Polly who just happen to find you? Where did you come from, lady?"

His unexpected insight and quick mind, the easy banter they'd stumbled into, reined in Mallory's meandering thoughts. Of all her neighbors, it was crazy that Pete Lombard was the person she felt most comfortable talking with.

She'd like to see Polly happier and more stable. But she'd shared far more than she'd intended to with anyone in Chandlerville. And becoming too attached to the Lombards' situation would be trampling on the same kind of personal boundary that had ended her formal career in social work. She had a habit of overidentifying with pet cases. That was another mistake she'd promised herself never to make again.

"I come from somewhere that gives me a leg up working with people like your daughter," she reminded herself out loud. That's all that was happening here. This was another impersonal connection she'd spin into something good, because helping and letting go once her job was done was supposed to be her specialty.

"And you think you can work with us?" He didn't sound convinced.

"That's a question you're going to have to answer for yourself. I've considered sending Polly back to her class when she comes to my office, but I worry about how she'll take that kind of rejection. And I could lock my doors here..." She ignored the cringe deep inside, a flashback of being hemmed in as a child, unable to leave. Not until morning when daylight made it safer, though never completely safe, to be out and about. It was a claustrophobic, panicked place she hated each time her mind returned to it. "But if Polly came back another night, she'd be—"

"Locked outside in the dark, and there'd be no pretty Christmas tree for her to hide behind. No one to alert me that she was gone." Pete seemed to age before Mallory's eyes.

"I don't have definite solutions to give you." Thinking that she did was a slippery slope. "I suspect I'll end up asking you more questions than anything else."

"Questions I'll like about as much as you giving Polly puffed air for a late-night snack?"

"Get back to me on that one. My guess is she'll sleep better with it in her stomach than she does the harder-to-digest, wholesome fare you're giving her for dinner."

"Because you served her the nutritional equivalent of crack?"

"No, because she ate it from a chipped princess bowl."

Mallory waited for him to get that she was kidding. He didn't blink. So much for distracting him with playful sarcasm.

"The cereal's a base for her stomach." She felt ridiculous lecturing him about dietary dos and don'ts while looking like a waif that barely came up to his chin, wearing oversize thrift store pajamas she suspected might not be entirely covering her breasts. Only she wasn't drawing attention to the situation by clutching at the lapels of her nightshirt. "Even with the appalling amount of sweetener coating it, something like puffed corn is a good option for bedtime. Like rice, it's easier to digest than more complex grains. Have you heard of the BRAT diet? I recommend it for many of the kids I work with. There's a lot of anxiety to deal with for little ones who're constantly moving around with displaced parents."

Pete blinked. "There are kids like that at Chandler?"

Mallory inhaled.

"No..." she backpedaled. "I was speaking of other places I've worked. What I'm trying to say is digestive problems are common in kids who experience upheaval too early in life."

"The BRAT diet?"

"Bananas, rice, apple sauce, and toast. Four of the most easily digestible foods you can find, and there's substantial dietary value to each. When you're rebooting a little one's system, I'd start with BRAT every time."

"I'll try to remember that."

It was the nicest thing he could have said to her, even if his acquiescence came out rusty, like the scrape of a door that didn't want to be opened.

"Friends, then?" The suggestion tumbled from her mouth as if she hadn't bungled each attempt to make a similar offer to other families in their community.

She extended her hand, officially committing to their cease-fire for Polly's sake. And why not? To this man a friendship with her would mean nothing more than being casual acquaintances. And *casual* was a crystal-clear boundary Mallory could work with.

"If Polly continues not wanting a tree of her own," she said, "maybe the two of you could come back one afternoon to visit it together. I'll stay out of the way. You can have a little holiday, at least, without her feeling pressured to want what you've always done with her mother."

"You're hard to figure out." He shook and held on longer than any casual friend she'd ever had.

"You're better off not trying." Mallory slipped free and yanked her pajama top tightly closed. "Tougher characters than you have given up in frustration. I'm a nut that defies cracking."

When he laughed she felt a rush of pleasure race through her.

"Daddy?" a tiny voice said. Then a tiny body emerged through the butler's door. "I'm tired."

Pete knelt and cuddled Polly close. As he held her and stood, his daughter's head fit beneath his chin as if she'd laid it there a million times. The bond between them no matter how much they'd both lost was clearly stronger than ever. They were still trying. Maybe they were failing a little, but they were trying.

Watching them Mallory felt alone beneath her glaring Christmas tree for the first time since putting the thing up.

"How's your tummy feeling?" Pete ran a hand down his daughter's hair.

"Better," Polly whispered around a yawn. Her eyes drooped, then shut completely.

Pete scowled at Mallory's unapologetic smirk.

"Night." Savoring her victory, she led the way to the patio.

"We should give you back your robe."

"Next time," she heard herself say.

Pete stepped outside. He turned back. The look he gave her clouded with unvoiced questions. "Next time," he accepted, sealing their deal. "Thank you."

"You're welcome."

Too welcome. She stepped away and caught herself wondering which afternoon that week the pair might be back.

She had way too much personal experience with what it was like for a little girl to dream of a Christmas that wouldn't break her heart to be inviting Polly and Pete Lombard deeper into her rebooted life. She slid the glass shut between them, her tree's lights reflecting her image like a mirror. With a flip of the switch beside the patio door she disappeared, her tree going dark for the first time since she'd decorated it.

The world beyond her window re-formed, shadowy and frigid. Her neighbors were already gone. The door in the corner of her fence was shut. Peace had reclaimed her view. But the crystal perfection of it no longer tempted her to smile.

As quickly as she could she cleaned the kitchen, reset the thermostat, turned her tree back on as she passed through the living room, and crawled into bed. Much, much later, she fell asleep, worry for the Lombard family joining her until dawn painted ribbons of lavender across a gray sky and Mallory's own childhood grabbed for her with greedy fingers.

Chapter Three

My life closed twice before its close...

W hen you got nothin', you're invisible.

Mal had her mama, but not really. And her crazy mama had left everything but Mal behind three months ago when she'd taken Mal away from Grams and Papa. They had nothin' now except what they could carry each time they moved on from whatever place they were, before someone realized that Mal should be in school or that Mama and her had nothin' of their own. Not even Christmas.

Being invisible had been okay at first. It was trying not to get caught that got old fast. And scary. It was scary to never belong and never stop the way Mama kept saying they would one day. Mal didn't believe her anymore. And now that Thanksgiving had come and gone and they were still movin' from one shabby building to the next, hardly ever sleeping at the kind of shelters that gave away free turkey dinners and pumpkin pie, Mal had started to wish someone would finally, really, see her.

If they got found out maybe it would stop. Maybe the one day Mama kept promising would happen. Maybe Christmas and Mal's grandparents would find them after all.

"Come on, Mal, we have to keep goin'. It doesn't hurt that bad. We'll make it in time."

Mama never called her anything but "Mal." No "Mallory Jane," the way Grams called her. And she never worried like other moms, even the other street moms, or stopped to see how tired or cold or sad Mallory was. Mama felt too much already to worry about stuff outside her head. Most of the time she needed Mal's help to stop feeling—Mal, and whatever Mama found to drink that made everything better for a little while.

It was Christmas Eve. The TV news had said so on the overhead screen in the stuffy, crowded drugstore they'd walked around in until it closed. Now instead of finding some vacant place to stop for the night or even a shelter with free presents, they were walkin' to the next town like they did all the other nights when Mama couldn't sleep.

An image filled Mal's mind of two homeless Energizer Bunnies with crazy hair and bad teeth and grimy coats that didn't keep them warm, drumming down a no-name city street. She laughed out loud.

"Shhh…" Mama warned.

A jagged cough grabbed Mal's insides as she tried to shush. She let it out just like the laugh, and it went on and on until the pain got so bad she squeezed her arms around herself and held her breath and swallowed the next wheeze, trying not to cry. She hated to cry. Mama couldn't stand it either. It made her crazier, which made people look at them weird while Mama paced and talked to herself and cried, too, because she was scared of everything, but mostly of Mal bein' taken away from her.

"Someone will hear," Mama said in her scared voice.

But there was no one, not ahead of them or behind. It was late. Probably after midnight. Christmas morning. The world was deserted. Tall buildings and trash and filth and winter wind was all there was for miles. No one would hear her cough. No one would see Mal tonight.

She remembered a story from kindergarten, from back when she'd lived with Grams and Papa. A story about kids with yards and play sets and Christmas trees and real families. Those kids liked the cold that came with the holidays. Leaves changed in their perfect yards. They played games in piles of them after their parents raked their lawns. They had toys they left outside that got buried by the fall. They didn't have to hold onto everything that was theirs, carrying it with them wherever they went or someone would steal it. They had jackets and hats and warm soup and turkeys at Thanksgiving and loads of presents each Christmas. They had everything, and when you had everything the cold didn't matter so much.

Because of her mama, Mal's family had never been like that. And now all Mal had was her crazy mama and a cough. They'd coughed up crud for days while they kept goin', because the shelters in this city weren't like the one they'd left in the last small town. She and Mama couldn't be invisible here, not if they needed a doctor. Doctors and nurses in big cities made you sign stuff, and the different shelters talked to each other. They kept track of kids like Mal, especially if they were sick. Someone would call the police, who'd take Mal away and put Mama back in the hospital.

Mama said she'd rather die than lose the only thing she'd ever really had—Mal. She said they had to get to somewhere else before they could stop, no matter how bad Mal's cough hurt. No matter how hard it was to watch Christmas come and go like it was just another day. Like they really had no one. Nowhere. Nothin' of their own. Nothin' but each other.

It began to snow.

Mal pulled their hats from her backpack, making sure Mama put hers on. Mal was always making sure. Without Mal, her mama would forget to eat and sleep and get clean whenever they had the chance. Mal had stolen cough syrup before they left the drugstore. She'd make sure she and Mama took it—every four hours, the bottle said—until it was gone. Then when Mama finally let them stop, Mal would steal more.

A fresh start, Mama called each new town. Except Mal remembered Gram's soft, clean sheets. They'd been fresh, not the nasty boxes and stuff they slept on most nights now. She'd drank cold orange juice for breakfast at Grams's, in cartoon glasses, not whatever the next shelter served lukewarm, or something a store threw out because it was no good to anyone but people who'd dig it out of a Dumpster. There was no fresh for people carrying their life around in wet plastic sacks and a backpack that Mal had stolen long before the cough syrup.

There'd be no fresh waiting for them in the next town, either. Or the next. Two or three more cities from now, Mama would finally drink enough to crash. She'd stop movin' completely. Like the last time and the time before that, Mal would find them a place, maybe a good shelter, and Mama would wind down like her batteries were empty. She'd get too tired and drunk to keep goin', and for a while they'd stop, even though there was nothing Mal hated more than bein' trapped inside one of those places with other people like them.

There'd be only grimy windows to see out of. There'd be gray all around them. Whatever colors the shelters painted on their walls, it all looked gray to Mal. There'd be no leaving behind the awful smell of rooms filled with cots and other dirty people where they'd be told to sleep. Not until Mama got better. Mal would stay by her, guarding their stuff day and night till they could keep goin' again. And by then there'd be no Christmas for another year. The magic she'd been dreaming the holidays might bring would be long gone.

Mal lost her hold on the next cough.

Pain streaked up her side.

Mama kept walkin' through the snow.

"We'll make it," she was muttering.

Mal palmed the quarter hidden in her frayed coat pocket. As long as she had her quarter there was a number she could call to make this all go away. A phone number her teacher had made her remember over and over until she'd stopped forgetting it. There was a Christmas, another life, waiting for her to go back to no matter how long she'd been gone or how invisible she was or how messed up that world had been, too.

"You're such a smart girl, Mallory Jane," Grams had said when she'd heard Mal repeat their phone number. "Now you can always reach us, no matter what."

But Mama would never go back there, even if Grams and Papa still wanted Mal. The police and then the hospital would take Mama away for stealing Mal from her grandparents. Then who would take care of Mama the next time she wound down? If Mal stopped being invisible because it was Christmas and she was sick and dirty and freezing, would she ever see Mama again?

She kept walkin'.

She sucked down another cough and her dreams of the yard and the trees and the perfect house and family she'd wanted her whole life.

"We'll make it," Mama said, louder than before, as the night got colder around them and the snow closed in until there was nothin' but blinding white and darkness. "It doesn't hurt that bad, Mal. You'll see. The next town's not far. We'll find you your Christmas. If we don't stop, if we keep goin', we'll make it in time…"

Chapter Four

Success is counted sweetest
By those who ne'er succeed...

"How are you feeling this morning?" Julia Davis asked her cul-de-sac neighbor and dear friend Sam Perry, of a mind to work some Mimosa Lane magic.

At a quarter past eight in the morning, the North Georgia air around them was crisp but rapidly warming. The neighborhood kids were just back to school from Thanksgiving and less than a month from Christmas break. They'd been an overexcited, chattering swarm as they'd run through the neighborhood toward the bus stop. Happy and loud and anxious to share their Thanksgiving stories, they'd headed off for their first day of biding their back-to-school time, until winter break arrived with its two more weeks of freedom.

Not that the weather itself had succumbed to holiday fever. Chandlerville's youngest would have to wait a bit longer before breaking out the coats and sweaters that the rest of the country already wore. Georgia this December was still clinging to the last echoes of a hot, dry summer—their warm, humid fall days stubbornly refusing to fade to winter. For many the delay was putting a damper on the traditional countdown to presents and holiday treats. The grown-ups especially were digging deeper than ever for a seasonal spirit that should have been effortless.

Each night since Thanksgiving more and more Christmas decorations appeared in the yards up and down the lane. Still, it was hard to enjoy stringing twinkle lights on bushes and trees when most families had needed to run their air conditioners during Thanksgiving dinner and were still wearing shorts and sandals each afternoon and barbecuing dinner outdoors. The leaves had already changed and fallen, but full-on winter was so far a no-show. The weatherman had forecast temperatures to rise into the seventies again today, though the overnight chill kept slipping closer to freezing than ever and a cold snap was due by the first of next week.

Julia knew Sam would be working religiously in her yard each blissfully mild morning, basking in the sun's healing rays and the breathtaking blue skies that fed the flowers and bushes she nurtured with such care. For just a while longer, for far longer than people north of the state line would believe possible, Sam's yard would be the sanctuary that anchored her to their community.

But once cold daytime temps did come it would rest particularly hard on Sam's petite, frail shoulders. Over the winter she would sit outside on her back patio wrapped in blankets and her heaviest clothes, staring blankly into the hibernating, silent world she would no longer interact with. Gone would be Julia's opportunity to casually drop by and chat while Sam dug into fertile soil and coaxed fragile beauty to flowering life.

Remaining indoors for long periods of time was hard for Sam. Being surrounded by walls would forever make a part of her feel as if she were trapped within the Manhattan high-rises she'd been too close to as they'd first burned and then crumbled to the ground. But until spring came this still-traumatized 9/11 survivor would be lost to both her yard work and their community. Taking regular part in their neighborhood's social activities had always been difficult for Sam.

It was as if even their picturesque world hurt too much for her to embrace for more than a few panic-riddled moments at a time.

"It'll be a pretty day." Sam stood from where she'd been weeding the flower bed beside her mailbox. She pushed back her straw hat with a gloved hand, her arms too thin, the shadows beneath her hazel eyes too dark. She smiled, seemingly pleased to have Julia there but not answering her question about how she was feeling. Sam never did when someone asked. "Cade was asking if this afternoon's practice could be on the outside courts again."

"He's loving his basketball. Will you be there tonight?" Julia sipped the decaf two-Splenda latte that she'd poured into her travel mug. She smiled hopefully at one of the women she felt closest to in the world, even though they saw each other less frequently than Julia did the rest of her circle.

To look at them even now, a stranger would have thought she and Sam barely knew each other—Sam seemed to already be inching closer to her house and away from Julia's questions. In reality, over the years Sam had graced Julia and Emma Lombard with the most priceless of gifts—opening up to them about her deepest hurts and dreams and the fragile hope Sam clung to that she would one day resume the active, happy life she'd taken for granted when she'd lived and worked in New York City.

Most everyone pitied this young mother, understanding enough about what had precipitated the Perrys' move to Georgia eleven years ago to give both their past and Sam plenty of space. Julia, however, knew the depth of grit that lay beneath her friend's tightly wound personality. Yes, there was pain, always simmering below the surface. But Sam had the spirit of a fighter. She was a woman refusing to give up on the world that had nearly destroyed her. And Julia was equally determined to fight alongside her friend, even if she sometimes had to play dirty.

"Brian's going to be there tonight," Sam said, speaking of her husband and shaking her head at the thought of helping corral overactive boys into organized athletics. "I have dinner to put on the table as soon as everyone gets home."

"Maybe Brian could pick up takeout on the way back from practice? That would free up your afternoon. I know your boys would love to have you watching them. Their skills are getting so much stronger. Just last night Walter was talking about both Cade and Joshua's progress." Julia placed a hand on her friend's shoulder and squeezed. "We'd all love it if you'd join us."

Brian Perry and Julia's husband, Walter, coached the Rockets, the neighborhood rec basketball team. Walter and Julia's boys were in high school now, but Walter hadn't let go of working with the youngest of the community's players. And Julia was one of the team moms every season, a customary job for the head coach's wife. The welcomed responsibility kept her in touch with the families who flocked to Chandlerville for quality schools and a middle-class suburban lifestyle. But Sam, even though it was clear that she doted on her boys, never joined her family on practice nights at the YMCA gymnasium. Group gatherings were particularly difficult for her.

She was missing out on so much.

Time seemed to stop whenever Southern communities drew together to mix and mingle and share their lives. Individual identities expanded to include the realities of the people living around them—creating an extended family who cared for one another as fiercely and effortlessly as they did their own kin. It was the exact kind of connection that Julia was determined for Sam to embrace this holiday season. She'd watched her friend sink into debilitating depression for too many years now, from early fall through the colder winter months. This holiday, solitude and isolation simply wouldn't do—for either Sam or Polly Lombard.

"I really want to make more practices." Sam began packing her trowel in the caddy she used for her gardening tools. Her movements were jerky and hurried, her hands trembling just enough to be noticeable.

"Did you see little Polly at the bus stop this morning?" Julia asked, shifting tactics before she found herself standing alone at the curb. "I'm worried about her. She's not getting any better."

The one neighborhood tradition Sam never missed was walking her boys to the school bus, then meeting them there again every afternoon. And each morning Julia watched Sam give Polly Lombard a little extra attention, even though the child never outwardly responded any more than she did to the other parents.

Polly's complete withdrawal from her neighbors was hardest on Julia and Sam. They'd been such close friends with Emma. But no matter who approached Polly now, the child simply clung tighter to her daddy and pretended no one was there. It seemed to distress Sam most of all that there was no comforting the little angel.

"She must feel completely alone," Sam said. The turbulent green of her eyes deepened to a stormy gray, her empathy for Polly sounding hauntingly personal. She set her bucket of gardening tools down on her still-green grass and clenched her hands together in front of her body. "I imagine it feels like no one in the world could possibly understand what she's going through."

Julia knew for certain that Sam didn't have to imagine how Polly felt as the child dealt with emotions that were too overwhelming to cope with. And that morning as Julia had watched her reclusive friend attempt once again to engage Emma's daughter, she'd felt a plan begin to form. One to help both lost souls come out of their shells.

"Polly has the world on her shoulders," Julia agreed. "Even though I'm sure Pete and her teachers at school are doing their best to help her deal with losing her mother."

"Sometimes there's nothing anyone can do." Sam cast a long look at her garden, as if her own answers lay there rather than with the people who lived nearby. "Sometimes dealing with something that horrible simply isn't possible."

"It's like Polly's decided that the way she's feeling is the way she's going to feel forever, and there's nothing anyone can do about it. Not even Pete."

"Of course she feels hopeless." Sam's scowl suggested that Julia had shed fifty IQ points. "Do you blame her?"

"I don't think it's healthy, the way she's pulling away. Neither do you, or you wouldn't keep trying to talk with her."

Julia cleared her throat around words that suddenly didn't want to come out. She knew how much this conversation must have been hurting her friend.

"I was thinking just this morning," she said, rushing to make her point, "that you might be the right person to push a little harder and break the ice with Polly."

Walter had warned her to back off not just the Lombards' problems but the Perrys', too. But this was what Julia did, both at her job on the county school board and as head of the Mimosa Lane homeowners' association. She helped people every chance she got. She connected lives. She strengthened the community bonds that made their world better for all of them. She didn't know how to stop, and she didn't want to try.

She loved Sam and Polly so much, the same way she'd adored Emma. Two beautiful souls like Polly and Sam deserved better than living reclusive lives amid the vibrant chaos of everyone else's reality.

"I'm the last thing Polly needs." Sam glared at Julia.

"I think you could be a wonderful friend to her," Julia pressed, "if we could somehow get the two of you to spend a little more time together."

"That child lost her mother while we all stood there watching it happen. Emma and I were the same age. We even looked a little alike. I imagine I'm a reminder to Polly of what she's lost, no matter how much I'd like to help her. And no one needs to face horrible memories like that every day, especially not a little girl."

"Running away from what's happened doesn't seem to be helping either one of you," Julia pointed out, knowing as she did that she was taking an enormous risk. Even a friendship as strong as hers and Sam's had its limits. "Being alone with your memories isn't protecting either of you."

A flash of heat, of hatred, lit up Sam's mercurial eyes, reminding Julia that she was talking to a woman who'd, amid the first large-scale terrorist strikes on American soil, watched her world literally explode around her. Then just as quickly, Sam's expression cooled, and she was staring blankly at Julia as if she didn't know her.

"I need to take care of something inside." Sam turned and walked through her garden, a broken survivor—a former elementary school teacher missing her students but no longer capable of functioning within a classroom.

Julia watched her go, more determined than ever not to give up on her friend. She'd see Brian tonight at basketball practice. Maybe if she took a different tack she could get through to him.

Each year someone on Mimosa Lane threw a Christmas party to ring in the holiday season. And the Perrys' sprawling two-story Colonial would be the perfect location for this year's celebration. People would arrive and leave whenever their schedules allowed. Some would linger and mingle. The bonds that communities like theirs had been designed to foster would deepen, and Sam would at least be able to enjoy her neighbors from a distance while she hid upstairs in her office the way she had the few other times the Perrys had hosted get-togethers.

The world she no longer needed to fear would come to Sam this Christmas, refusing to let her hide away entirely. And maybe, just maybe, Sam with her own bouts of silence and debilitating attacks of shyness and fear, as well as her experience working with children, would find a way to do the same for Polly. *If* Julia could talk Pete into attending.

She checked her watch and headed for her car, sipping the last of her first cup of coffee from the mug she'd refill on the way to the county courthouse and the office hours she kept three mornings a week.

She loved her community and the life she and Walter had built in Chandlerville. She believed in the power of neighbors and friendships and the value of shared experiences—both joyous celebrations and heartbreaking losses. To her soul she'd already accepted that there was a reason the Lombard and the Perry families had found their separate paths to this place, and why her closest friends now needed so much of the same kind of healing.

Mimosa Lane had some magic to make this Christmas season. All it needed, Julia thought as she backed out of her driveway and rolled down her window to enjoy the morning breeze, was for someone to help the situation along just a bit.

She'd talk Brian into hosting the party. Then she'd wrangle a promise from Pete to attend for Polly's sake. The man was almost as determined as his daughter to keep to himself. But Julia would get through to him.

This Christmas, she'd get through to them all.

***

"Flu?" Mallory said. "Already? Tell me you're kidding. It hasn't even dropped below freezing at night."

She hadn't yet made it to her office in the clinic at William B. Chandler Elementary. And already it was proving to be a two-Tylenol morning—with a pot-of-coffee chaser thrown in to get her to lunch. When she'd taken the gig as a school nurse, she'd known finessing flu outbreaks would be part of her job. But she'd managed to dissociate herself from that reality so far, hoping she'd escape its clutches until after the holiday season.

Mornings, particularly Monday mornings, were supposed to be Mallory's downtime. The school would soon be teeming with eager voices and nonstop energy, but for a while longer no one would typically need her for much. Today, battling a tension headache after her late-night visitors and the dream about her first Christmas on the streets with her mother, she'd needed some time to shrug off her emotional hangover. She'd also wanted to review the school's medical records for Polly

Lombard and the latest recommendations from her pediatrician for managing the child's diet and anxiety.

"Fourteen parents e-mailed teachers over the weekend," Kristen Hemmings said. "If it's anything like last year, half our students could be out sick by the end of the week."

The assistant principal had caught up with Mallory on her way into school. They were due back outside for bus call. In less than ten minutes children would begin arriving in an endless swarm that wouldn't quiet until the morning's first bell rang for everyone to settle down in homeroom.

Mallory hitched one shoulder to resettle the straps of her tote bag.

She'd already seen enough her first few months on the job to have an idea of what was coming. Parents always wanted to believe that a harmless cough or a sniffle was nothing more than a cold. That was until their sick little darlings ended up in Mallory's office running a fever, infectious to everyone they came into contact with.

She'd spent the month of November sending out e-mails and class notes lobbying for flu shots and parental agreement to keep sick kids at home, particularly viral ones. She suspected her requests for preemptive action had fallen on mostly deaf ears. People with the means to take their children to family doctors anytime they wanted to were prone to creating an environment ideal for spreading illness. It was a blind kind of recklessness that Mallory couldn't wrap her mind around.

A flash of residual panic from her own childhood shouldered its way to the surface.

When you spent your formative years on the streets with no way to get well once you were ill, you learned to pay attention to early warning signs. Living somewhere like Chandlerville, not only did families have insurance, they had the luxury of state-funded nurses like Mallory to alert them when there was a problem. And no matter how long a virus festered before action was taken, kids sick with something as seemingly insignificant as the flu would almost always get well again after resting in warm, clean homes and being cared for by doting parents.

Not so much for people who circulated from one homeless shelter to another the way Mallory and her mother had. Or for the financially strapped families living in overcrowded public housing like many of the people she still helped on the weekends, volunteering in Atlanta's assistance community. You didn't let yourself get sick when you didn't know where your next round of medical care was coming from or how you'd pay for it if it were available. Every adult worked just to stay afloat, sometimes shouldering two and three minimum-wage jobs. There was no one to stay home with you and push fluids and meds and food, or to deal with the secondary complications that could follow poor treatment—things like bronchitis, walking pneumonia, and even permanent lung damage.

Those harsh realities were so far removed from what life was like in a middle-class suburb, it was ridiculously easy to rationalize sending your kids to school with flu-like symptoms that might or might not turn out to be anything to worry about. If you were wrong, there was a built-in support network to care for children until parents could take over. At Chandler Elementary, that network was Mallory's job to manage.

So much for her taking it easy until dealing with happy, shiny people didn't make her feel like screaming.

"There goes the rest of the day," she said.

"There goes the week." Kristen flipped through the file she held, a compilation of the atom bomb last year's flu blitz had set off amid her orderly bastion of learning. The woman had a file for everything. "We'll be lucky if this doesn't consume the better part of the calendar between now and Christmas break. Our disaster recovery plan includes placing calls out to the community asking for volunteers to help with the overflow if more kids than you can handle flood the clinic. Lots of moms and friends of the school can pitch in, taking temperatures and handling minor things while you oversee the worst of the cases until the parents can get here to pick children up. You'll want to send a memo to the teachers about sterilizing as much of their common areas and materials as they can, as often as they can, until this runs its course."

Elementary-age kids crammed together into classrooms or playing like bands of roving puppies on playgrounds were a breeding ground for a tenacious virus. Even with tried-and-true containment protocol in place, the flu would spread unchecked. Some of the staff would likely fall prey, too. They were all required to get flu shots, but not every strain of the virus was covered by each immunization.

Chandler Elementary was in for a bumpy ride.

"Ms. Mathers and Mrs. Arnold's classes seem to be the epicenter," Kristen said with harried professionalism, looking down from the six-foot-two height that must have served her well as a college basketball all-star. Younger than most of her teachers, Kristen ruled her domain with a gentle voice and a quiet gift for achieving the staff's commitment to the highest of standards. "Come see me after the bell. I'll have worked up a short list of volunteers the school administrative assistants will call as soon as you think you need them."

"Today," Mallory said, mentally rallying. "My guess is I'll need them before lunchtime today."

Good thing she'd donned her brightest, most obnoxious scrubs in the hope of jump-starting her attitude to something perkier than *Don't screw with me.* It was harder to be cranky when you were covered top to bottom with Tweety Birds.

With a distracted nod Kristen peeled off, ducking into the front office with the grace of an all-conference MVP sprinting down a basketball court for a layup. Mallory considered sprinting herself, but kept her pace calm and unhurried. She smiled at the teachers she passed on the way to the clinic. As unhinged as she felt, this was work. And she could always, always handle herself at work.

Once inside the clinic, however, she longed for a dark, cool spot to hide until the ache behind her right temple eased. She bustled farther into her brightly lit domain and stared at the cot she kept freshly made in the corner. It was ridiculous, fantasizing about spending the morning there tunneled under the covers. By lunchtime she'd likely have to cart in spare sleeping mats to handle the anticipated flood of sick children.

She fired up the coffeemaker that she'd inherited from the previous school nurse who'd left after having her first child. She rolled her shoulders and told herself she was used to not sleeping. She regularly found it difficult to ease into the relaxation and recharging that nighttime was supposed to nurture. But the exhaustion vibrating through her today was different. She felt hollowed out and echo-filled. More empty than she had in years.

Shadows from her dream were still clinging, settling in with a slimy, sickening after burn, owning pieces of her that didn't fit in with the cheery sunlight streaming through the clinic windows or the gaggle of community volunteers that was about to descend.

She'd trained to be a social worker after years of volunteering in homeless shelters and assisted-living centers, telling herself since she was a teenager that those places were where she still felt most at home. She'd wanted to make a difference where she could do the most good for people in the most need. In the end spending all her time with lives still trapped in the world she'd escaped had made it impossible for her to either do that job well or move on with her own life. That's when she'd set her sights on making a home somewhere else.

She'd started over in Chandlerville. She was done looking back, no matter how hard letting go was turning out to be. She was strong enough to do this, just like her grams had said…

Mallory secured her tote and lunch bag in her bottom drawer, sat in her desk chair, and dropped her head into her hands. The intercom chimed all over the school, giving a two-minute warning to bus call. Behind her closed eyes flashed a picture of her mama's dirt-smudged, emotionless visage, then of Polly Lombard's pale, beautiful features. Guilt bubbled through Mallory from each image.

You can't fix everyone, her supervisor had said at her last appointment as a social worker. *And if you don't stop overidentifying with your cases, you're going to eventually wreck more than your career.*

Mallory pushed out of her chair and, on her way to intercept the buses, stopped at the mirror beside the clinic door. The face that smiled back at her was as much a stranger as always. Where was the competent, successful woman who'd moved on from every mis-start and mistake and mess and arrived safely on the other side, ready to settle down? The past, not her future, filled her eyes, tainted as always with a predatory hunger for peace.

She could handle a run of the flu. She could handle the Lombards. If she had to, she could handle this Christmas feeling just as forced and empty as all the rest, no matter how much she craved a taste of holiday magic all her own. She could handle anything. But she was tired of it—the constant, careful dance of pushing away who she'd been, so she could navigate the world she lived in now.

Polly Lombard didn't have a patent on avoiding painful holiday memories. Mallory had lived that same choice most of her life—never celebrating Christmas all out, no matter how much she'd longed to as a child.

She'd triumphed, according to her childhood therapist, her grams, and her own once-upon-a-time social worker. She'd escaped the world her bipolar, alcoholic mother had dragged her into. She was free, they'd insisted. Free to be happy and make everything she wanted a reality. This first Christmas of her fresh start she'd planned to put their assurances to the ultimate test.

She'd intended to revel in the holiday season, not merely survive it. Nothing in Chandlerville was supposed to remind her of her childhood. Hadn't that been the point of moving somewhere so different?

Except despite her cushy job and pretty house and the twenty hours of volunteer work she still donated in Atlanta each weekend to keep her hand in paying back all that had once been done for her, an unrelenting part of her was still walking down that freezing-cold, dead-end road with her mother.

It doesn't hurt that bad...

The intercom chimed again. She walked slowly out the door when she normally would have hurried along with her coworkers, through hallways that smelled of crayons and books and glue and happy childhoods.

Each day that went by, she counted it a blessing to have found her way to this nurturing world. A world where good people like Pete and Polly could have their lives ripped apart, but know that their community would rally around them until they fought their way back from the shock and pain. Chandlerville was a hopeful, healthy place, and Mallory had made herself a part of it.

Yet she knew her colleagues at work only as much as she needed to do her job. And she couldn't string two sentences together with her neighbors—except for the grieving ones. There were no presents under her fake tree and no holiday cards on her blue refrigerator. And a silly flu outbreak was threatening to torpedo even more her chances of manufacturing the jolly Christmas she craved.

As she walked toward the buses she could feel the bite of a long-ago winter pushing at her back, whispering to her of another, darker reality she understood so much better.

It doesn't hurt that bad, Mal, she heard her mama saying. *One day, this will all be over...*

***

Polly had never been more excited to ride the morning bus to school. All school year long she'd sat alone in her seat at the front, trying not to cry or scream or want to disappear. The other kids looked at her like everyone else did, expecting her to be something she couldn't—to be better or happier or more like she used to be. And she hated it. She hated being with almost anyone now, going anywhere where she had to fake being okay, where people talked and acted like they understood, only they didn't.

But this morning was different. The bus was noisy like always, with kids talking and playing and screaming like she used to. And it still smelled like the driver's, Mrs. Appletree's, medicine that she put on her hand and arm sometimes when they were waiting for a stoplight to change. And the kids who used to be her friends had still stared at her when she got on, then when she didn't say anything to anyone they'd ignored her. But today she didn't mind feeling lonely while Mrs. Appletree drove them through Chandlerville.

This morning she couldn't think of anything but her plan— the one she'd been thinking about for days now. She finally knew how to save Christmas and get her daddy back, the way he'd been a real daddy before Mommy left them.

Every day it was like more and more of him was gone— more of the daddy who'd used to hug her and Mommy like it was the best part of his day, and kiss them and join in the fun games Mommy always made sure they played whenever he wasn't working. He never played now, and they never went anywhere anymore because he was so worried about Polly and how she'd act.

Not that Polly wanted to be someplace, anyplace, but at home. Not that she really wanted to be home, either, when all her daddy talked about there was eating and sleeping and school and Polly feeling better. He'd used to want to go do fun things almost all the time. Now he didn't want to do anything. Not with Polly—not when she was so upset she made herself and Daddy and everyone else act so weird everywhere she went.

She made her daddy sad now, and she'd give anything to stop. She'd give anything to go back to being normal so he could go back to loving her the way he used to before.

He never talked to her anymore. Not about important things. He was too worried. She wasn't a good girl anymore when other people tried to talk to her about how she felt. Every time she'd cry and tell them to go away even though it made Daddy get even more quiet around her—and he was the only person she really wanted to talk to at all now, even when she couldn't.

It made him mad, too, the way everyone treated them. Polly could tell he wanted people to go away and leave them alone, too. *"I don't need anyone's damn help,"* she'd heard him say to Ms. Phillips last night and under his breath one morning at the bus stop just last week when everyone had been asking all over again how it was going and what they could do to make things better.

It wouldn't be good for Polly, he'd said when the next day she hadn't wanted to wait for the bus anymore with everyone else. She and Daddy needed to stick to a normal routine, her doctor said. So they had to try harder to be with people on Mimosa Lane and at school—when Polly kept wishing Daddy would just try harder to be with *her* even though she was upset like all the time now.

She'd messed up Thanksgiving at her grandparents'. She'd *really* messed it up. Daddy hadn't wanted to be there, either, and he hadn't wanted to think or talk about Mommy the way Mommy's parents always did. But he'd said they had to go, they had to try. And then Polly had freaked because it had felt like her mommy should have been everywhere she looked at her grandparents' house, only Mommy wasn't going to be there for another Thanksgiving ever again.

Everyone kept acting like everything was okay and they were all just as happy as ever and it didn't matter that Mommy was everywhere, only she wasn't there at all. And Polly couldn't do it. She just couldn't. She'd run away in the middle of dinner— right out the front door and down her grandparents' brick steps. When Daddy caught her in the front yard and tried to get her to stop crying for Mommy, he'd right away said they could go home, almost like it was what he'd wanted, too.

That was when she'd begged him not to have Christmas at all. Not if it was going to be like Thanksgiving and every other day since Mommy died—Polly not being able to forget or sleep or eat or be with people the way she was supposed to, because she couldn't stop remembering the way everyone else could. He'd agreed, even though he'd sounded even sadder and had acted even more worried and gotten even quieter ever since.

She'd hurt his feelings, and she'd sorta lied. She really *did* want Christmas, more than anything in the world. A *real* Christmas, not a scared one the way Thanksgiving had felt.

Mommy had always made the holidays so fun and full of music and decorations and cookie baking and present wrapping. Polly wanted all of that back. The daddy she remembered, too, as much as he wanted the Polly she'd used to be. He'd always watch them being silly, then he'd laugh that way he did that made her feel all shimmery and perfect inside, and suddenly he'd be dancing with them and doing silly things, too, like hanging too many ornaments on the tree or too many lights outside on the front porch, or trying to figure out what was inside the presents Mommy had wrapped and put under the tree.

She wanted all of that back.

It was all she thought about anymore, especially when she stared out her bedroom window at night at her neighbor's shiny tree. How did she make herself feel better in time? How did she stop being so sad, so Daddy could stop feeling bad, too? How did she act normal again so he'd start treating her like a real daddy did, and so everybody else would leave them alone and stop doing and saying the things that hurt so much?

She hugged her lunch box to her chest and watched the streets pass by outside her window. She tried not to, but all she could think about was before and how her mommy used to drive her to school down the same road. She tried not to think about how Mommy had always been so happy to see Polly leave for school and come home again, or how Daddy treated the bus stop like homework now—it was something Polly had to do, so he could check it off his list of things that were going to make her better. She tried not to think about how Mommy used to always be talking with the neighbors in the mornings and afternoons when the bus came, being friendly to everybody even though she drove Polly back and forth to school. Now all the neighbors talked about was Mommy and how Polly and her daddy were doing without her.

"How are you feeling?" they always asked, expecting Polly to say she was better, and she wasn't, so she didn't say anything at all. And then Daddy didn't say anything, either, not to any of their friends the way he used to talk to all of them.

She had to fix this. She had to stop her head and her chest and her tummy from hurting, especially the way they had at Thanksgiving. She had to stop thinking about the way things were before. She just had to.

Before was ruining everything.

She thought of Ms. Phillips and her silly new tree and her fun kitchen and pretty pink cereal. Daddy had said he and Polly could go back to Ms. Phillips's house. Ms. Phillips had said she wanted to help make Christmas better for them. And Ms. Phillips never felt like pretending and faking or needing to run away. Would it be the same way with Polly's plan? Would Ms. Phillips help with that, too?

The driver pulled up to the curb outside the school. Polly was in the first front seat since she was the youngest kid on the bus. She sat the tallest she could now, scanning the school staff who waited at the curb to make sure kids got to class okay without wasting time before going inside. Ms. Phillips was right where she always was, wearing her Tweety Bird uniform today and looking just like she always did, like no matter what a kid did or said it would be okay with her.

Before she changed her mind, Polly reached into her Cinderella lunch box and grabbed what she'd brought from home. The bus door swung open. She slid off the seat, her fist clenched around her treasure, her other arm squeezing her lunch box to her tingly chest. Her backpack felt like a million pounds weighing her down as she stepped onto the curb and hurried over to the school nurse. Ms. Phillips smiled down at her. One of the other kids knocked into Polly's backpack and pushed her closer.

Ms. Phillips had asked her what she wanted over and over again, instead of telling her what to feel and do to get better. Polly shoved what she'd hidden away for so long into her neighbor's hand, desperate not to be afraid anymore the way she bet Ms. Phillips was never afraid of anything.

"I want to forget my mommy," she said, "so I can stop making everyone so sad. Will you help me save Christmas this year for me and Daddy?"

Then before Ms. Phillips could answer, before Polly could explain what she'd given to her and why and how they couldn't tell Daddy until Polly had forgotten everything she needed to, she chickened out and raced inside the school that she hated, too, because all she could remember whenever she was there was how her mommy had volunteered almost every day, helping with absolutely everything.

Polly had run from what she'd really wanted to say, just like at Thanksgiving. She hadn't told Ms. Phillips all she'd planned to or asked her to keep her secret until Polly was better. What if Ms. Phillips called Daddy because she didn't understand? He'd be even sadder. He'd feel even worse. And maybe he'd be mad at Ms. Phillips the way he'd sounded like he was for a while last night.

What if instead of making things better, Polly had just ruined this year's Christmas for good?

Chapter Five

To comprehend a nectar
Requires sorest need...

Today of all days wasn't the time to have Polly camped out in the clinic.

But Mallory didn't have the heart to shoo the little girl away. At least her records indicated Polly's pediatrician had administered a flu shot a few weeks ago. The kid hadn't made it through her first lesson that morning before showing up with a note from Ms. Caldwell that her stomach was upset—amid Mallory's triage of what seemed like the entire third grade's descent into the creeping crud.

None of the ten kids curled up on mats in her office knew Polly, so no worries that any of them might make fun of her for sitting in the corner alone, looking pale and lost, with the biggest, saddest eyes Mallory had ever seen. Not that any of her coughing, sneezing patients were curious about anyone else in the room.

By mere proximity Polly and her weakened immune system were running the risk of catching the virus, despite her immunization. Still, after last night's visit and the bizarre moment they'd shared that morning, how could Mallory send the child back to class until she knew what was wrong?

"Pete Lombard, please," she said into the phone once the call connected at Pete's station house. "He's an EMT with your company."

Parent and community volunteers had been trickling in since nine thirty to help care for the growing number of plague victims waiting for parents to pick them up, freeing Mallory to document and triage each new student. Only her current priority was getting Polly out of there, while she longed to make an excuse to flee herself.

She stared at the mint-green walls of the clinic, at the cartoon posters of boys and girls happily eating veggies and brushing their teeth and getting shots from equally beaming doctors and nurses, and felt herself losing even more ground. No matter how competently and in control she was functioning, each happy volunteer's smile and offer to do whatever she needed whispered that she had to get away, that any minute they'd all see that she didn't belong there any more than Polly did.

"Pete's out on call," said the masculine voice on the other end of the line. "Is this an emergency?"

Mallory wasn't sure she'd call it an emergency, but something important had most definitely changed for Polly.

How many times had Mallory made this call, saying she would keep the little girl in the clinic until Pete could come by the school? What must her constant interruptions be costing him at his job? But her little friend was finally opening up. Though Mallory didn't fully understand what had happened, Polly looked on the verge of a breakdown. Today of all days she needed her daddy there as quickly as possible.

"Please have him call the clinic at school. It's important." She hung up before the man could say anything more.

"Poor little thing," one of the community volunteers said, a Mimosa Lane neighbor Mallory had spoken to once or twice in passing as they'd plucked their mail from their boxes. Each time, Mallory had of course been wearing the same raggedy shorts and tie-dyed T-shirt.

Forty-something Julia Davis sat on the county board of ed and had been the PTA president when her kids attended Chandler. When Kristen Hemmings's plea had gone out asking for extra hands, Julia had been the first volunteer on the scene. Within minutes of arriving at the clinic she'd literally rolled up the sleeves of her conservative navy business suit and blended into Mallory's process as if she'd always been there—reassuring and cheerful and boundlessly confident in that way all successful working mothers seemed to master.

The woman had whispered her *Poor little thing* just now, presumably because she didn't want to disturb their dozing patients. The problem was she wasn't talking softly enough to prevent her observation from being overheard by either Polly or the parents milling about the clinic and the hallway beyond.

"Pete Lombard's doing the best he can," she continued, "but it's such a difficult time. I've never seen a family that needed more help, even though men like Pete can't fathom there being anything they can't do for themselves."

Mallory chanced a glance to the corner to find Polly still teary eyed and glaring silently toward the other woman. Mallory could relate. Well-meaning people had reacted the same way to her back in the day, through a parade of cramped, colorless shelters. They'd talked about her and her mother, they'd talked around them as if she couldn't hear or understand just how tragic everyone thought her life was.

It hadn't taken Mallory long to realize the difference between what people pandered to her face and the things they whispered to one another. Once she had, she'd never again trusted adults' smiles and assurances that they were her friends. They'd been lying when they talked about things getting better. And the worst part had been how much they'd needed *her* to drink down the BS they were spouting, so they could feel better themselves.

It was exactly the kind of crap she'd made it a point as an adult never to dish out to children. It was precisely why even now she took whatever people said with a grain of salt.

Mallory saw the same kind of cynicism shimmering in the eyes of the little girl huddled in the corner, as distant from everyone else as Polly could get. Mallory was fine with her staying out of the way of the sick kids and the volunteers who were regularly checking temperatures and offering patients watered-down fruit juice. She *wasn't* fine with anyone putting pressure on the kid to do or feel or be anything she wasn't ready to be. Especially not after what Polly had said to her in the bus lane.

I want to forget my mommy, so I can stop making everyone so sad...

"Mr. Lombard is fighting to make a new start for his family," Mallory said loudly enough to reach Polly.

Last night her confidence in the man's determination to help his daughter had grown exponentially. If Mimosa Lane's resident expert on everything wanted to gossip about the Lombard family, let her natter on about that.

"The man clearly needs help." Julia bent to pull a blanket up over one of the sleeping kids, patting the little boy's back and smiling a motherly smile that softened a bit of Mallory's impatience. "There are so many families from the neighborhood who've tried to be there for them both, but he won't hear of it. He's always been so quiet and controlled. Friendly, but in a standoffish way. Emma was the social butterfly who made sure they kept in the flow of everything and that Polly had all the wonderful things a community like ours can give a child. That's up to her daddy now, and the man seems more resistant by the day to any efforts to give him a hand. They're doing fine, he keeps saying. He's doing just fine."

"They're grieving." Mallory looked pointedly at Polly, a less-than-subtle hint that Julia should at least lower her voice. "He's protecting his child from even more upset."

"They're drowning before our eyes." The well-meaning woman's exasperation made her sound like an insufferable ass. "No one's trying to upset either of them. You just moved in, so it might not be as clear to you—"

"Half of *them* is listening to every word you say about her father." The hell with being subtle. "What's *clear* is that it's not a good idea to—"

"Ms. Phillips?" Tiny fingers wrapped around the fist Mallory had clenched at her side. Polly was standing beside them, tears streaming down her face. "I want to go home."

Julia knelt down before Mallory found her voice. She gazed into Polly's bottomless eyes, her heavily made-up face softening with pity, making Mallory cringe.

"How are you feeling, sweetie? Are you having a bad day?" Julia smiled, her voice pitched in that patronizing timber that well-mannered kids in the South were trained from birth to endure even though it made you want to hurl.

Polly shied away from Mimosa Lane's self-appointed matriarch. Her nails dug into Mallory's hand.

"She—" Mallory tried to say.

"Misses her daddy?" Julia reached to cup Polly's face, which Polly promptly hid as she shrank against Mallory's side. "He works a lot, doesn't he, honey? Being a single parent is so hard these days. Why don't I take you home and get you some lunch? I've got the rest of the day off since my office hours are over. I'm sure Ms. Phillips can manage better without us here distracting her. Maybe we can stop for some ice cream on the way and have a nice talk outside in the pretty sunshine…"

Polly shook her head, her silent tears wetting Mallory's scrubs. She was clinging like a monkey, her arms wrapped around Mallory's waist when she'd never before that morning so much as held Mallory's hand.

Polly's struggles felt so close, so mixed up in the avalanche of personal memories pressing down on Mallory, it made her want to push the little girl away and pretend she wasn't walking the same fine line. But Mallory wasn't budging, not now. Not like this. She waited until Julia's gaze rose from where the woman still knelt in front of Polly.

"The school has nothing in their records designating you as an alternative guardian to pick Polly up," Mallory pointed out.

"I've known the Lombards since they moved into the neighborhood." Julia rose to her full height. A smattering of annoyance peppered her tolerant expression. She reached a reassuring hand toward Mallory as if they were fast friends themselves and by simple touch could unite their conflicting viewpoints. When Mallory shied away just like Polly, Julia said, "Emma and I were close long before Polly was born. We walked together every afternoon at sundown, even after she got sick. I'm sure she'd approve of me—"

"Her husband's approval is the one the school has to be concerned with." Mallory could have kicked her neighbor for being so completely oblivious to how her words and actions were hurting the very child they were supposed to be helping.

"Pete's not ready to make those kinds of decisions," Julia argued, "or he wouldn't have let things become so precarious with Polly while he pushed everyone else away."

"He's dealing with circumstances I'm sure none of us can fathom. He's taking care of his daughter the best he can."

"And he's failing, because he thinks he has to do it on his own. All the more reason for the community to come together to help him. It's time to move on, to start over, and he's not—"

"My daddy doesn't need anyone's damn help!" Polly shrieked, confirming Mallory's suspicions that she'd been eavesdropping last night when Pete had yelled the exact same thing near the kitchen door. Polly glared up at Julia, her tears making her little girl rage all the more magnificent. "Why can't you all just leave us alone? You're so stupid. You don't know anything! We don't want your help. Why don't you just leave us alone?"

"Sweetheart." Julia knelt again. "Your mommy and I—"

"My mommy hated you! I hate you. All of you…" Polly was a ball of motion and energy, hurtling toward her neighbor, pushing Julia away as she screamed, "Why won't you go 'way and stop butting in and making everything worse, talking about me and my daddy and my mommy? I hate you. HATE you. HATE YOU!"

Julia stumbled backward, at a loss for words about five minutes too late.

Mallory grabbed for Polly, the bustling activity of the other adults around them coming to an abrupt, silent halt as if someone had hit a mute button. She picked up the child. Polly continued to scream and kick and struggle, all the while clinging to Mallory, making a scene everyone on the first floor of the school could no doubt hear.

"Oh dear." Julia covered her mouth with her hand. "I'm so sorry."

Mallory just bet she was.

She could have told Julia that Polly's outburst had likely been inevitable given the emotions that had been building inside her since last night—since her mother's death. But the other woman and her idea of what community should look like were finally backing off, so Mallory ignored her and rocked the wailing child in her arms, wishing she could join Polly and vent a little herself.

Her phone rang before she could figure out what to say to the adults staring at the two of them. She pressed the intercom to answer the call hands-free.

"Chandler Elementary Clinic," she barked.

"This is Pete Lombard." Polly's sobs and her nonstop *I hate yous* raged on. "Is that my daughter? What the hell's happened?"

Mallory sat in her chair, settled Polly into her lap as best she could, and picked up the receiver.

"Can you stop by the school, Pe—Mr. Lombard?" He wasn't *Pete*. Not while she was at work. "Polly's okay, but she's had a bit of an episode. The clinic is slammed with sick kids today, and we're pretty sure it's the flu. The sooner you could get here, the better."

"We're about to transport a patient. It'll probably be another hour before I can break away."

The strain in his voice was heartbreaking. He'd missed a lot of work picking Polly up early from school, several afternoons a week at least when she was having a particularly hard time. And Kristen had said he'd formally requested since his wife's death not to work night shifts, which must be causing waves with his coworkers. Yet he'd always come for Polly as soon as he possibly could.

Mallory wanted to tell Julia just that. And about how lost he'd sounded last night as he'd grudgingly accepted Mallory's help, this man who clearly didn't know how to fail. Yes, he might be misguided about a lot of things, but he was fighting with all of his might to save his child. He didn't need the community Julia Davis seemed to think was a cure-all judging his every move.

She glanced at Julia while he said, "If I weren't already on-scene, I'd come right now. But—"

"We really can't wait this time." Mallory wished she could take their conversation somewhere private or do something more herself. "I've never seen her so agitated."

"Da...Daddy?" Polly's body shuddered with a stream of hiccupping breaths that were just as disturbing as her uncharacteristic shouts had been. "Daddy..." She began coughing on her own tears, her crying escalating again.

"Shit..." Pete whispered into the phone.

The sirens of one of the rescue vehicles working the emergency scene shrieked over the connection. The man was protecting and caring for the citizens of Chandlerville. Meanwhile being the single parent of a traumatized child was ripping his private life to pieces.

Julia was right about one thing. He absolutely couldn't keep doing this alone, not if he really wanted to give Polly the support she needed. And he'd listened to reason last night, back when

Mallory had thought she was done inflicting her own warped perspective on his decisions for his daughter. Getting more involved would mean challenging all their comfort zones even further. But could she really walk away from what might happen to the little girl in her arms if she refused to try?

Her gaze locked with Julia's. The reality behind the other woman's nosiness united them in a startling moment of clarity. The Lombard family was falling apart. They needed whatever help they could get. And right now Mallory was the only person Polly seemed to trust.

"I'll take her home with me for the afternoon," she heard herself decide out loud.

Polly needed someplace quiet and nonthreatening where she could process the emotion swamping her and talk through the truth behind her outburst. That was the only priority now. Kristen Hemmings would eventually agree, after the AP flipped at the prospect of losing her nurse in the midst of a medical crisis. Julia's silent nod of approval bolstered Mallory's confidence as she rode out Pete's prolonged silence.

"I'm not sure that's such a good idea," he finally said. "It sounds like you're having a busy day, and—"

"I have more than enough volunteers to take temperatures and wipe noses and call parents to come pick up their kids. I'll let the assistant principal know that I'll be back as soon as I can. She'll agree that the most important thing is for Polly to have familiar surroundings now that she's letting some of her emotions out. I know she sounds bad, and I do think you should hurry as quickly as you can. But this could be a really positive thing once you get home and talk with her. Let me help make sure she's ready for that, okay?"

Mallory's chest tightened at the feel of Polly's body softening against hers. The child's outburst was quieting. The others in the clinic, including the kids who'd sat up from their mats to see what was going on, were once again ignoring the mini-drama playing out in their midst. It might be a good time to try resettling Polly in her own chair, but Mallory couldn't imagine letting the little girl go.

The rest of the school day would be a circus for the staff. But Kristen had excellent procedures in her files for dealing with sickness and dispensing whatever meds a child was allowed to take. Teachers as well as administrators were approved to follow the same steps Mallory would. And *this* was an emergency—a chance to make a very real difference in one of their students' lives.

Polly curled into a tighter ball in Mallory's arms.

"Trust me," Mallory said to the child's father, feeling more than a little panicky at the thought of him refusing.

"I do trust you," Pete said.

"Get to my place as soon as you can, then. We'll be waiting for you."

She hung up, suddenly terrified.

What was she doing?

"I'll be back as soon as possible," she told her neighbor. Before she could talk herself out of it she stood and grabbed her tote from the drawer and headed for the door, lugging Polly's limp weight with her the way she'd clearly have to all the way to the office to sign out and let her boss know she was bailing on at least the rest of the morning.

She turned back, her former supervisor's warning echoing through her mind.

If you don't stop overidentifying with your cases, you're going to eventually wreck more than your career…

"Don't worry about a thing." Julia winked and picked up the clipboard Mallory had been using to track kids' temperatures and parents' estimates on when they'd arrive for their children. "Take care of that precious bundle in your arms. We'll be fine here. I'll make sure Ms. Hemmings understands that. We go way back. Don't worry about taking the whole afternoon off if you need to. I can stay as long as Kristen needs me."

Mallory hesitated at the whiff of genuine inclusion in the other woman's reassurance.

"Thank you," Mallory mumbled, walking away.

It was irritating, confusing, how she was even more agitated than she'd been when she'd woken up that morning. In the space of less than a day her simple if floundering new beginning had expanded to make room for a traumatized little girl, a harried single father, and a meddlesome neighbor who was now a coconspirator in Mallory's entrenching herself even deeper in the Lombards' problems.

Let me help you…

What on earth had she gotten herself into?

***

Mallory's door opened, startling Pete with how quickly she'd responded to him ringing the bell.

"Polly's settled," she said, sounding relieved. "She's much calmer."

She was dressed in yellow scrubs with cartoon birds all over them. He felt himself smile. Some of the tension that had hounded him all the way home eased. The same thing had happened last night once he'd calmed down enough to see how concerned she was for his child. Speaking with Mallory, letting the truth in her words soak in when he'd resisted advice from so many other people, had been the first nonthreatening experience he could remember since hearing his wife's terminal diagnosis.

The fact that Mallory looked just as cute in her boxy work clothes as she had in her clingy pajamas had the same effect as last night, too. She was evidently just the distracting enigma his body needed after all these months to decide it wanted to feel close to a woman again.

"Is it a nurse thing?" he had to ask.

"Excuse me?"

"The make-believe theme. The animated characters and the rainbow-bright colors all over the place, even at home. You're as addicted to them as Polly."

"A girl needs something to make her smile now and then." The curve of her lips was one shade shy of saucy, but the careless laugh she gave him didn't make it all the way to her eyes.

"I'm sorry we're being so much trouble." He found himself wishing he'd made the time to get to know her better, so every conversation they'd had wouldn't have been about Polly.

"It's no trouble, really," she lied.

He'd sensed her hesitation over the phone. He'd expected her to relent as soon as he'd said he didn't expect her to inconvenience herself. Instead, she'd offered to take his child home.

"Polly's in the kitchen." She stepped sideways to allow him entry. "She's eating a tuna fish sandwich." Her smile turned impish. "I was thinking about Pixy Stix and Pop-Tarts. But you've had a busy morning saving the masses, so I cut your nerves some slack."

Polly was eating honest-to-God protein? "Any chance this visit isn't going to end with you raking me over the coals again?"

"I'm not that charitable."

"Is it just me you enjoy giving hell to, or is this another charming facet of your disposition that you insist defies understanding?"

"Don't take it personally." This time her laugh sounded more like an apology. "I'm a smart-ass with most everyone."

"You're…" It came to him from out of nowhere—exactly what he needed to say in case this was her last grand gesture before backing away from his family for good. He couldn't let that happen without clearing the air. "You're really something, to be taking such a personal interest in Polly. I don't know how I'll ever repay you."

Mallory swallowed whatever quip she'd been about to say next. "Did you realize she was still so upset this morning?"

He stepped into her house, their bodies brushing. It wasn't much. It was nothing at all. But the instant connection was disturbing, at least to him, memorable in a way that he knew would be haunting him later that night while he stared across their backyards at her ridiculous tree the way he had until dawn that morning.

She closed the door and struck off across the oversized family room toward the kitchen.

"I wanted her to stay home." He followed until they stopped in the empty dining area. He was struck again by the sparseness of her furnishings. The minimalist decor didn't match either the boldness of her personality or her rainbow-bright kitchen. "I tried to change Polly's mind about going to school. I was ready to call in sick, but she insisted she was okay. That she had to go. She's been so skittish at the bus stop all fall. I thought it was a good sign that she was eager for this week to start."

They were standing near her swinging kitchen door, a replay of their midnight encounter. Except in the daylight, with the sun falling over them through her uncovered windows, Mallory's features looked even softer, more inviting, her complexion almost translucent in that rare way some fair-skinned women had of making a man want to touch them to be certain they were real.

"Polly came to school to see me, I think." Mallory picked up his hand and placed something cool and shiny in it.

His body tensed at her touch, his senses clamoring. It took several seconds for him to realize what she'd handed him. Her fingers slid away. He stared down at the sparkling object and froze from the inside out.

"Where did you get this?" he managed to ask.

Mallory flinched at the harshness of his voice, but she stood her ground the same as she had when she'd faced down his anger last night.

"It belonged to your wife," she said. "Didn't it?"

"Where did you get this?" he demanded again, his hand shaking. "I haven't seen it since before Emma…"

He couldn't finish the sentence.

For six months, he hadn't been able to utter the words.

Mallory didn't rush to cover the uncomfortable pause that followed, the way others would have. It settled easily between them, the overwhelming grief and the silence most people who knew him couldn't tolerate. He exhaled into that void, feeling as if he'd been holding his breath forever.

Last night he'd been furious at the way Mallory's questions kept triggering memories of his wife. It felt almost natural now, standing there beside his neighbor with his heart pounding and disjointed pieces of his life flashing across his mind's eye like an out-of-control slide show. Him. Emma. Polly. All of them happy. Then sad. Then broken in ways that might never mend.

Mallory didn't smile or tell him it would be okay. But she didn't back away either, her quiet acceptance helping him weather the wave of emotions sucking him down. Just as her calm, in-control demeanor on the other end of the phone earlier had helped him make the decision about work that he should have come to weeks ago. It was as if when he was with her, talking with her like he hadn't with anyone else on Mimosa Lane, he could see his life clearly for the first time since everything fell apart.

She waited as if she knew for certain that his next strangling breath would come, and then the next. He inhaled, filling his constricted lungs, then let the breath out so loudly his ears rang with his battle to regain control. He nodded, hoping she'd understand it was an apology he couldn't put into words.

"Polly gave that to me at school," she finally said. "Before she ran inside from the bus lane, she handed it to me and told me she wanted to forget her mom so you two could have Christmas this year."

She didn't ask about the vintage pin in Pete's hand. She evidently wasn't going to, not this elusive, complicated woman whom his child was opening up to. Pete looked down at the tiny metal cat he held. It was only a piece of costume jewelry, but it was a treasure. Fashioned out of gilded brass or bronze, its gold finish was worn around the edges, darker metal peeking through from beneath. Its eyes, red dots, were fashioned from paste. Its black nose was a sweep of some type of composite. Tiny wire whiskers were bent in several directions at once, giving the creature a slightly maniacal expression.

Emma had worn it every chance she got, gladly sharing the priceless story behind how she'd inherited it from her grandmother with whomever noticed it and asked where she'd gotten such a unique piece. She'd cherished it and all her antique pins for as long as Pete had known her, accessorizing with them in her own whimsical style. She'd begun passing them to Polly almost from birth, eventually hoping they'd become a way to keep the two of them connected even after she was gone.

"My wife was allergic to animal hair, all kinds of it." He remembered like it was yesterday the way her eyes had swollen practically shut not long after he and Emma had begun going steady in junior high, after she'd petted the new puppy his parents had brought home. "She desperately wanted a cat but could never have one. Her mom and dad would get furious when she wasn't able to keep her hands off some creature she passed on the street. It made her sick every time, but that never stopped her. Her grandmother had a million trinkets like this, all kinds of animals. Every holiday and birthday a pretty box from her nana would show up under the tree with Emma's name on it. Inside was a beautiful animal that Emma could wear. When Caroline ran out of her own jewelry, she and Emma scoured flea markets and garage sales looking for more. When we were sixteen, Emma's nana died the week before Christmas, and Emma's mother found one final present in Caroline's bedside drawer, wrapped in holiday paper and tied with a big red bow—it was this little guy."

"He must have been very special to her." Mallory's smile was as sad as it was wistful.

"She treasured her collection. This one pin especially. It made her feel like her nana would always be thinking of her, spoiling her, making sure she had whatever she needed to be happy. Emma told Polly the story so many times, every holiday and celebration when she'd give another piece of her nana's jewelry to our daughter. Once we accepted how sick Emma was, she started inventing everyday reasons to give even more of them to Polly. They'd sit together for hours sifting through the ones in Polly's jewelry box, and the ones still in Emma's. This cat was supposed to stay with Emma. She wore it every trip to hospital. In the end…She liked having it pinned to her nightgown or her robe, especially when company came over for a visit. Of all the jewelry she owned, this was her most prized possession."

"She was giving Polly a piece of her heart to keep always."

There were tears in Mallory's eyes when Pete came back from the past. Instead of pity, which was all his friends seemed to feel these days when they looked at him and Polly, in Mallory's gaze he saw longing.

"I looked for it after…" He cleared the lump that had risen in his throat, holding the pin higher so that it twinkled as brightly as Mallory's tree. "I wanted Emma to wear it when we buried her. But I never found it. I guess I should have known Polly had taken it, that she wouldn't want to let it go. But I haven't seen her go anywhere near her mother's things since Emma died. I don't even know where her own jewelry box is. It's disappeared, too."

"Like Polly disappeared when she came here last night?"

His gaze narrowed at the odd correlation. "Why would Polly give this to you now?" he asked. "What did she mean about forgetting her mother?"

"I don't know." Mallory's expression clouded up, striking him again with how much this seemed to be affecting her personally. "She seemed almost panicked when she got off the bus and ran over to me. I was surprised to see her smiling. She handed me the pin, and her words rushed out as if she'd been waiting all night to say them. She seemed so sure that I would help her."

"Help her forget Emma?" Pete's knees threatened to buckle.

"I know how that sounds. But at least she's talking about her mother. Has she done that before now?"

"Neither of us has," he said. He'd give anything not to be talking about it even now. "Nothing I say helps. It only seems to do more harm. The doctors recommend keeping things positive and trying not to upset her until she settles down."

Mallory's nod of understanding helped keep some of his guilt at bay. She'd mastered the same calm detachment as the fire and rescue professionals he worked with. He got the sense that no matter how difficult an obstacle, this woman simply faced it—or more likely climbed over it to get to whatever she wanted on the other side.

"Something you said last night has been on my mind all day," he admitted.

"If I was out of line, I—"

He silenced her with his finger, pressing just the tip of it against her lips. He dropped his hand when her words stuttered to a stop.

"You were right"—he grinned at the smirk of triumph that blossomed on her face—"about how I've been messing up at bedtime. Instead of listening to Polly when she gets agitated and can't sleep, I've been pushing her to get better. I've *needed* her to get better so I could stop worrying about her. She's changed so completely, and I want my little girl back. I haven't been listening to her at all, not the way you do."

"Because I'm not dealing with the same loss," Mallory said in a near whisper. "Don't be so hard on yourself. She needs you to want her the way she is now, that's all. You'll figure out how. You already are. Just keep fighting for her, and you'll make it. I promise."

"I asked for an extended leave of absence from work," he admitted. "I should have made Polly my only focus before now. I'd convinced myself that keeping to our regular routine was best. But I...needed the work, I think. It's an escape, and I wasn't ready to surrender that, too."

"Is...?" Mallory's brow wrinkled. "Can you afford to...?"

"How can I afford not to?" And his captain had said to take all the time he needed. "My daughter wants to forget the mother who loved Polly more than her own life."

"She has to be ashamed of how she's feeling," Mallory said, gutting him all over again. "Whatever is going on, don't let her think you disapprove of anything she says or feels. She has to figure this out, not worry about how it's affecting you. Has she seen a therapist?"

"Her reaction when we tried was similar to what I heard over the phone this morning." They'd gone twice, before the therapist had agreed that Polly wasn't ready to talk. They needed to give it a little more time. That had been at the beginning of the summer, and Pete hadn't bothered to schedule a follow-up visit. "Do you really think she's been trying to erase Emma from her mind all this time? Thanksgiving with Emma's parents was impossible for her. Emma was all anyone was talking about. Her parents want to be sure Polly doesn't forget her mother."

"It's not that unusual a reaction for a child her age. Kids read others' emotions in a very personal way. They feel responsible for things they shouldn't, including making their parents feel better. There's something about you mixed up in all of this, not just her mother."

"Me?"

"Why else would she think she had to forget Emma so the two of you could have your Christmas? She loves you so much. You should have heard her yelling at Julia Davis when the woman criticized you. She's scared and angry. Finally letting some of that out is a good thing. But it's easier just to wish ugly feelings away, instead of dealing with what's causing them. Neither of you can afford to let that happen."

"Yeah." He rubbed a hand over his face, dreading the conversation he'd have to have with Julia eventually.

"You can't let Polly think she has to keep everything inside and give her mother's things away in order to be okay. She has to need what she needs and trust the people around her to help her."

"She trusts you," he pointed out. And last night he'd despised her for it.

Somehow she understood his daughter's trauma infinitely better than Pete did. He gazed at her crazy Christmas tree, then around what he'd assumed was a carelessly unfurnished home. He found himself wondering at the real meaning behind the way his neighbor chose to live her life.

"I'm not as vital to your daughter's sense of well-being as you are," Mallory said.

"I'm not so sure about that."

"You're everything for her, Pete. You're all she has left. Dealing with losing her mother, especially if she's wondering if she's somehow upsetting you by how she feels, must be overwhelming. It can make a kid do and think all sorts of things. Her coming to me first with this isn't a sign that she doesn't need you or that you're not doing everything you can to help her. It's a symptom of how much Polly's entire world is wrapped up in the two of you being okay."

"It's a sign that you can give her something she isn't getting at home." He fought back another surge of petty jealousy.

She shook her head as if she weren't going to respond. She was looking over his shoulder in the direction of her tree, only her gaze seemed much farther away.

"I've just listened until you two found each other again," she said. "Until she was ready to start figuring out what she really wants. She's found a way to be brave enough to do that now. She had to know on some level that I'd call you." Mallory gestured absently at his hand and Emma's pin. "This was her cry for help. All you have to do is take it from here. Don't try to fix Polly's feelings. For now just listen to them and help her understand what's happening."

Without Mallory, she seemed to mean.

Pete experienced a moment of panic at the idea of once again dealing with his child alone. An answering look of regret crossed Mallory's face as if she wanted to keep helping them regardless of the distance her words were creating.

"Whatever happens next," she said, "know that there are adults in this world who can't face what Polly's trying to. Some people never consciously work through the kind of trauma a child endures when she loses a parent. Be proud of her for trying. Then be there for her, no matter what, and you'll both be fine."

Her rock-solid confidence made Pete almost believe he *could* manage the rest of this on his own. It was utter bullshit—he was a medical professional who'd lost his wife to a disease that no amount of prayer or expensive treatments or holistic alternatives could defeat. He was a man who understood that the world was primarily beyond anyone's control—especially his. And he hated everyone for that reality, himself most of all.

He needed help, he accepted fully for the first time. But if this was as far as Mallory could go, if she still needed to back away as much as she seemed to last night, then he'd be forever grateful that she'd done as much as she had.

"I've pretty much been a blind bastard." It felt good to say it, and to see her easy smile of agreement. "And Polly's paying the price."

"She's an angry little girl." Mallory winced. "You could have heard her all over the school, yelling at Julia how much she hated everyone and wanted us to leave her alone."

"Even you?"

"I was holding her in my lap. I don't think she was aware of it, but she was holding on, too. She wasn't running or shoving at me or trying to get down, but she definitely didn't want to be there. Has she had a problem with Julia Davis before?"

"Julia is—was—one of Emma's best friends. Sam Perry from down the lane, too. Polly used to love both of them as if they were second mommies, and they're terribly worried about her. But she won't even look at them now. She's afraid of them, just like she is of everybody else."

"You should ask her why when the time is right. She's probably finished her snack. Any other kid would be crawling all over us by now, trying to interrupt because they're bored or feeling left out."

"She's afraid of me most of all."

It was unforgivable how he'd let Polly's grief drag on unchecked for so long. A million years could pass, and he'd never want to deal with what losing Emma had done to them. He'd promised his wife she didn't have to worry. Now he was petrified to open a door and try to pull their precious child into a hug.

"What if she still won't talk to me?" he asked.

His wife had been his entire world since he'd been little more than a boy himself. According to the well-meaning friends who'd come to her funeral and the house afterward, he'd lost her so she could go on to a better place, so he and Polly could move on from the horror of watching her suffer. He should be grateful she was finally at peace.

But how could you move on when you were the one left behind? Where was the gratitude in knowing his daughter thought she had to forget Emma so they could have Christmas? As if she knew a part of him wanted the holiday to go away, too, and leave him alone to curse every sacred thing he'd once believed in.

"She'll talk," Mallory assured him, "once she knows you're really listening."

"Wanna tell me how I'm going to convince her that I finally am?"

Mallory's touch closed over his fingers, covering Emma's vintage pin.

"I think she's already told you how."

Pete's gaze locked onto their hands. It was on the tip of his tongue to beg her to keep helping them. But something about all of this was clearly unsettling her on a personal level. She had a right to do what was best for her, while he manned up and became a better father all on his own.

If he didn't convince Polly to let him share her sadness and help it get better, he might lose her for good.

No more running.

No more hiding.

For either of them.

Chapter Six

If recollecting were forgetting,
Then I remember not;
And if forgetting, recollecting,
How near I had forgot...

M s. Phillips hadn't talked much on the way home from
school. She hadn't given Polly Mommy's pin back, so
they could pretend she hadn't said anything. She hadn't asked
Polly about what she'd said, even though Polly knew the school
nurse was probably talking to Daddy about it right now, since
Ms. Phillips had left the kitchen to answer the door and hadn't
come back yet and it had been a really long time.

She hadn't said she'd help Polly forget, either, even though
she'd brought Polly home with her. Maybe what she was telling
Daddy was that Polly wasn't going to be able to visit her anymore,
at home to see her tree or at the clinic.

Polly drank another gulp of milk from a glass with some
blue cartoon character on it. Ms. Phillips had smiled when she'd
given it to Polly, like she really believed this was all going to
be okay. Except as Polly rubbed her finger over the blue guy's

white beard and droopy red hat, she could hear the grown-ups talking. They were closer now, on the other side of the kitchen door, maybe, but keeping their voices down so she wouldn't hear them.

Her stomach was starting to burn. And she suddenly wanted to throw the happy little smiling man glass across the room so when Daddy got to the kitchen he would talk about the mess she'd made with her milk and her crying at school and yelling at Mrs. Davis, and not about how Polly had said out loud what she never should have said at all.

She'd thought for sure Ms. Phillips would understand. Only Polly hadn't asked right, and she hadn't been able to stay and hear what the school nurse said, and then there'd been so many people in the clinic, and…

She took another bite of the sandwich Ms. Phillips had made her, just as the door swung open and Daddy was standing there, Ms. Phillips right behind him. He looked so upset, the way he never was before Mommy got sick. Bread and tuna wadded in Polly's throat, choking her. She fumbled for her drink. It slipped through her fingers and crashed into shards of milk and glass on Ms. Phillips's white floor.

The tears were coming again, the ones Daddy couldn't stand and only Mommy had known how to stop. The really scary ones, not like when Polly was fake crying because she wanted something she'd been told she couldn't have or had gotten into trouble or was mad.

These were the ugly tears she hated, pouring out of her eyes and down her cheeks. Feeling them was like being in the middle of a bad dream she couldn't wake up from, like watching Mommy go away. They hurt so much, but they were always there, and they never stayed inside anymore no matter how hard she tried to make them. She was choking on them now, on her food and the thought of Christmas getting closer and it being awful.

Then suddenly Daddy's arms were around her, holding her, squeezing—and somehow his hug didn't make her feel so alone this time. Because while Ms. Phillips cleaned up the glass and the milk he wasn't telling Polly *shhhh*. Or fake smiling and saying it was okay because he needed her to believe it was. Or wiping away her tears wishing she'd make herself stop. He was holding on, like Mommy used to, like he used to hold Mommy when they didn't think Polly was watching. Like she was the most important thing no matter what, and he'd never let go.

He smelled so good, felt so good, so much like before, Polly's tears got worse. She wanted him to tell her she could just cry and stop pretending. She wanted to feel Daddy holding her back and crying, too, like he had that night, the night he'd said Mommy was gone forever.

After that night he'd never just let her cry and keep crying the way Mommy had let her so many times in the end. Not until today. Only he had to stop. He had to turn Polly loose now or she was going to mess things up even more.

"Let me go." She pushed him away, thinking about that last night and how she'd missed Mommy every day since and how it was never going to be the same. "Let me go, Daddy."

She was kicking, screaming the words, shoving at him like a baby, like a bratty baby the way she had at school when Mrs. Davis had wanted to be nice, but her *It's okay* smile made Polly remember how Mrs. Davis and her mommy used to laugh and smile for real. The way Mommy and Daddy used to laugh and smile and tickle each other and Polly, too.

"Go away," she begged her memories while Daddy knelt there next to her, staring at her, and still he didn't say anything.

His face wasn't fake smiling at all. It was just what she'd thought she'd wanted. It was Daddy, feeling just like she was instead of what he wanted her to be. But now that he was, it was awful, and she was the one who wanted to pretend. She was the one who wanted him to stop, needed him to stop.

She flew to Ms. Phillips, afraid instead of happy. She felt confused instead of safe. She felt alone, even though Daddy was there being a real daddy again and wanting her just the way she was, messing up and all.

Her neighbor caught Polly and held her, kneeling beside the table and Daddy, too, rocking Polly and somehow making it feel good and easy to be in her arms because there were no memories there. There was just the great way she always smelled, like chocolate and cotton candy, that wasn't like anyone Polly had ever met before. It always made her want to smile, even when she couldn't do anything but cry.

"I don't want to," Polly heard herself saying, over and over again. "I don't want to. I can't. Tell him I can't. It'll ruin everything…"

Remembering made everything awful, and not just because of other people. *She* didn't want to remember. Polly didn't want to ever remember anymore if it was going to feel like this. She wanted all the awful things to go away so all the good things would come back, and if she remembered that would never happen.

"You can't what?" Daddy was beside them sounding like he'd been crying just like Polly, though he never cried. Not once. Not since that awful night Polly wanted to forget most of all. "I'm right here, Polly. You can tell me yourself, and I'll listen this time. I promise. We have to start talking again. About all of it. No matter how much it hurts. Talking, not forgetting, is the only way Christmas and everything else are going to get better. There's nothing you can't say to me, sweet pea."

That name. The one she hadn't heard in forever. *Sweet pea.* It made her remember so much more. It was what he'd called her every night before, when he and Mommy tucked her into bed. She didn't want him to call her that now. Hearing it made her tears worse. But she wanted him to say it again, too. Over and over again. It felt so good inside, like hugs and Christmas and her grandparents and school and the other kids and even Mrs. Davis used to feel good.

It felt like Mommy was there with them when he said it, hearing him call Polly the name only he called her, which was making her nickname feel awful now just like everything else. Because Mommy *wasn't* there. She would never be there again.

"I can't." Polly peeked from where she was crying all over Ms. Phillips's nurse clothes from school. "I can't remember…It hurts. I don't want it to hurt anymore. I don't want to remember…"

"You don't want to remember your mommy?" Daddy sounded as bad as Polly felt.

He was so strong. He saved people every day. And when he'd used to pull the covers up under her chin at night, Polly used to believe he was a prince, her and her mommy's prince, who'd never let anyone hurt his princesses, not ever. But the cancer had hurt Mommy anyway, and she'd gone away, and so had the old Daddy as if he didn't know how to save anything anymore. Only now he was saying they had to remember to get better.

He reached for her hand, uncurling it from where she was holding on to Ms. Phillips's. Polly tried to jerk away, thinking he was going to pull her back into his arms. Instead he was giving her something cool and smooth and familiar. Then he let her go.

"Whiskers," Polly whispered, looking down at her mommy's favorite pin and remembering every single time Mommy had worn it, and how Daddy had always teased her, and how easy it had been back then to be with him and Mommy and everybody.

"Your mommy always wanted a cat named Whiskers," he said. "I'm sorry it's been so long since we've talked about her, sweet pea. I never meant for you to think that you shouldn't."

He covered Polly's hand, reaching around Ms. Phillips to do it, like they were both holding her. And somehow it didn't hurt so much, not like when he'd hugged her before. It felt tingly and warm like it used to.

"She always wished you could have had a pet," he said. "She knew how much you wanted one. A cat more than anything. She told me how you loved this pin the most. She talked all the time about getting you a kitty of your own, no matter how much it would make her sneeze."

Polly shook her head, not wanting to hear but not wanting Daddy to stop talking, either, like Mommy could still be there with them somehow and it didn't have to hurt.

"Ms. Phillips tells me you were pretty mad at the clinic," Daddy said. "That you were upset with Mrs. Davis. But Mrs. Davis isn't who you're really mad at, is it?"

Polly buried her head against Ms. Phillips's shoulder.

Ms. Phillips had given Whiskers to Daddy like she didn't want to help. But she was holding tight to Polly now. The walls of her pretty kitchen were too close, and Polly couldn't hear anything but the ringing in her ears and the empty sound of everything she didn't want to think and feel. But she didn't want to be anywhere else, either. Her neighbor felt so good. She felt like the last time Polly had cuddled with Mommy and believed it was all going to be okay.

"I get so mad sometimes," Daddy was saying, "I can't hear anything else. I hate the world and everyone and everything in it, because Mommy's gone. But I don't want to let anyone else see how much. And that makes me do things I wish later that I hadn't done. It makes me want to say I'm sorry to all the people I'm hurting when I'm so mad. Especially you, sweet pea. I'm so sorry I haven't made things better for you."

Polly was sorry, too, even though she couldn't say it. All she could do was hold on while Daddy talked.

"Is that why you asked me to help you forget your mommy?" Ms. Phillips asked. "Because you're feeling things you don't think you should? And you're scared to let it out like you did today, because of what people will say and think and what it will do to things like Christmas?"

Polly kept shaking her head, trying to make the words go away. Because she *was* mad, just like Daddy. She was so mad she wanted to scream at Ms. Phillips like she had at Mrs. Davis. Only it wasn't the school nurse or their neighbor or the other kids at school or even Daddy who she was mad at most.

It was Mommy.

She had to stop remembering Mommy, because she hated her most of all for going away—and herself and the stupid pin she was squeezing too hard right now so her hand would hurt instead of the awful things inside her. She wanted to throw Whiskers across the room. She wanted to throw all her favorite memories away forever.

"I get so mad sometimes…" Daddy's voice sounded like he was choking on Polly's sandwich. He sounded like he had when he'd told Polly that Mommy was gone. "Because…It hurts. Everything hurts, and I didn't want you to know, Polly. I wanted you to get better, and I was worried you wouldn't if I didn't get better first. So I tried to forget what's making me hurt and mad, only I shouldn't have. I never should have made you think you had to do that, too."

Polly clutched Mommy's pin even tighter. Or was it Daddy's fingers pressing around hers that were tighter? Or Ms. Phillips's arms squeezing Polly closer? Or Daddy's arms wrapping around them both so he could hold Polly, too? It felt so good, even with the memories coming so fast now.

"I know I've let you down," he said. "I know I'm not helping enough. But please don't think you have to give Mommy up to make me or anyone else happy. You should never have to let go of anything that you remember about her."

"Don't want to remember anymore!" Polly screamed, holding tighter to all the arms around her, and pushing them away harder, and curling closer to Ms. Phillips and away from Daddy while she secretly hoped he'd never let her go ever again. Everything was swirling so fast in her mind. "Don't want bedtime stories or dinner or playtime or her dumb, stupid jewelry or *anything*. I just want to forget it all so Christmas will be better. I hate it. I hate her. She ruined everything, and now everything's broken and messed up and I don't want to remember any of it ever again!"

She went to throw the pin, Mommy's favorite thing in the whole world. But the hand holding Polly's stopped her.

"What if you don't have to remember for a while?" Ms. Phillips said. "But you don't have to throw your mom's things away, either? You don't have to hate her, Polly, to let go for as long as you need to. I'll hold on to Whiskers and any other memory you don't want for as long as you and your Daddy need me to. But you don't have to give any of it up, sweetie. You can be as mad and angry as you need to be, for as long as you need to be, until you can remember all the things about your mommy that you loved—until thinking about her feels good again. It'll all be waiting here for you when you want it back…"

Polly stopped struggling, stopped crying, stopped everything.

She looked up at her neighbor, with her kitchen full of magical colors all around them, and stared. Because Ms. Phillips was saying exactly what Polly had wanted all along, deep inside. What she hadn't known how to say, but Ms. Phillips had understood anyway.

Polly hated feeling like she hated her mommy. 'Cause she really didn't. She really didn't want to forget her, either. She just wanted it to stop hurting, and she wanted Daddy and everyone else to treat her normal again, and act normal again, and she wanted Christmas most of all, like she'd have had Christmas if Mommy hadn't died.

"I'll keep it all safe." Ms. Phillips took the pin and winked, even though she looked sad, too. "You can leave anything here you need to. I have tons of room. It's—"

"Are you sure you want to do that?" Daddy pulled Polly a little closer. "You've already done so much."

Something inside Polly screamed. Something so soft, so hopeful, she was afraid to let it out. She'd die if Ms. Phillips took back what she'd said.

"It's not an imposition," Ms. Phillips said, whatever *imposition* meant. She was looking down at Polly and then at Whiskers and smiling, like helping them was making her feel better, too.

"You left work early today," Daddy said, "because I haven't been around enough to help my little girl." He hugged Polly. "I'm going to be here from now on, for as long as it takes. Today won't happen again, whatever I have to arrange at work to make sure I'm here for Polly."

"My office was the last place I wanted to be today," Ms. Phillips said. "Really, coming home early was a treat."

"We kept you up late last night."

"I don't sleep that much..."

"Well that definitely makes you perfect for us, since Polly and I have practically turned into creatures of the night."

Polly giggled at her daddy's silliness, and so did Ms. Phillips. And Daddy was smiling now instead of frowning.

"How about if Polly helps me out around here with some things I've had piling up?" Ms. Phillips said. "Would that make you feel better about her coming over when she thinks she needs to?"

Polly held her breath, holding as still as she could. *Please let Daddy say yes. Please...*

"It might make things easier," Ms. Phillips said. "She'd have a break, and then going home would feel better than both of you staying cooped up together all the time."

Polly looked at how Ms. Phillips was holding on to Whiskers so easy, like it was no big deal. "Please?" she begged, turning to face her daddy. "Can I? Please?"

"Polly..."

He was going to say no again. She could tell. But then he was reaching for her face, too. His finger rubbing her cheek the way he used to every time he'd called her a princess at bedtime. Only now he was wiping away the tears, and he hadn't asked her to stop crying.

"Please, Daddy? I'll be a good girl, I promise. I won't cry or anything."

"Sweet pea," he said. "Even if it's okay with Ms. Phillips, you're so tired when you get home from school. You're still not feeling well, and there's dinner that you need to eat sooner than I'm sure Ms. Phillips eats at night, and—"

"She can eat here," Ms. Phillips whispered, as if her voice had gotten tired or something. Then she took a deep breath and smiled a smile Polly had never seen her make before. The kind adults used when something was wrong only they didn't want you to know it. "If we're in the middle of something and she gets hungry, it won't be a problem for me to whip up a healthy snack."

"I'll eat whatever she says I should," Polly quickly promised. "I won't be any trouble at all. You'll see."

"Sure," Daddy said, "as long as whatever Ms. Phillips serves is coated in sugar."

"No, anything. Even broccoli." It was Polly's least favorite vegetable, but if broccoli meant seeing Ms. Phillips whenever she needed to and bringing over more of Mommy's things and feeling better at home without having to give Mommy up for good, that's what Polly would eat. What else could she promise to make them both see how much she wanted this? "You won't have to get me anything else for Christmas, either. I won't wish for anything at all from Santa."

"Really?" Ms. Phillips's grin was softer now and more like her real one. "We'll be fine," she said to Polly. "And I'll have slave labor for some of the work I can't get done on my own around here."

"She might be too tired after school to be much good to you as an indentured servant." Daddy looked funny at Ms. Phillips, like he used to at the puzzles he'd helped Polly work when she was little.

"Then I'll help on the weekend, too," Polly rushed to say. "I'll go to bed as early as you say on Friday night, Daddy, and help Ms. Phillips all day Saturday."

"Well...um." Ms. Phillips's weird smile was back. "Saturdays are when I go into Atlanta, and..."

"And?" Daddy asked.

He was smiling now, too, bigger than Polly had seen him smile in a long time. And his eyes looked that way they did when he was having a good time teasing one of the friends he and Mommy used to have over to the house all the time. Polly looked back and forth between the adults, more confused than ever.

Daddy wasn't saying no anymore. It was really going to happen. So why was Ms. Phillips acting so strange all of a sudden?

"What exactly do you do every weekend?" Daddy asked, his hand rubbing Polly's back, causing her to lean even closer because it felt so good. "No one around here has a clue where you disappear to between sunup Saturday and sunset on Sunday. Why is that?"

***

"I..."

Mallory had to be out of her mind.

Pete had already taken leave from his job. He was reconnecting more with his child with each passing second. The Lombards were going to be fine, even though Polly's determination to escape her grief by obsessing about saving Christmas would take more than today to sort itself out. Pete had practically given Mallory his blessing to back away gracefully.

Except she'd stood in the dining room and heard the pain in his voice when he'd talked about Emma. And she'd felt Polly's second meltdown of the day deep inside, then had watched her excitement bloom at Mallory's impulsive suggestion that she could leave some of her worries here for a while if it would help her and her daddy sort things out.

What if you don't have to remember for a while...

Mallory stared down at Emma Lombard's pin. The metal cat glinted under the overhead light, winking at her. Her mind flashed with memories of her own mother all but throwing Mallory away, then with images of Mallory struggling each Christmas since to feel the same joy and excitement everyone else did.

Her gaze shifted to Polly's expectant smile, then her father's teasing grin. He looked like a cat himself, ready to pounce. Because he wanted to know more about the life Mallory had kept separate from Mimosa Lane for a reason. This wasn't supposed to be how her reboot worked. From now on, she was keeping the two halves of herself in separate worlds. She needed clear boundaries. There would be no more confusion about who and what she was each time she left behind the work she did away from Chandlerville.

But Polly finally wanted something Pete could give her. It was a breakthrough Mallory couldn't squash. Maybe if Pete knew the truth, he'd decide for himself that he and his daughter were better off hanging in the burbs this weekend than trailing after Mallory.

"I volunteer at several midtown assistance shelters," she said, a weight she hadn't been fully aware of releasing with the admission. "They need someone with basic medical skills. I help out as often as I can."

"All weekend?" Pete asked. "Every weekend? Is that where you were over Thanksgiving?"

"Homeless and assistance services need volunteers the most during the holidays, especially in this economy."

"What's services?" Polly asked. Her cheeks were streaked with tears, her upturned nose red and running. But she'd relaxed against her father in a beautiful way that made Mallory want to give Pete a high five.

"It's how people help people," she explained. "Except these people don't have family and friends who can step in and take care of them. So they have to depend on strangers for a while. People who'll be there for them until they can do more for themselves."

"Like you're helping me and Daddy?"

"Sort of. Except we're not strangers anymore." A reversal Mallory hadn't a clue how to deal with any more than she did the admiration that was consuming Pete's teasing grin.

"We're friends, right?" Polly blinked between Mallory and Pete, her green eyes solemn.

"Making new friends is one of the best parts of all my jobs," Mallory said, nodding her agreement. "And working with people who need the kind of help I can give them makes it seem less like work, especially this time of year."

"So when you're done helping kids at school, it makes you happy to help more people all weekend?"

Mallory pushed Polly's bangs out of her eyes, wiping at the last of the moisture on her face. "It makes me happy when people learn how to help themselves again after they've had a hard time. Lots of people go through bad things, sweetie. We all have to figure out how to come back from that. Even grown-ups can't sometimes, when things have gotten really messed up and it's the holiday and it seems like you can't deal with anything. We all do our best. But some people need a little more help than others do. Those are the people I see on the weekends."

"Then I'll help you help people have their holiday." From the look of wonder spreading across Polly's face, you'd have thought Mallory had just described a trip to Disneyland. "And then Daddy won't feel so bad about you helping us have ours. That way we'll all feel better."

"I'm not sure your dad would want you in town in the middle of the places I work in." And Mallory was certain she didn't want a family from Mimosa Lane venturing into the world she identified with far better than she did Chandlerville. "We should figure something out for after school instead. If you promise to catch up on your sleep and eat better, then I bet your daddy would rather you come over and—"

"No," Pete said. "We'll be there Saturday. Maybe I can find a way to make myself useful after everything you're doing for us. And besides, don't tell me you're actually capable of disappointing Polly, because I'm not buying it."

"I don't know…" Mallory hedged.

"I'll figure out a new meal plan," Pete reasoned, "one both Polly and her doctor can live with. We'll spend this week settling into a new routine that suits us better. By the weekend, we should be ready for a break. She can come see you anytime she wants after school, as long as it's okay with you. But give me the address, and we'll be there Saturday to pitch in for as long as you need us."

"Yes!" Polly bounced up and down in her daddy's lap, squeezing and kissing his neck. "Will they have a Christmas tree?"

Pete looked a bit startled at her rush of happy enthusiasm. Then he grabbed his daughter even closer. His chuckle was a warm, inviting vibration that rushed through Mallory, full of wonder and patience and unconditional love.

He and Polly were going to be okay. One way or another this Christmas was going to bring them the healing they deserved. And Mallory wanted to be part of that, she accepted, more than anything she'd wanted in a long time. But was she willing to expose them to a part of herself that she didn't think *she* could handle them seeing?

"If…if you're sure…" Mallory's heartbeat skipped as Pete's gaze met hers and held. His unreadable expression pulled her in deeper until she found herself wondering if she ever wanted to find her way out. Because she felt at home there, suspended in time, connected through their concern for a motherless little girl neither one of them would allow to give up.

He kissed Polly's cheek and smiled down at her, wiping out the last of Mallory's misgivings. Pete's love for his child was a drug she could find herself addicted to.

"I'm sure there will be a tree," he said. "We'll bring presents to put under it, okay? I bet there will be lots of kids wherever Mallory's going this weekend, and they're all dying to have a good Christmas, just like you."

Polly nodded her excitement, the grief that had driven today's meltdowns gone. For now there was only a father and daughter committed to a week of getting to know each other again, and now they had a Saturday adventure to look forward to. Right there in the middle of the kitchen Mallory had filled with ridiculous colors so she'd feel less lonely.

"O-okay, then," she said, agreeing to spend an entire day with a child who reminded her too much of herself at the same age and a deeply feeling man Mallory had to tear her eyes away from before she started drooling.

She took Emma's vintage pin to the Mickey Mouse cookie jar she kept on the counter by the toaster. There were no treats inside—she was never home long enough to keep snacks from going stale. But she hadn't been able to resist purchasing the chipped thing, along with a collection of Smurf juice glasses she'd found at a downtown flea market one weekend on her way home from work.

She lifted Mickey's head and carefully placed Whiskers inside, then closed the lid and patted the mouse's tubby belly. She turned back and found Polly watching her with inquisitive eyes.

"This'll be your special place," Mallory promised—committed now, regardless of the temporary insanity she'd clearly succumbed to. "Whatever you want to put in here is okay by me. I won't look unless you want me to. We won't talk about any of it until you say it's okay. You can forget whatever you put in here for as long as you need to. And I'll keep it all safe until you're ready to take your things back home."

A safe place. A place to stop running from the things that were damaging her. An open-ended place totally removed from limits and rules and conditions, where Polly couldn't shock or disappoint anyone with whatever she needed. That would be Mallory's Christmas gift to this family.

Polly and Pete could work out the rest on their own, she promised herself.

"You can come over," Pete added, "as long as Mallory's here. And as long as you knock and let her know you want to visit, and I know you'll be here. That's what big girls do. You've got to help me out here, Polly. I couldn't take it if anything happened to you. We'll figure out school and friends and what you like to eat and even Christmas. But you've got to stop running away from me. You don't have to talk about or feel anything you don't want to, I promise. But I don't want you to forget us or Mommy, either, not even if it hurts for a while. You've got to give me a chance to work through this with you. Okay? Please let me help you."

Polly nodded, her bottom lip trembling. "I'm sorry, Daddy. I didn't mean to be mean to you or Mrs. Davis or the kids at school. I just…"

"You needed someone to listen." He pulled her close. "And we're going to make sure you have that from now on." His voice caught on his promise, making Mallory want to wrap her arms protectively around them both. "Then you and I are going to help Ms. Phillips out to pay her back for being so nice, right?"

"Right." Polly stared up at her father as if he'd just slain every last one of her dragons.

Mallory knew just exactly how the kid felt.

"So we have ourselves a deal?" she asked, pushing her dangerous thoughts aside. *We…*There'd been a time when being part of a *we* would have been Mallory's dream come true. Now it felt like yet another opportunity to learn how much of an outsider she'd always be. "Let's shake on it, and then you only have to promise to do one more thing for me. I really can't handle hearing *Ms. Phillips* all the time at home. When we're here, we're friends. And my friends call me Mallory. Deal?"

"Deal!" Polly nodded and shook, her ponytails swinging beside the charming set of dimples she'd inherited from her father.

"Thank you," Pete said. He kept his tone light. But in his expression Mallory saw his silent acknowledgment of the precarious path they'd set themselves upon.

"Save your thanks for Saturday," Mallory warned. Lying to herself only made things worse for everyone. Big girls learned that as soon as they were old enough to stop believing in fairy tales. "I'm betting none of us realizes what we're getting ourselves into."

Chapter Seven

We grow accustomed to the dark,
When light is put away...

"**M**ama, we have to get some help." Mal sat next to her mama on a tattered cot in a run-down shelter, in a run-down town she didn't know the name of somewhere outside of Memphis. "You're too sick this time. The medicine's not working."

"It'll be warmer tomorrow," Mama said. Then she coughed for another minute, or maybe two, the way she'd been coughing for days. Weeks. Almost a month, actually, getting worse every day. "Then we'll head out again. I just need you to be a big girl for one more night. Don't be scared, Mal. You promised you'd stop being so scared."

It had been Thanksgiving since Mal hadn't cringed every time Mama started coughin', worrying that it would get as bad as last winter. Now it was nearly Christmas, and this year's flu was making Mal wish it were last year again. Or the year before that. Because then she'd still believe this wasn't the way it was always gonna be.

Turned out her mama hadn't wanted Mal as much as she'd wanted to keep goin'. Otherwise, they'd have found someplace to stay by now. *They wouldn't still be invisible, with nothin', in a world with no colors and no real Christmas and no home of their own.*

Mama's next cough lasted so long Mal patted her back, then rubbed it the way Grams used to. The way she'd wished Mama had rubbed her back their first year on the streets, when it had been Mal who'd felt so bad. She'd been such a baby back then—six forever years ago—dreamin' of Christmas trees and the perfect kind of holiday she'd always wanted with Grams and Papa, when hers was always gonna be cold and rainy and searching for some way, any way, to get out of the weather. Like a baby she'd thought she was gonna die that first Christmas if she didn't get what she'd wanted.

This year was their worst Christmas yet, and Mama needed her more than any of the others. She'd been getting sicker since last winter. She was never gonna be right in her thinking or in the way she spent what little money they had that Mal didn't hide on drinkin' stuff to make her feel better, only it always made things worse once she ran out.

That's what had landed them on the streets in the first place, because Mama wouldn't go to the hospital that Grams and Papa said she had to, or take the medicine that would make it where she didn't have to drink to get by. She'd said it was to keep Mal. But it hadn't been.

People went to the thinkin' kind of hospital when they didn't see the world right and couldn't live like other people—that's what Mama always said while she drank. And who wanted to live like other people, anyway? So she'd run instead of going there, and she'd loved Mal so much she couldn't leave without her. And that kind of love was the most important thing in the world. It made her and Mama richer than everyone else, Mama said, no matter how little they had. It was why Mal had to be a big girl now, so they could stay together.

But Mama had needed Mal more than she'd loved her, Mal had figured out when Mama wasn't thinkin' right and when she was drinkin' and when she was sick. Without Mal's help, Mama never would have made it this long. Which meant to keep their family together, Mal had to stop dreaming about the baby stuff she'd wanted when they'd first run. Even if they always had nothin', even if they stayed invisible forever, if Mal kept goin' she'd still have her mama.

But six years of not staying anywhere long enough to find a place of their own, or to get clean for more than a few days at a time, or for Mal to go to school or see other kids hardly any at all—it felt like forever. Especially after it started snowing again this winter.

Mal used to love snow. It hardly ever snowed in the South. This was only the second time in her whole life she'd ever seen it, and walking around in it the last few days should have felt like living in a snow globe. Like a Christmas dream she could have for real, where everything was fresh and perfect, and they were finally gonna have a magical holiday.

Only they were stuck inside now, where Mama never wanted to be. And they were so dirty, Mama was so sick, that even in a shelter everybody kept staring at them like they wanted them to go away. And if Mama's cough didn't get better, a volunteer might get too close, wantin' to help, and start asking questions and maybe notify the people Mama said would take Mal away and put Mama in one of those places for people who didn't think right.

That's why they couldn't go to a free clinic or an emergency room no matter how sick Mama got. Free stuff, even medicine, wasn't really free. You had to sign papers and explain who you were, and kids like Mallory weren't supposed to be on the streets wandering from one place, one season, one year to another, hiding from the world because that's the only way she could stay with a mama everyone thought was crazy.

Nowhere was safe—not anywhere there were normal people. So they'd stuck to smaller towns with nice churches and local shelters that weren't connected to anyplace else. And Mal got to keep her mama, which was all the safe she had left.

But Mama's cough was worse than ever. They'd heard the people at the last place they'd moved on from say that people like them with nowhere to get dry and warm and better were dyin' of the flu this year. On the streets you got used to not feeling so good. It was no big deal, until it was. Until it was life and death, and you forgot about havin' no holidays or birthdays or school days or summer breaks or grandparents—because what did any of that matter when you couldn't breathe your chest hurt so much?

No matter how much food and medicine she stole this winter, it hadn't been enough. Mama's fever wasn't goin' away, and she hadn't really eaten anything Mal had found for her, not for days. Then it had gotten too cold for Mama to keep walkin'. Mal had found a shelter in an old church where so far nobody was looking too close at them. But it wasn't helping. Mama was already talking about goin' outside again, saying over and over that people were too close and they would take her and Mal's clothes or the other stuff they were dragging around.

Six years of stuff—treasures, Mama called it, even though they didn't have much, not really, just a pile of tattered nonsense that smelled as bad and looked as shabby as they did.

Mama refused to part with any of it. They had a bag of clothes they washed whenever they found a bathroom with soap and a lock on the door. Another bag held trinkets they'd mostly pulled *from other people's trash, except for Mal's one and only posses-sion that was all hers—a doll a nice lady volunteer had given her the week after that first Christmas, when Mal had been crying because she'd realized she'd never get another present again. The lady had said it had been left there special, just for Mal.*

For some reason this year, Mama was obsessed about someone taking it most of all—a doll Mal had never even let herself name. It was like keeping the doll was more important to Mama than Mal or getting better had ever been—more important even than not dying of the flu because she wouldn't let Mal take her to a doctor.

"Maybe Grams and Papa would help," Mal said to herself.

She rubbed Mama's back when she coughed again, and tried not to panic. She had to do somethin'. She couldn't let Mama stay sick. She reached into the plastic shopping bag that stored her stuff, careful not to untie one of Mama's special knots that kept everyone else out. She found her doll and tucked it under her arm, even though it was stupid for a twelve-year-old to need a baby doll to calm herself down.

"Just for a while," she said, "maybe Grams and Papa would come and help until you're better." She didn't know what else to do, and she really, really didn't want her mama to die. "Or they could send us money. Or maybe—"

"They'd make us go back." Mama coughed again, harsh and scratchy and makin' Mal's chest hurt, too, as she tried not to cry. Mama huddled deeper into the old orange coat she never took off, even when it got warm outside. "We don't want to go back, and they won't help if we don't. We're doin' just fine. This is where we belong. We don't want to go back."

Mama thought they could do this forever.

But Mal was twelve now, and twelve wasn't six. She could see things better. The craziness. Mama's sickness. It was worse. All of it was more worse than ever.

Even if Mama hadn't caught the flu, things were never gonna be fine no matter how many Christmases went by, or how many memories and dreams and trashy dolls Mal held on to. There was no fixing what was scaring Mal most—that feeling safe was never really gonna happen for them. Not unless she went back on the promise she'd made Mama the day they'd run away—that they'd stay together always and never go back to Grams and Papa's.

She dug her hand into the pocket of her too-short jeans and closed her fingers around the quarter she kept hidden there instead of in their bags, where Mama would find it when she sifted through everything looking for money or to make sure nothing had gotten stolen. She clutched her doll close. She wanted to scream as Mama coughed into her arm to muffle the sound so no one would hear.

"Of course we don't wanna go back," Mal said, still patting her mama's back. She leaned her head against the wall behind the cot, making a thudding sound. She squeezed her eyes shut, then opened them and stared through the dark room full of cots and other street people who'd come out of the cold, looking out the grimy window high up on the wall she was facing, at the snow still falling through the moonlight.

The tiny window made her feel better. It made the little town's night seem more like a fantasy than a scary place where she kept wondering if her mama might really die this time. It almost made Mal want to sleep, so she could dream and forget how bad things were and how scared she felt and how much she wanted this to end.

What would it be like? Christmas morning with Mama and Grams and Papa again. Clean and safe and nothin' to worry about, even though Christmas had never really been like that with her crazy mama messing things up, not even before they ran.

But in her perfect Christmas dream, everyone she loved would be there with her, and there'd be nothin' but smiles and presents and everything special Grams would buy for Mal to eat, even the silly pink cereal Grams thought was bad for her but got anyway. There'd be no worrying about now or tomorrow. Just family and belonging and no one being sick ever again, because Mal had been brave enough to call, and Mama had loved her enough to get better and stay.

Except Mama would run if they went back, and she wouldn't take Mal this time, not if Mal acted like a baby and went back on the promise she'd made.

So Mal stared into the snow globe world outside the shelter's dirty windows. It all looked gray now, the same as the walls around her. The white of the snow wasn't for her and Mama. It was for other people with better windows to look out of and real homes to live in and no worries about whether anyone would ever steal their treasures. She held on to her doll and her quarter, and she tried to believe that she could get through this Christmas, too, like a big girl.

Mal didn't need Grams and Papa. She wasn't gonna be scared, not anymore. Maybe it would get warmer tomorrow and the snow would go away, and when they had to go back outside Mama would be able to breathe better. Maybe they could keep doin' this forever.

They were gonna make it.

Mal was gonna make sure of it.

Chapter Eight

We dream, it is good we are dreaming,
It would hurt us, were we awake...

"How are things going this fine Saturday?" Julia Davis asked as she rushed across the cul-de-sac.

She picked up speed when Pete didn't immediately respond, practically sprinting toward where he was strapping Polly into her car seat in the back of his four-door Jeep Extreme. The woman's taupe-and-brown, leopard-printed tracksuit made swishing sounds with each stride.

"Daddy?" Polly eyed their neighbor nervously. "We're going to be late to meet Mallory."

"Just a few minutes, sweetie." He gave her cheek a kiss and made sure her heavy jacket was tucked snugly around her so the colder weather that had moved in didn't give her a chill before he could turn the heat on. Then he shut the door and turned to greet the friend he'd been avoiding since Emma's death, along with everyone else in their neighborhood.

"Hey, Julia," he said, taking in her tastefully applied makeup and perfectly arranged hair. He'd never seen her without makeup. He wondered sometimes if Walter ever had. How often had he and Emma wondered if their friend actually slept that way—in case a community emergency required her attention in the middle of the night? "It's gotten cold, hasn't it?"

Julia wrapped her arms around herself and gave an exaggerated shiver. She smiled in agreement, but the aura of perpetual sparkle that usually surrounded her wasn't there.

"I've stopped by to check on Polly a few times," she said. "Everyone's missed her at the bus stop. Sam's boys say they've seen her at school. I can never seem to catch you at home, even though your Jeep's in the drive all day now. We were hoping everything's all right."

"It's been an unusual week, but we're fine." He'd been home each time Julia had rung the doorbell. Then knocked. Then phoned after she got back to her place. "Polly's fine," he added, checking behind him to find his daughter staring at him like she had so many times before when he'd said the same thing to people, not realizing the pressure he was putting on her to be okay. "She just needs a little time to herself right now when she's not at school. We both do. I hope everyone understands. The whole lane's been amazing to us. But I've decided to take the rest of the holiday off from work, just for us, you know? I want her to have as good a Christmas as we can."

"I…I didn't mean to upset her the other morning in the clinic." Julia looked close to tears, reminding Pete of just how big a heart lay beneath her well-intentioned pushiness.

That was the thing about communities like theirs. You became so entrenched in one another's lives, the lines people drew around their worlds to keep some things in and other things out began to blur. You became an extended family, which was an amazing thing in an increasingly cynical world.

He and Emma had moved to Mimosa Lane because they'd wanted to be in a place where everyone cared for and understood everyone else. But the downside of that kind of life was the temptation to see things only the way everyone around you did. It could grab at your consciousness before you really noticed it—until it felt normal to be doing and enjoying and experiencing practically everything as a whole rather than as an individual.

Which worked just fine, until your world blew apart and that commonality began to feel like a threat instead of a blessing. Because you were on the outside looking in at it, and even people you'd known for years started to seem like strangers.

His thoughts flashed to how Mallory, from the moment she'd moved in, had seemed uncomfortable with all of them. He marveled all over again at how he and his daughter seemed to have more in common with her now than with the neighbors they'd once socialized with on a daily basis. Lost without Emma's knack for charming and befriending anyone in any situation, he'd pulled completely back from the safety net the lane could have been for him and his daughter—depriving his child of seeing that the people who loved her would always love her, no matter how hard a time she was having.

"I'm going to need your help this Christmas," he said to the friend Emma had trusted implicitly, when trust wasn't something Pete came to nearly as easily. "I think we're all going to have to get used to Polly being upset for a while." He made sure his voice was loud enough for it to carry to the brave little girl behind him. "You actually did us a favor Monday, by letting her vent some of what she's been holding inside for too long. I wish I'd realized what she needed sooner. I'm sorry if she made a scene at school and embarrassed you, but I need you to help everyone on the lane understand that it might happen again, and it's exactly what Polly needs to do so she can deal with losing Emma."

"Embarrassed me…" Julia's eyes filled with dismay. "Pete, please tell me you haven't been avoiding me all week, for the last six months, because you think I'm going to scold you about your child missing her mother so badly she can't be nice to a nosy woman who doesn't keep her opinions to herself when they're not wanted. Of course Polly should feel and say whatever she needs to. We're all here for her. For you. Whatever you need, you don't have to ask. It's yours."

He reached out a hand to squeeze her shoulder. The smooth material of Julia's tracksuit was ice cold, rustling beneath his touch. Her hand came up to cover his before slipping away.

"Is that why you two haven't been at the bus stop all week?" she asked. "Because you're worried what everyone's thinking?"

Pete cleared his throat, beating back the instinct to say that he wasn't worried about a thing.

"I'm not sure what anyone's thinking anymore," he admitted. "Least of all me and Polly. But that's going to change, starting now. She asked me to drive her to school Tuesday morning, like her mother used to. It's one of the only times she's asked me for anything since Emma died. I've been so busy rushing around taking care of everything I haven't stopped to see what she really needs."

"She just needs her daddy. That's all." Julia's heartfelt encouragement was another type of hug, full of the pride his wife used to shower him with as he doted on her and Polly. "You sound better than I've heard you since Emma passed. That's wonderful, really."

"Yeah," he said, staring down at the crack in the driveway where grass would sprout again come spring.

In a single week their new morning routine riding to and from school, mostly in silence, had begun to feel more real than anything they'd shared since losing Emma. Dinner and bath time and bedtime were no longer rushed ordeals, since he wasn't crashing into them at the end of a long day or after picking Polly up early from school, which he hadn't once had to do. They were slowly building a new life together to replace what they'd lost. All because of an enigmatic woman his daughter saw every day at school and found a reason to visit before dinner each night.

He'd only caught fleeting glimpses of Mallory through the gate in their back fence, never grabbing her attention for longer than it took to wave a friendly hello. He'd phoned her once or twice to say it was time for Polly to come home for dinner. But other than that he hadn't pushed her for more interaction, no matter how badly he'd longed to see her again.

"She's beautiful," Julia said.

"What?" Pete's attention snapped back his neighbor, who was oblivious that the beautiful face springing to his mind belonged to a leggy blonde with a healer's nurturing soul, a spitfire attitude, and a penchant for bright colors and clothes spotted with cartoon characters that he'd never think of the same way again.

"Polly's so beautiful. She looks so much like her mother. So things have settled down since Monday?"

"A little."

Neither of them was getting much sleep still. But thanks to Mallory's insight he and his daughter were curling up on the couch each night, where instead of reading stories like always they'd found a new pattern—watching silly cartoon videos, both of them finally nodding off until the morning alarm started blaring. They still had a long way to go, but they were finding their way through it together now.

"Is she eating better?"

He nodded. "Mostly when she visits Mallory in the afternoons," he added, wincing as soon as the words were out of his mouth and he saw the combined look of astonishment and interest on Julia's face.

"Mallory Phillips?"

"Polly's grown very attached to her through school. She's spending afternoons at her house now. It seems to help—having someone to talk with who isn't part of everything that happened with Emma."

"Well, that…That's wonderful, too." Julia stole a glance toward Mallory's house.

Wonderful?

He thought of her urgency to help Polly when she couldn't seem to handle the rest of the community, then her obvious panic at the thought of them visiting her in town today. He was beginning to wonder if having Polly barge into her isolated life might not be doing Mallory as much good as it was his daughter.

"She's more than any of us expected," he admitted.

"It would seem so." Julia's smile widened at his offhand compliment.

"We're headed into the city to see her now, as a matter of fact. Polly's excited to get down there."

"Downtown Atlanta?"

"Midtown. She volunteers clinic services on weekends for some of the shelters."

"*Every* weekend?" Julia's expression filled with the same admiration Pete had experienced.

"She was down there over Thanksgiving."

"She pulled out of her driveway around six this morning," Julia reported, "just like every other weekend. After tangling with the flu all week at school."

"Polly's dying to see what she does in the city—I'm pretty sure our neighbor's achieved superhero status in her mind. She's determined to help out. Which will probably create even more work for Mallory. But I hate to discourage anything that gets Polly this excited…"

Julia squeezed his arm again. Wind kicked up, circling dried lives around them—a brusque reminder that they were well into what should be winter months, even if everyone on the lane had been wearing shorts and T-shirts up until a week ago.

"She sounds absolutely wonderful," Julia said. "I was hoping…All I was hoping all this time was to be a friend, and maybe a distraction for Polly, if she'd let me."

"I know. I'm sorry we've been so distant. Just give us a little more time to sort things out, okay?"

"You're doing just fine."

Pete's throat tightened at her simple praise. "We'll see how today goes, and the last week of school before break."

Something told him that the closer they got to Christmas, the more precarious his and Polly's unspoken truce might become.

"I've almost talked Brian Perry into hosting the neighborhood holiday party," Julia said. "I was hoping you and Polly would come."

Pete couldn't respond. It was the community event Emma had loved most. Beautiful memories came back to him, every one of them dripping with the acid of knowing their life together had been cut too short.

"I know it can't be an easy time," Julia pressed on. "But you said you wanted to give Polly a good Christmas. And everyone—"

"I don't think so," he bit out.

The rage and hopelessness rushing through him must have registered on his face, because Julia was moving closer, an unwanted hug looming. He brushed against the side of the Jeep, stepping out of her reach. Julia stopped dead in her tracks, clearly hurt.

"Why don't you and Polly talk it over?" she said. "The party won't be until next weekend, so you have time. Maybe she can invite Mallory if that would help Polly enjoy things more. I know people would love to get to know our new neighbor better and to hear more about the wonderful things she's doing in the city. You don't need to RSVP or anything," she rushed to say. "Just pop over. It wouldn't be the same without your family there."

His family. The family he still had, instead of the one he'd lost—a family that included loving, understanding neighbors who'd known Polly her entire life. That's what he'd promised himself he'd stay focused on now. That's what his daughter needed him to make his priority.

"All right. I'll let Polly decide what she wants to do," he said, loud enough to make sure his daughter understood the choice was completely hers. "Thank you for inviting us, Julia. Really. And thank Brian and Sam, too, if they end up hosting."

Julia smiled. "I'll be thinking about the two of you. I really do hope things are getting better. There's not a family I know who deserves a happier holiday. Why don't you bring Polly by the bus stop next week, before you drive her to school? She used to love doing that with Emma."

He turned from watching her walk away to find his daughter staring at him, her eyes wide with worry instead of the excitement that had been shimmering through her since she'd woken up that morning and wolfed down the sugary whole-grain cereal that was her new favorite, even if it wasn't cotton candy pink like Mallory's.

His first instinct was to pretend Julia's disturbing invitation hadn't been a big deal. Instead, he opened Polly's door and soaked in her frown.

"How are you doing, sweet pea?"

"Do we have to go?" Polly pulled the strings to her jacket's hood until the material bunched behind her head like a pink pillow. "To the Christmas party?"

"Like I told Mrs. Davis, that's entirely up to you. We won't go if you don't want to. This is our first Christmas without Mommy, and Thanksgiving was hard. I have to stop expecting all the old stuff we used to like to be just fine. We don't have to do anything for Christmas that you don't want to, okay?"

"But you want to go."

Pete did, no matter how badly he'd reacted just now. Despite the inevitable conversations about Emma he'd be dragged into at the Perrys', talking with Julia had reminded him how much he'd missed his friends, his community. He wasn't certain he was any more ready than his child to face his neighbors again, but their life was too damn empty without them.

"I want you to have Christmas the way you need to have it this year," he reminded them both. "If that means keeping to ourselves except for when you visit Mallory's tree, that's fine with me. But I think it might be fun to see everybody else."

"Do you think Mallory would go?"

Pete doubted it. "I guess you'll just have to ask her," he hedged.

"When?"

"We'll know when it's the right time."

He imagined having Mallory beside him at the Perrys' house instead of Emma. He had no clue what to do with the fact that it felt right somehow, in some way that he didn't yet want to name. Except that he'd love for the rest of the community to get the chance to appreciate her quiet intensity and free spirit and honest understanding, when she wasn't busting his balls for not being able to see the nose on his own face.

Would she come? Would having her become an even bigger part of their holiday plans make Christmas just a little better for him and Polly, and maybe Mallory, too?

***

"Is it like school, Daddy?" Polly chirped from the backseat, about halfway into town. She'd recovered quickly from their encounter with Julia—far quicker than Pete had after realizing how much he wanted Mallory to stay a part of their lives.

"Is it like school?" Pete considered Mallory's inviting, welcoming clinic at Chandler. Polly and the other kids had been more than a little afraid of Nurse Karen. But evidently none of them could resist Mallory's smiles and the cheery, colorful touches she'd added to the clinic, not even when they were sick and it was her job to give them medicine.

Then he thought of the few assistance shelters he'd seen spotlighted on TV news segments. The prevailing sadness of those programs didn't bode well for Polly's fairy-tale image of what they were about to walk into.

"No," he said, giving the same answer he had all week. "I don't think it will be anything like school. Remember us talking about what a shelter is?" His daughter was still acting as if they were on their way to an amusement park. "It's a place for people who need help."

"People like me." Polly was playing with a Barbie, twirling the doll's too-perfect hair around and around. Platinum strands the texture of straw swirled in every direction. The miniature woman's ridiculously proportioned body parts were unabashedly bare. Polly kept losing the clothes, all except for Barbie's hooker heels. "Do you think there will be lots of people?"

It was good that she was playing with some of her toys again, he reminded himself, even if she was obsessed with the most politically incorrect doll she owned. Emma used to keep up with Barbie's bits and pieces. She'd been a pro at nurturing Polly's love of make-believe, taking each unexpected twist and turn of their child's imagination in stride and making the most of every adventure.

That was Pete's job now.

"Daddy?" Polly said.

"Yes," he said. "It sounds like Mallory helps a lot of people in the city."

"Kids like me, right?"

"Sure," he conceded, knowing his child was too excited to hear any answer but the one she was expecting.

Kids like me...

Some of Mallory's patients would be homeless—some of them Polly's age. Others would be living below the poverty level, even if they had a place to stay. Even in his and Polly's county, Pete had seen a lot of sad things on his rescue calls. Pockets of poverty dotted the rural communities on the outskirts of Atlanta and beyond. And when those who had very little, none of it insured, lost it all in a fire, it tore him up to think of how they were going to start over again.

And in an urban metropolis like the city of Atlanta, it was a heartbreaking reality how many people in today's economy couldn't afford even the basics of day-to-day life. Those in the most need tended to flock to the midtown area, where free services like the centers where Mallory volunteered were in abundance, doing whatever could be done with their limited funding.

"So, it's just like school," Polly insisted.

"Yeah," Pete agreed absently. "Just like school."

Why would a woman who was no longer a practicing social worker keep immersing herself in others' struggles the way Mallory was? Every weekend. The entire holiday. That mystery hadn't let him go since she'd admitted where she spent practically every minute of her free time that she wasn't doting on his child.

Polly had rolled out of bed each morning this week determined to have a better day at school so she would get the chance to see Mallory in the afternoon and then to work with her today. Ms. Caldwell had phoned to say Polly's overall mood had lightened, she'd begun participating more in class, and she was even joining some of the Christmas craft projects that had upset her so badly just a week ago.

She continued to eat lunch in Mallory's clinic, but she no longer sulked to get permission to go. She simply asked for a hall pass like the other kids. And in fits and spurts she was talking to some of her old friends. She was making it through the entire school day now until Pete picked her up in the car pool line. It was a transformation just short of miraculous, even though Polly was still underweight, eating mostly sugar and white flour, and was still exhausted from not getting enough sleep.

He just hoped today turned out to be another positive *Mallory* experience, instead of whatever they were about to walk in on setting Polly's progress back.

He exited the highway and took Peachtree toward Ponce, passing the glistening skyscrapers and deserted Saturday sidewalks snaking into Midtown. He could have stopped on any corner for designer coffee, made his way to the Center for Puppetry Arts for a matinee, or be heading to eat greasy burgers, hot dogs, and onion rings at the Varsity. Instead, they passed by everything that was remotely familiar, heading to the heart of the seedy, hidden underbelly over which Atlanta's nationally lauded *progress* had been constructed. All while Polly hummed and sang and chatted away with exhibitionist Barbie.

Like warm soda pop bubbling over the rim of a glass, there was no curbing her enthusiasm to see their visit as a kind of playdate. A little girl's tea party with teddy bears. The kind of Saturday she'd enjoyed so often with her mother. He pulled into the well-kept, nearly deserted lot beside the Open Arms Shelter and prayed to Emma and whomever else was listening that he wasn't making yet another colossal parenting mistake.

"There's Mallory's car," Polly said, pointing and bouncing up and down within her seat belt.

Mallory's ancient yellow Beetle had faded pansies tied to its radio antenna. She'd combat parked the heap near the side entrance of a dated redbrick building. Two young men in jeans and pullover sweatshirts were huddled just outside the doors, shivering in the morning chill and smoking.

Pete parked near the front of the lot. While he helped Polly from the car and pulled out the bag of wrapped toys they'd brought, a shabbily dressed man in overalls and a threadbare coat loped up to the younger guys, pushing a grocery cart that bulged with what looked like a trove of discarded items.

The man gestured wildly amid the shadows the shelter was casting, the sun not high enough yet to clear its low-built walls. Something wasn't quite right about him, but the young men—Pete assumed they were volunteers like Mallory—ground out their cigarettes beneath the heels of their sneakers and companionably gestured for him to precede them inside. An attempt by one of them to help the guy up the entrance's brick steps was shrugged off. An offer to assist him with his cart when it got stuck on the top step earned the other volunteer a generous hip check as the street guy swerved his things out of reach.

The second kid glanced back at his buddy, nonplussed, then opened the door and waved the man through.

It should have been a sad, pathetic reminder of all the worst-case scenarios that had been running through Pete's mind. Instead, witnessing the volunteers' offbeat respect for their cantankerous visitor made him smile, then chuckle. Their acceptance of a homeless man's pride reminded Pete of Mallory's just-the-facts demeanor when she'd faced him down that first night, when he himself hadn't exactly been on his best, most neighborly behavior.

He chuckled again.

Thank God the woman was formally trained in dealing with annoyed, oblivious bums.

"Come on, Daddy." Polly grabbed his hand and began dragging him inside.

***

Polly couldn't wait.

She hadn't been able to sleep at all last night. But it hadn't been the bad kind of not sleeping that used to make her want to run away, because lately she and Daddy were cuddling up on the couch at night so neither one of them would feel so alone.

She'd wanted to walk to Mallory's house again last night, to ask if Mallory was for sure going to be volunteering today. But Polly had promised she wouldn't go out again after dark, so she'd stayed there with her daddy on the couch with a princess movie on the TV turned down low, so excited she could barely pay attention.

She'd done everything she'd promised that week so she could keep seeing Mallory after school and so this get-better Saturday could happen. And in the afternoons she'd gotten to hide more of Mommy's special pins in Mallory's cookie jar. Then when she wasn't helping load the dishwasher and fold towels and sweep the floor of Mallory's awesome kitchen, she'd gotten to look at Mallory's amazing tree and all of the cool lights and ornaments on it that didn't remind her of anything but what she wanted this Christmas to be about.

Her stomach still hurt sometimes, and her head, too, and her heart, when she forgot that she wanted to forget and thought about Mommy and how perfect things used to be. But mostly this week she'd been too excited to be sick, because she was going to get to spend today with Daddy and Mallory. She'd even played with Sally Mathews and Ginny Strom and the other girls at playground time yesterday, like she was as happy as them, when they had their mommies and Polly never would again.

The sick school feelings had come back after they returned to class and there were so many normal kids around her, happy that it was almost Christmas while Polly remembered she wasn't like them anymore. She hadn't felt bad enough to go see Mallory in the clinic and call Daddy to come get her early. She hadn't had to do that all week.

She'd known all along this was going to be a magical day, just like the ones the characters in her favorite movies had, when everything that was wrong would with the swirl of a magic wand suddenly feel like it could all be better. And now it was finally here.

She held tight to her daddy's hand as they walked into the big building, her tummy twisting the way it did when she worried at school because she was never sure anymore how she would feel about normal things. Would this be one more place she didn't fit in? Would Daddy be able to see whatever he needed to see to say they could stay? He was worried, she could tell. And, magical or not, Mallory was worried, too, that this might not be good for Polly. And everything that wasn't good for her had to go, Daddy had kept insisting before this week.

They'd stopped just inside the door. Polly had been looking up at her daddy's face, wondering if he'd frown and if that would mean they'd have to leave. When he smiled, she didn't know why until she looked at where he was looking.

Ms. Phillips?

Mallory?

Polly was smiling now, too, because instead of the princess Polly had always pictured her school nurse would play if she were in a cartoon, Mallory was dressed as Glinda the Good Witch from *The Wizard of Oz*.

She had the crown, the magic wand, the glittery, poufy dress that was a cloud of white and blue sparkles, and everything. And there were kids piled all around her in the big room they'd stepped into, on the floor in front of the chair she was sitting in. All of them were laughing while she gave a Cabbage Patch doll a shot and the Transformer she had in her other hand shied away from the fake needle.

Polly wasn't close enough to hear all that Mallory was saying. She let Daddy's hand go and ran down into the group of kids.

"So what do you think happened," Mallory asked them, "after Cathy Crabby got her flu shot and He-Man Henry didn't listen to his mommy and went home without one?"

"Cathy kicked his butt," yelled the boy sitting right in front, and the other kids and Mallory laughed again.

"Now, I'm not so sure Cathy Crabby could have done much of anything to Henry at first," Mallory said. "But you're on the right track." She tapped the boy with her wand. "Because once the flu blew through their town…"

She reached under her skirt, under her chair, and pulled out a huge wad of bubble wrap that was rolled into a ball and tossed it into the crowd of kids. The boy batted it up into the air first, then Polly swatted at it next, and then they were all reaching for it, squealing and keeping it flying.

Polly felt it coming. She didn't know what the feeling was at first. Then it shivered up her middle, making her tummy flutter in a good way for a change. It burst out of her throat, and only then did she realize that she was laughing, too. For the first time since she could remember she was laughing along with everyone else, and it felt like she could keep laughing forever.

She glanced at Daddy to make sure he didn't mind, and he was smiling at her now the way he'd smiled at Mallory before. Like Polly was the pretty princess and she made him happy just looking at her. So she kept laughing, soft and then louder as she batted at the ball when it was her chance again, sending it up and over the boy at the very front. Mallory caught it and pushed the ball behind her.

"Once the flu blew through their town," she said again, "all the kids knocked it back and forth for weeks the way they do in your schools and neighborhoods here in Atlanta. And of all the kids like Cathy who had their flu shots and the ones like Henry who didn't, who do you think ended up in bed sick?"

"He-Man Henry," everyone yelled, including Polly, when she hadn't answered a teacher's question at school all year.

Only no one was looking at her here as if she were different. No one was looking at anyone at all but Mallory. Polly was just like the other kids at Mallory's shelter, just like she'd known she'd be. Like nowhere else in her life anymore, this was where she could be normal.

"Everyone used to be afraid of He-Man Henry," Mallory said. "He used to be so strong and fast he'd swoop down on Cathy"—she flew the Transformer in front of the doll—"and ruin her tea parties, and all the girls would scatter."

Mallory reached under her chair again, then there were miniature dolls flying into the crowd of kids, the kind that came with the hamburger meals Polly used to love. The girls, all ages, grabbed for them, while the boys groaned and shrugged away like they'd get cooties.

"But once He-Man Henry came down with the flu and the girls didn't, because they'd listened to their mommies"—Mallory pointed her wand at the parents standing all over the lobby—"and to their nurses"—she swirled her wand over her crown, just like the good witch in the movie—"guess what happened?"

"They kicked his butt!" all the girls yelled. And when they laughed, Polly giggled with them.

Mallory nodded, the little stars and glitter on her crown sparkling. "Superheroes aren't always the ones with the most muscles, but they're still the bravest and the strongest people you know. Because real superheroes take care of themselves and other people even when they're scared. So later today when your parents tell you it's time to have your flu shot, or if you come to my office and I wave my wand-of-all-knowing and I say you're due for a booster shot for something that might not sound so bad to you if you got it, what are you all going to say, even though a shot can be really scary?"

The kids just sat there, all of them, including Polly, who hated shots but had already had her flu one because Daddy had been so worried. All the kids were just as scared of shots as Polly and He-Man Henry.

"Are you going to say yes or no when it's your turn to make sure you and your family don't get sick this year?" Mallory reached under her chair again and pulled out a fistful of candy wrapped in Christmas colors. "Did I mention that everyone who's a superhero gets something sweet? So, what are you going to say?"

"Yes!" they all yelled, then they were laughing again when Mallory tossed the candy into the crowd.

Kids scrambled for a piece, Polly, too. Mallory threw more, and Polly dove into the crowd, snagging one with a red wrapper away from another kid. No one warned her to be careful or worried that she'd get hurt because she'd been so sad and sick since Mommy got cancer. It was like a dream, a good one, an awake one, about when she used to feel this way all the time.

She ran toward the good witch, jumping into Mallory's arms to show off her candy. She was caught out of the air and held, and even though she was crying a little now thinking how Mommy would have loved Mallory's story, she was also still laughing a little, too. Because today remembering didn't hurt, not much at all. She wasn't scared or wanting to forget how it had been with her mommy. Not here where no one would ask her to think or talk about anything she didn't want to.

"Can I volunteer with you every weekend?" she begged, burying her head against the good witch's neck and holding on tight. "Please?"

Chapter Nine

The gleam of an heroic Act
Such strange illumination...

Mallory's morning had become a swamp of anxiety and sleep deprivation. One jarring moment after another kept leaping across her path, thanks to her latest trip down memory lane in last night's dream. The past had never seemed more determined to collide with her present.

She'd volunteered in shelters since she was a senior in high school, once she realized she felt more at home in these places than anywhere else. Her grams had let her go. It wasn't until years later, after it was too late, that Mallory realized her obsession with helping strangers had broken just a tiny bit more of Honey Phillips's heart.

On some level she'd always known she'd been searching for her mother, too, as her volunteer work continued through college and the start of her career as a social worker on staff at an assistance center just like this one. Her mama might have been long gone, as if she'd never existed, no matter how many feelers Mallory had put out or contacts she'd made with shelters all over the country. But Mallory would always have places like this where she could feel needed and useful, and where she saw instant results when she succeeded in helping someone the way she'd once tried to help her mother.

When she'd burned out on social work she'd decided no more losing herself in other people's desperate situations. No more searching for her mother, period. Her plan had been to build a life far, far away, but her volunteer work still kept her from escaping completely. It was too vital to the community for her to turn her back on it. Or had it been too much a part of who she would always be—the person she became all over again each time she headed for midtown?

This morning it felt as if she were seeing herself in every face she encountered. It had been the flu week from hell at school. But this close to the holidays, even with her dreams hounding her, she couldn't be anywhere else but at a shelter this morning. And holding the sweet, happy weight squirming in her arms now, seeing Pete Lombard's megawatt smile from all the way across the lobby where he'd hung back with the other parents, were the added assurance she'd needed that she'd made the right decision.

"Anytime your daddy wants to bring you down to one of my visits"—she smiled as Pete approached—"you're more than welcome. We can use all the volunteers we can get."

"But how do we help?" Polly asked, leaning back in Mallory's arms and chatting freely when just a week ago she'd barely managed a few words at a time. "My daddy knows medicine stuff, too. And I'm good at helping. Really, I am."

Pete, who'd stepped closer, ran a hand down his daughter's curls. "Yes, Glinda." A teasing smile curled at his mouth. "How do we help, since you clearly have everyone in this place eating out of your hands?"

Mallory's breath caught. His praise was like a shot of caffeine coursing through her veins, awakening her and teasing her with pointless visions like the ones that came now each night as she tossed and turned restlessly. Those smiling lips brushing her hand the way Prince Charming would. Then his kiss all over her skin. Pete's touch chasing away loneliness and her desperation to belong places that a scared little girl who would forever be on the run couldn't belong...

Polly giggled at her dad's silliness, dragging Mallory back from her daydream to the reality of her threadbare, ancient costume, which suddenly seemed to be mocking her. Still, Polly's laugh was like the candy Mallory had thrown to the children. Sparkling and shot through with color and fun.

Forget the fairy tale, she told herself sternly. It was going to be a good day. Having these two there for as long as they'd stay was just what she needed to banish the last of her dreams about the past.

"Follow me." She put Polly down, feeling a bit ridiculous as she and her poufy dress led the way to the clinic.

But then Polly's little hand reached out to stroke the sparkly fabric, and she said, "Wow..." It was the best compliment Mallory had ever been given. She'd pulled the old thing from her bulging costume wardrobe full of outfits she'd collected over the years, hoping that it would tickle this one special child's fancy most of all.

The shelter kids tended to prefer the clowns and pirates and cartoon animals she could transform into. The boys didn't always respond as well to the girly finery she'd selected this morning from the bottom of a moving box wedged in her closet.

But Mallory had been determined to make glitter work today, whatever antics she'd needed to resort to. With Polly skipping along beside her, Mallory no longer cared about how her costume itched or how much of her mother and her own past she still felt lurking around every corner.

Pete and Polly hung inside the clinic doorway at first as Mallory began working with the line of families that had queued up in the hall. Pete wound up leaning against the wall just inside the door, watching her every move while Polly fetched whatever nonmedical things Mallory needed to help a patient. Parents had been filling out medical history forms during Mallory's skit, allowing her to quickly review them and ask additional questions before treating their kids. The tenth flu shot of the day had been administered within twenty minutes, with Polly beaming beside her daddy because helping Mallory seemed to be the best thing ever.

"You're all set, champ," Mallory said to the little guy who'd sat practically under her feet during story time.

His frowning father loomed beside the exam table, looking pissed as usual that so much of his morning was being consumed by their visit. But he'd decided, he'd said, that a flu shot was his best chance not to have to take time off work or pay for cold medicine down the road.

"Do I get a toy from the box?" Charlie Cooper asked, a return customer who knew the score. So did his single dad who worked sometimes fifteen hours a day at whatever minimum wage job he could snag to keep them in a nearby one-room apartment they rented by the month. The man crossed his arms and waited impatiently for Mallory to come up with the goods.

"Well, that depends"—she kept the clinic toy boxes in each of the shelters stocked with donations people dropped off, and when those dried up, she purchased whatever she could afford from dollar stores all over Atlanta, but she didn't need to rifle through the box for the toy she'd set aside for this special patient—"on whether you have room at your place for a down-and-out superhero."

"He-Man Henry!" Charlie grabbed the plastic action figure she'd held out to him. Then the tough little guy was hugging her as tightly as Polly had.

"You're a brave boy." She hugged him back. Charlie hated shots, and his diabetes—the condition that was a nonstop strain on his father's finances, despite public assistance—required him to take shots at home every day. "You were a huge help with the other kids. I can't think of a better place for Henry to recuperate from the flu."

Charlie jumped off the exam table, sprinting away to show his new favorite toy to the other kids, Henry raised high over his head flying He-Man proud. His dad, Dennis, looked and smelled half-drunk already, and it wasn't even noon yet. This was his one day a week off from work. The man glared at Mallory, unapologetically aggressive with his arms crossed over his chest, shrugging his shoulder at the thirty-year-old chip that seemed permanently attached there.

"We done here?" He ran a condescending eye down her getup. Then his sneer veered toward Pete and Polly. "I don't have all day for make-believe like you rich people. These places want to get their hands on my boy and ask all kinds of questions every time we come in for a handout. He's fine. I take care of him good. Give me whatever you sign when you see him, lady, so I can get my groceries and get the hell out of here."

"Have you been testing his glucose before and after every meal?" she asked, taking his belligerence in stride. She understood how hard it was to accept help when you'd do anything in the world not to need it. "I know it can be difficult to remember. What about first thing in the morning and again at bedtime?"

"Of course I'm checking his levels, lady. You think I'm buying all that expensive testing shit for my health! I know what I'm doing, and my kid is fine. They said last time I was here that Charlie had to get a flu shot from you today. He has his shot. We've got a doctor to deal with the rest. Butt the hell out."

Mallory's gaze narrowed. She bit her tongue against the impulse to ask, since they were doing just fine, why Dennis smelled of booze every time she saw him. And if he'd be sober enough to remember to pack his son's toys the next time they were given twenty-four hours to vacate an apartment they'd been evicted from because he spent too much money on his addiction. And if he had any idea how worried his boy must be for him, when whatever he drank made him sick and Charlie had to see that and wonder if his dad was going to get better.

That was something Mallory understood far too well, too.

"Everything okay?" Pete asked, appearing behind Dennis, his well-developed upper body easily twice as wide as the other man's.

"Everything's fine," she assured both men, cursing herself for letting her issues get in the way of dealing with a father who was at least trying to do right by his kid, which made him a better parent by far than her own mother had been.

She grabbed the clipboard from Polly, who was also standing there watching. It held the clinic release forms. She scribbled her initials in the correct box and handed the slip over.

"I'd like to see Charlie again in a month for a booster shot," she said, "when school starts back up after the holiday."

Dennis crumpled the form that would score him increased benefits when he stopped at the donation center on his way home.

Mallory had lobbied at each of the clinics where she volunteered hours for a special benefit program. Parents who brought their kids by on her volunteer Saturdays and participated in the free clinic services being provided received a supersize donation of whatever clothing, food, and household supplies they needed to supplement their own efforts for their families.

"I got no idea where that school's gonna be." The flicker of defeat that passed over the man's features did hateful things to his already angry expression. "My work's drying up. We don't make rent this month, by January we'll be someplace else that's got more to offer than this nowhere city."

Somewhere in the southeast that had more employment opportunities than where he was now, no matter how hard Atlanta had been hit by the recession?

"But Charlie's lived here his entire life," she said without thinking. "And you have a network of excellent medical care set up to help you with his condition."

Dennis's simmering resentment erupted. "And livin' here ain't done jack for him or me, if we gotta go beggin' for help all over town from know-it-all bitches like you!"

Pete stepped around the man, intimidation oozing from every pore.

"Look—" he said, stopping midsentence in response to her raised hand. There was murder in his eyes, but he stopped.

"I'm sorry," she apologized. She glanced at Polly and gave her a reassuring smile, then did the same for the parents and kids still milling in the hallway outside the clinic. She stepped closer to Dennis when what she really wanted to do was hide behind her big, strong neighbor. "You're a hardworking father. I know you're doing the best you can under impossible circumstances. I know you want what's best for Charlie just like everyone here.

I respect every hard choice, every sacrifice, every impossible decision you've made to take care of him and keep him with you—including coming here every month and accepting help that no proud man wants to need."

Dennis's anger fizzled. Enough at least for the tension to release from Pete's shoulders and his gaze to flick from the other man toward Mallory. Then he nodded, a silent gesture she was beginning to recognize as a sign that he'd made up his mind about something important.

"Do you have a car?" he asked Dennis.

Charlie's father rounded on Pete. "What business is it of yours, what the fu—"

"I'm a paramedic, and the cleaning company that services the fire stations in my county is expanding," Pete replied, meeting the other father's gaze squarely. "They need extra hands, particularly the crew that deals with my station every Monday night. As long as you have evening child care for Charlie and dependable transportation to the suburbs, I'd be happy to make a recommendation to the service on your behalf. I have a contact inside the company. It would mean steady nightly work, just at different locations depending on where they need you. If Ms. Phillips vouches for you, that's good enough for me. What do you say?"

Pete held out his hand to another struggling father, the easy gesture brimming with respect. Dennis looked down at where Polly was now clinging to her daddy's waist, then over his shoulder at Mallory who was clenching her clipboard to her chest and praying that he would listen, really listen, to the unbelievable opportunity Pete was offering.

Is he for real? was written all over Dennis's face.

"You already work nights, don't you?" she asked him. "Do you have someone who can keep helping with Charlie?"

"My neighbor's a grandmother with her daughter's three kids to watch," Dennis said. "She loves Charlie. Gets him on the bus in the mornings. Then I'm there to pick him up after school"—he looked back at Pete—"in my car."

"Sounds like a solid setup," Pete said.

Dennis paused, as if confused by the compliment.

"You can trust him," Mallory insisted, "just like you and Charlie have learned to trust me no matter how much you hate having to."

Dennis stared holes through her. A war was going on within his sharp, intelligent, and slightly buzzed gaze. Then he snatched the clipboard and pen from her and wrote something on the form on top before silently handing it back and heading after Charlie.

Mallory looked down and smiled.

Tearing the slip away from the others beneath it, she handed the form to Pete and said, "Here you go, He-Man."

"His address and phone number?" Pete asked, ignoring her jibe. "I don't suppose you have a name to go with it."

"Dennis Cooper. He's a good man, even if—"

"Even if he looks and smells like a walking hangover and was scaring you to death a few minutes ago?" Pete hugged Polly closer. "I told you I'd find a way to make myself useful to you."

Useful?

All kinds of jittery sensations were coursing though Mallory as she marveled at what he'd just accomplished. And he made it sound as if he'd done it all for her. A bemused smile was spreading across her face, the confusing connection between her and Pete and Polly growing even stronger, filling her up and scaring her more than Dennis's blustering had. How was this happening? And what on earth was she going to do with the whiplash of fear that came with wondering if it was going to end badly somehow for all of them?

"Um…" She reached for Polly's hand and drew her to her side. "Why don't you go find some coffee in the break room," she said to Pete. "We'll get back to work before the rest of my parents revolt, and catch a break in an hour or two once we have the flu shots out of the way. You can come back for Polly then. I'll show you both the rest of the center."

Pete's attention stayed focused on her for several of the deep breaths she was taking to keep herself from rushing into his arms and shouting, *Thank you, thank you!* He nodded as Polly curled against Mallory's side.

"Take all the time you need," he said. "I'll show myself around the place. I'll be here when you're ready for me."

***

"I'll be here…" Pete had said to Emma the night just after Christmas last year when they'd received the final test results from her oncologist telling them that there was nothing more that could be done medically for his wife.

Emma had been terrified in that moment. Not of dying or even of more pain. The doctors and hospice people had promised there were ways to ease her along the path she was following. No, his brave Emma hadn't been able to face the thought of leaving him and Polly alone, of another Christmas coming and going without her there to make it special for them. She'd been shaking at the image of her daughter grieving and there being no mommy there to take that pain away.

So Pete had lied and promised that he'd be strong enough for both of them, that he'd make things okay for their child no matter how much losing Emma would destroy him. The last Christmas present he'd given his wife had been a promise to go on without her. And it had taken him six months to feel capable of fulfilling that oath—half a year, and a run-in with an unexpected, unfathomably complex Mimosa Lane neighbor who hadn't even been part of their world then.

He was sitting alone in the shelter's break room, a foam cup full of steaming, barely drinkable coffee warming his hands. He'd first put his and Polly's wrapped gifts under the shelter's tree, then he'd spent nearly an hour not-so-subtly asking around the place, grasping for any information the other volunteers would share about Mallory. As if he could have stopped people from gushing as soon as he asked the first question.

Atlanta's homeless services community was as tightly knit a group as fire and rescue and the families on Mimosa Lane. And Mallory was clearly in her element here. Had been since she was a teenager from the sound of it, continuing to volunteer time even after she'd become a social worker and now as a nurse, offering free weekend clinic hours year-round.

And the woman never showed up empty-handed, he'd been told. She collected donations from all over—clothes and house stuff and toys and furniture and sometimes things like referrals for free dental appointments and once to a nutritionist for little Charlie Cooper right after his diabetes had been diagnosed. Whatever someone needed most, it magically appeared the next time Mallory rotated through that shelter.

Her connections to generous donors who'd pony up just about anything were legendary—a woman who was so insecure at the thought of meeting new people in a picturesque place like Mimosa Lane that she'd resorted to hiding away from the lot of them. When Pete considered her beaten-up car and sparsely furnished home, he suspected Mallory herself was financing much of what magically appeared at each shelter. Turned out she was a pro at giving away hope and the promise of things getting better to not just his lost child but needy people all over the city.

No one at the shelter knew what drove her almost desperate connection to her work in Atlanta, or why she'd moved to Chandlerville when she was still so tied to the life she'd built in town. It made Pete's pulse race to think about the seeming randomness of that decision, and the reality that if not for Polly's nocturnal wanderings Mallory might never have become a part of their lives. Or maybe it hadn't been so random after all.

I'll be here, too, always... Emma had promised that night, a night just after Christmas when Polly had been sleeping peacefully in her bedroom of just-opened presents because they hadn't yet helped her understand what was coming. *Even when I'm gone, I'll be here. You'll find me again in someone else. So will Polly. One of our friends, someone you and Polly will know instantly you can depend on. Someone who'll show you the way to go when you can't find it yourself. That'll be me, Pete. You'll see. When you find that person, you'll know I'm still here...*

A person Polly had known she could depend on long before Pete had opened his eyes and wised up.

He remembered asking his wife for guidance that first night he'd walked over to Mallory's place. Tears filled his eyes as he accepted what had been pressing toward the front of his mind since the moment he'd crossed their backyards to stomp into her world. At first he'd thought that it had been his daughter's wandering and Polly's desperation for a place to heal that had thrown him and Mallory together. Then that their shared concern for his child had been why he couldn't keep his mind off his neighbor—as a woman, not just as a helpful new neighbor.

Now he wondered if it hadn't been Emma all along.

He could sense her again as he sat in a shabby break room drinking stale coffee and feeling the grueling loneliness of last spring give way to a peace he hadn't thought possible again. Emma was there in his heart and mind as he smiled and thought of Mallory's antics with the shelter kids and her clear devotion to Charlie's well-being and her courage as she'd first stood up to and then helped Charlie's down-on-his-luck father believe in another chance to do better for his child.

You'll find me again, in someone else...You'll know I'm still here...

Chapter Ten

※

Too bright for our infirm delight
The truth's superb surprise...

"You okay?" Pete asked as Mallory stared down at the plastic grocery bags someone had left on the floor beside the door of the Kid Zone, the children's activity area at the shelter.

She nodded, unable to form words, the cloud she'd been floating on for the last few hours popping like an overfilled balloon. Her mind was playing tricks on her. That's what this was. That's all it had been all morning. She was dealing still with the lingering memories from her latest dream about her mother, and she was exhausted, and she was simply overreacting.

Yet the handles of the three bags were tied in slipknots that closed off their bulging contents from prying hands. Knots just like the ones her mother had taught her to make around the same time that Mallory had learned to tie her shoes. They'd still been living with her grandparents the way they had Mallory's entire life because her mother was in and out of hospitals, and when she was out her hold on reality had been tenuous on a good day. It was long before they'd run away, but Mama had already been hoarding nonsense things, hiding them and using intricate knots that only she and Mallory knew how to open without tearing the bags.

"Mallory?" a deep voice from the present said, pulling her back and making her realize that she was still staring at the floor.

"Sure, I'm okay." She turned away from her neighbor and looked up and down the hallway outside the Kid Zone.

There was nothing there. No one. At least not the long-ago someone her mind had been feeling too close that morning. This was precisely why she'd left her career as a social worker and moved away from the city. Her mother was gone. She'd been gone for over fifteen years. When was Mallory going to accept that?

The bags were just another coincidence, at the tail end of a string of them she'd been stumbling across all day. When she'd first arrived just after the shelter opened, she'd found on one of the lobby tables a rubber-banded, scratched-up-from-endless-recycling ziplock bag full of newspaper clippings. Her mama had saved articles like that, all kinds of them about nothing in particular, yet she'd sort through them and organize them and check to make sure she always had them, over and over again.

Then twice that morning while Mallory had been trying to concentrate on her program she could have sworn she'd seen someone on the outskirts of the crowd of parents and kids who was too tiny to be identified clearly through the other people, wearing an old orange coat that looked just like the one her mother had their last winter together.

"Mallory?" Pete was looking at her as if she'd suddenly grown two heads.

"I'm fine," she said. "I didn't sleep well again last night."

Or maybe it was that she was still in full Glinda regalia while she grappled with ghosts every time she turned around.

She gave Pete her full attention and shrugged off her paranoia, accepting that having him and Polly immerse themselves in her natural habitat was ratcheting up her anxiety. Lord, she *had* to get some sleep tonight. She had another full day tomorrow at a shelter closer to the airport.

Squeals and shrieks of kids at play engulfed whatever Pete tried to say next. The innocence and exuberance of the shelter's Kid Zone was the irresistible boost she needed. She'd sent Polly there to play so she could finish the last of her paperwork, then had walked Pete over after he'd wandered into the deserted clinic from wherever he'd been passing time since she'd shooed him off earlier.

No matter what children like Charlie Cooper were living through at home, laughter and play and make-believe ruled in the Kid Zone. After a long morning of taking care of what everyone else needed, Mallory always stopped by to see if any of her favorite regulars were still around. And today, right there in the middle of the scramble of happiness, was a totally enthralled Polly Lombard running with the crowd, free and loose and for the moment exactly as Mallory imagined she'd been before her world had fallen apart.

Mallory laughed herself, marveling at a lost little princess coming back to her happy self amid the hastily scattered Christmas decorations Mallory had helped the shelter manager put out last week. She turned to Pete in triumph.

"Look at her," she said, exhaustion and worry falling away. "Flu season could have made this a drudge of a day for me. But you helping Charlie's dad and Polly having such a good time and me wearing my favorite work clothes…" She twirled, his wide smile making her feel as if she were wearing sparkling wings instead of a secondhand costume. "I'm so glad you two came for a visit."

Pete opened his mouth once more to say something, but the happy uproar of no less than fifteen kids rose another decibel. He placed a hand on her arm, the contact so startling she jumped with the memory of feeling his strength surrounding her as they'd both held Polly in her kitchen. She suddenly, desperately wanted to be there again. The look of surprise on Pete's face made her wonder if he were remembering the same moment.

When he'd returned to the clinic there had been a glimmer of sadness behind his handsome smile. But whatever had been troubling him had vanished as he'd watched the kids along with Mallory. And now he was leading her down the hallway beyond the Kid Zone, a new intensity to his expression, a new heat sizzling through her from his touch.

But that was ridiculous. They were simply caught up in the magic of watching Polly. The tension she'd felt sparking between them on Monday had been one-sided, just as any subtext to what he was doing now existed in her imagination alone. He simply wanted to talk with her in private.

She pulled herself together as they stopped walking, intending to make an excuse to slip away before she embarrassed herself. Only she couldn't. She simply couldn't. It felt too good to be standing so close to him, feeling him, having him focused on her as if there weren't space enough in that moment for anything else but them.

Pete rubbed his hands up and down her arms, which were bare compliments of her Glinda garb. Awareness and pleasure and chill bumps darted everywhere at once. He bowed his head. He was so close she could have stretched up on her toes and brushed her lips against his temple. She didn't. She didn't dare move for fear of unsettling whatever was happening between them.

He straightened.

The world around them faded away.

"What you've done for Polly…for us…" His hands cupped her shoulders. "This last week has been a miracle. Polly's getting better and better, and you've given her that power. You've set her free somehow, and I…"

His voice broke, and there were tears in his eyes. The muscles in his jaw clenched. He was so clearly trying to control himself. He'd been trying to keep it together and be okay for so long. And he was so much stronger and closer to being better than he realized.

"You'll be free of it, too," she promised.

Not that anyone was ever really free of the pain and damage and shock that losing someone you loved could create. But this strong man was going to make it. He had to know that.

"It will come back," she said, "the natural way you and Polly have always loved each other. It will feel good again."

His grip tightened, deepening the physical connection he was creating between them.

"As good as it feels with you right now?" he asked. "You've got to be half-dead on your feet. But the sound of my daughter laughing makes you light up like your Christmas tree. I could stand right here with you, listening to her having fun down the hall for the rest of the day. Do you have any idea how long it's been since anything has felt this easy?"

She shook her head, not knowing what to say or what to deny first. She'd been a confused, muddled mess most of the morning, not shot through with light. If she were so amazing, why was she selfishly longing to cling to him and lose herself in his compassionate gratitude, taking advantage of his weak moment so she could be held in this strong man's arms for just a little longer?

"I'm glad you both are doing better," she said. She gasped when his hands cupped the sides of her face. "But really, it's noth—"

"Don't," he said over her.

She shook her head, rubbing her cheeks against his palm. "What?"

"My family was speeding toward a cliff, and you've helped us pull back. Don't cheapen what you've done by shrugging it off, even if you're not feeling the same things I am. If you don't want to hear any of the rest, at least let me be grateful."

She blinked.

"What…?" She'd wanted to ask him to repeat himself, to explain. But she knew better.

Soon he and Polly would be fine on their own. The novelty of whatever he was feeling for Mallory would wear off, and so would his interest in the offbeat parts of her he thought he was beginning to understand. Or maybe she'd be the first to pull away. Regardless, she would be left alone once more trying to carve out her own place in Chandlerville. There was no point in growing dependent on the Lombards to help her feel as if she were as much a part of Mimosa Lane as they were.

There was only pain waiting for Mallory when this got too hard for all of them.

"You're helping more than just Polly with everything you've done for us," he said, his voice vibrating with need, tempting her. His gaze dropped to her mouth, torturing her. "And I—"

She was kissing him before she was aware she'd pushed up onto her toes. Reckless or not, it felt so good to have his lips pressed against hers. His harsh intake of breath said it was the same for him, that she wasn't the only one lost in the possibility of connecting instead of pulling back, wanting instead of shying away, feeling instead of shutting down.

He angled her head so he could deepen their kiss. This wasn't gratitude or appreciation or even a celebration of how far he and Polly had come so quickly. Mallory could feel his need, his desire, his wanting—for her.

And she could feel herself opening up to him the way her heart had always been wide-open with his daughter, no boundaries, no choice on her part. Her hands were sliding up his arms, then her arms were encircling his neck because she couldn't make herself stop. This was a day she wanted to remember feeling free and alive and needed, not lost to the scary shadows of a past she couldn't seem to escape no matter how hard she tried.

You just keep on bein' strong... Grams's voice echoed through her mind.

Pete Lombard was giving her something to cherish forever as their tongues found each other and began to dance. No matter what happened next, this was an amazing moment in time she refused to deny herself.

His powerful arms engulfed her, his hands sliding down and up her back, and then down again to the curve or her waist. He consumed her thoughts and her feelings and her awareness until there was nothing before, nothing beyond, just now.

"Daddy?" a tiny, trembling voice said.

Mallory and Pete sprang apart as if electrical current had arced through them. Polly was staring at them from the Kid Zone doorway, her bottom lip trembling.

"Sweet pea..." Pete said, his head down and his hands on his hips as he sucked in the oxygen Mallory couldn't get her own lungs to process.

"Mallory?" Polly asked, looking between the two of them as if they'd stolen her perfect day.

"Sweetie…" Mallory stepped toward her, her Glinda dress rustling. She reached her hand out, to do what she had no idea.

"Leave me alone!" Polly took off toward the lobby, leaving Mallory grasping at thin air.

"God," Pete said, starting to head after her.

"No." Mallory's touch stopped him. "Let me talk to her. You two have enough to deal with. Let me try to help her understand."

But understand what, exactly?

Mallory took off after the little girl who'd already disappeared into the lobby Mallory hoped was still deserted. A part of her accepted that she was running away from Pete, too, and her own shock at what they'd done. She bolted down the hallway, grateful that their focus was once more on Polly. She turned the corner and came to a skidding halt. She rubbed at her tired eyes.

But her vision wouldn't focus, or clear, or whatever it would have taken to transform what she was seeing into something else.

She was just standing there. In her hands were more plastic bags like the ones Mallory had seen earlier. And the woman standing beside Polly—both of them gazing up at the center's sagging, barely decorated Christmas tree—was dwarfed in the atrociously filthy, oversize orange coat Mallory had noticed blipping in and out of her sight line that morning.

Given the center's aggressive heating system, the gray-haired woman had to be sweltering in the garment. But she'd never take it off, Mallory knew. She'd never, ever take it off, or someone might steal it as soon as she wasn't lookin'…

It couldn't be.

Mallory couldn't be seeing her mother standing beside Polly Lombard, both of them staring silently at the shelter's artificial tree. Every adult, emotionally healthy, reasonable thing within Mallory froze. Her feet, her breaking heart, literally wouldn't move.

"Who is that?" Pete asked, rounding the corner beside her.

"It's..." She couldn't say it.

"Do you know her?" An edge of unease tightened his voice.

"I..." No. She didn't know the woman. She didn't know herself in that moment.

"Polly?" Pete called to his daughter. "Come here, sweet pea."

Polly looked back at them, her eyes sparkling, the tree's lights reflecting in her tears. Then she looked up at the woman and smiled, as if she'd made a new friend in just the few seconds it had taken Mallory and Pete to reach her.

"It's okay, Daddy," she said, reaching for the woman's hand and holding on when her friend didn't pull away.

"Mallory?" Pete asked. "Who is that? Do you know that woman?"

"I...I don't know." All she knew suddenly was that she wanted Polly with her and Pete instead of standing beside a ghost from Mallory's past. "Polly, can I talk with you for a minute?"

A little girl could look so grown-up when there was anger and disappointment and a sliver of betrayal flashing in her eyes. But this little girl, no matter how upset she still was as she glanced again at Mallory and Pete, had a soft spot in her heart for the people she cared about.

With one last glance at the tree, then up at the street lady she'd found next to it, Polly let go of the wrinkled hand she'd been holding and walked slowly across the lobby. When she was close enough, Pete picked her up and hugged her stiff little body close.

"I'm sorry Mallory and I surprised you that way," he said into her curls. "It...We were surprised ourselves, darlin'. And the last thing we wanted was to upset you when you were having so much fun. Please talk to us."

We.

Us.

Believing that she belonged had never been an easy thing for Mallory. It was as much of an impossibility for her now as when she'd been a little girl and had been treated like a pariah as she and her mother wandered in and out of dingy small towns and shelters. The instinct never went away, to feel safer on the sidelines where no one really saw you.

Through the years she'd carved out her happiness in other ways, watching the world she lived in more than she'd actually lived in it. Only now her world was full of people like the Lombards and Julia Davis and her colleagues at school like Kristen Hemmings. And a good man's kisses and his bravery and his determination to save his daughter's Christmas were making Mallory want to be part of a *we* more than ever, a connection she hadn't truly had with anyone since her mother, not even her grams, no matter how hard Mallory had tried.

It felt both terrifying and right to ease into Pete's arms as he reached for her, and to be pulled into a group hug with Polly.

"You were kissing her like Mommy." Polly's voice was fierce and frightened and confused.

"Not like Mommy." Pete held on when Mallory tried to pull back, preventing her from leaving the circle of his arms without making a scene. "I was kissing her like Mallory. Like I've wanted to kiss her since last weekend. I'm not trying to replace Mommy. And Mallory wouldn't dream of letting me do that."

Since last weekend?

Mallory's thoughts and senses spun, too fast and too full of conflicting emotions. Pete Lombard had wanted to kiss her all along.

Their embrace by the Kid Zone hadn't been an impulse, a moment of weakness she could shrug off once they calmed Polly down. It had meant as much to him as it had to her. And she had absolutely no idea why at the moment, or what any of them were going to do about it.

All she knew was that she was holding on—to him and Polly—and not just because he still wouldn't let her go. She simply couldn't make her arms drop to her side and have any confidence that she could remain on her feet on her own.

"I don't understand." Polly's voice was soft and muffled against Pete's shoulder.

"Will you let us help you understand?" Mallory asked, feeling her own confusion throbbing behind her eyes. "Let your daddy take you home, and I'll be there as soon as I can." As soon as she figured out who the woman in front of the Christmas tree was and where she'd gotten her coat. And the plastic shopping bags. And the collection of news clippings Mallory had found earlier. "I'll come by your house this time, and we'll talk as long as you want until we all understand this better."

Pete rubbed his cheek against his daughter's head. The hand that wasn't holding Polly squeezed Mallory's shoulder. They were in this together, his gesture said.

Polly nodded her head in agreement, closing her eyes and snuggling in.

"I think she needs a nap." Mallory smiled, because it was the most normal of normal-kid reactions, to be demanding and angry one minute and the next to be almost comatose from an exhausting, busy morning. Seeing Polly feeling and acting like a cranky, tired seven-year-old made her heart sing.

"She'll sleep all the way home," Pete agreed.

He'd grabbed Polly's jacket from the Kid Zone somewhere between their kiss and the lobby. He draped his daughter's shoulders in quilted pink nylon, not bothering to stuff her arms into the sleeves. He nodded toward the other side of the lobby, bringing a screeching halt to the warmth of belonging spreading through Mallory.

"Who was that?" he asked.

She shook her head, deciding that she wasn't going to answer and she wasn't going to turn around herself, not until Pete and Polly were on their way. She couldn't face the memories lurking in front of the shelter's Christmas tree until they were gone.

Then his words replayed and fully registered.

Who *was* that?

Past tense.

She whirled around...to find nothing. There was nothing there. No one. No bags. No stooping, gray-haired woman. No molting orange coat. Just a sad-looking tree that stood crookedly proud, defying visitors to think of it as anything but regal in its shabby splendor. And beneath it, lying on the tree skirt with the wrapped gifts people had donated, was a filthy doll that looked so familiar Mallory raced across the room to grab it up.

"How...?" She scrambled to the front door, pushing the thing open, her heart pounding in her chest. A scream of denial, of being abandoned all over again, rolled up her windpipe. "Where did she go?"

"Who?" Pete was right behind her. He looked up and down the street with her.

"The smelly lady?" Polly asked, rousing herself to look, too, then to stare at the dirty doll clenched in Mallory's fist.

Mallory experienced a moment of relief that Pete and Polly had been there to witness the woman's appearance—at least she knew she hadn't imagined the entire thing. Then, as she looked down at the doll and thought of all they'd seen, a wave of shame rolled over her. Would she have to explain it? Would Pete make the connection on his own between Polly's odd-looking, *smelly* woman and the bags Mallory had been staring at earlier?

The other shopping bags! The ones by the Kid Zone. And the ziplock bag full of clippings. They were likely still where Mallory had seen them. Did she dare hunt them down with the Lombards still there? Could she afford to wait even a moment to be certain of what her instincts were telling her had just happened?

"Mallory?" Pete asked. "Who was that woman?"

After all this time, the past Mallory hadn't shared with anyone in her adult life had returned for real. Of course it was happening in the midst of her reboot. In the middle of Christmas. Of course it was happening at the same moment that she'd found herself connecting with people who thought she was just like them.

Pete assumed she was someone he and Polly could want, because that's how things worked on Mimosa Lane. He thought they could be a *we*. All while the reason being part of anyone else's life had never worked for Mallory had been lurking somewhere nearby in a shabby orange coat.

"Hey," he said, stepping closer. "Are you okay?"

"That..."

She shook her head and took a deep breath, gazing back at him and Polly. They really were a beautiful family. She would be so blessed, so lucky, to be part of their Christmas this year, and anything else they were willing to share with her. Except she couldn't, not unless they knew everything.

Take your medicine, Phillips.

Then just keep goin'.

"I think that homeless woman was my mother," she said.

Chapter Eleven

I years had been from home,
And now, before the door...

Mallory's mommy?

Polly started looking extra hard up and down the street for the sad old lady who'd smelled so funny. The lady had been standing there under the shelter's tree, just staring at it the way Polly liked to stare at Mallory's tree. She'd been so sad and quiet, and she hadn't said anything about Polly crying, like she should stop and not be sad, too. And she'd held Polly's hand when Daddy had first said she needed to walk away, nice and tight, like the lady had wanted to be friends.

Mallory's mommy had wanted to be friends.

"What's homeless mean?" she asked.

Daddy hugged her closer, but he didn't answer. Neither did Mallory. They were looking at each other like they'd just met or something, even though they'd been kissing before.

"Daddy?"

The sick feeling was back in Polly's tummy, the one that had made her run when she'd found them in the hallway and it had felt so wrong. Not bad wrong, she guessed. She just wanted things to stay the way they'd been all week, with everything feeling better and today to look forward to and her not having to think about anything she didn't understand.

Only now she didn't understand what Mallory had said about her own mommy and the old lady with the weird-looking coat, like she didn't understand why Mallory and Daddy had been kissing or why they weren't talking to each other now. And Mallory looked really angry. Or scared. Or angry-scared, the way Polly had felt when she'd yelled at Mrs. Davis at school on Monday and then cried for so long.

She grabbed Mallory's hand the way she had the sad old lady's.

"Don't be scared," she said, wanting things to be better for Mallory, too. "I'm not mad anymore, and your mommy will come back. Won't she, Daddy?"

***

"That was your mother?" Pete asked, convinced he hadn't heard Mallory right.

"Maybe." She gave a shrug that might have looked nonchalant if her voice weren't shaking. "My memory from that time tends to be a little fuzzy. That's what can happen to a kid after she spends six years living on the street with only an emotionally ill parent looking out for her until she can't take it anymore."

"You and your mother were—"

"Homeless, yeah. It's the sort of thing you try the rest of your life to forget, only it's always there. It's always comin' back to you. It's never really over, you know, when you lose someone like that—the way I lost my mama when she turned back to the street instead of stayin' with me and my grandmother. You learn to deal with it and move on with your life. But it's never really over."

Pete wouldn't have been more stunned if Mallory had said, "Why yes, I actually am Glinda the Good Witch. Why are you surprised?"

The truth of what she'd said resonated, though, along with the damaged kind of pride that stole into her expression as she'd waited for his next response. She was clearly expecting him to pepper her with more questions, no doubt negative ones to reinforce whatever assumption she'd made about human nature that had convinced her to keep the circumstances of her childhood hidden from everyone.

Six years on the street. She'd been homeless as a child for six years, wandering around with no permanent place to stay, no security, no connections, except for—how had she put it?—a mentally ill mother?

How did someone survive an existence like that unscathed and move on to thrive as an adult? How did you tell people who only knew you as a well-adjusted, empathetic, compassionate person what your childhood had really been like? How did you do things like buy furniture and participate in cozy neighborhood functions and trust people with who you were inside and what you really felt like deep down where they couldn't see?

All this time, he'd assumed Mallory liked being alone. Everyone had. Looking at her now, with her arms wrapped around the middle of her glittering, threadbare costume, it made more sense that she simply saw herself as alone, period, and that was that. Meanwhile she'd made a life out of helping everyone who needed her, more than any other person would help, even to the point of spending her income on shelter donations instead of on her own comfort.

He glanced back inside, then again at the woman standing next to him who was coolly expecting him to judge her or make some kind of knee-jerk observation, or to back off from her revelation as if it somehow made her less appealing to him.

"You really are something, you know that?" he said, curling Polly's body closer and longing to do the same for the brittle woman standing in front of them, shivering as winter wind rushed across her bare arms. "You're amazing, Mallory Phillips."

Her mouth dropped open.

Her stunned gazed shifted to Polly, as if his child would have to be the one to toss her out of their lives because Mallory had survived the same existence as the neediest of those she now helped. Polly did him proud. Her head bobbed up and down in agreement that Mallory was by far the bravest, most inspiring person they'd ever met.

"Was she really—" he started to ask.

"I don't know." Mallory was shaking, so slightly he could barely see the tremble in the hand that self-consciously smoothed down her hair and clothes. Her too-bright gaze told him that she was shattering inside.

"Can we help?" he asked.

She clearly wouldn't believe him if he insisted that he thought even more highly of her now than before. Even though she'd initiated their kiss he'd felt her confusion as he'd held her, wanted her, needed her. He'd sensed her holding back something of herself, as if she couldn't accept how much he desired her in return. In her mind he clearly had even more reasons now to keep his distance.

Or was it the other way around?

"I…" She shook her head. "I need to look for her."

She was peering inside again, past him and Polly as if they were already somewhere else.

"We could—"

"No!" she barked. She inhaled, a good witch trying not to lose control. "Just take Polly home. She's had a big day, and I…"

She didn't want them there.

She didn't want a witness to whatever she was going through. Alone was likely the only way she could deal with running into her mother for the first time in God knew how long. As much as he hated to accept it, him and Polly being there was making this harder for her.

He nodded, not that he would allow her to think he was stepping away for good.

"I'd like to speak with you whenever you make it home tonight," he said.

"I understand." Her spine straightened.

She didn't understand anything about him. Not enough. Not yet. "Will you stop by, no matter how late it gets?"

She nodded. She opened the door to the building. Her costume swished around her as she disappeared inside without them.

"Where did her mommy go?" Polly asked. She tugged Pete's sleeve. "Daddy, is that really Mallory's mommy?"

"I don't know. But I think we should keep this just between us for now. Mallory needs some time to figure this out without anyone else knowing about it."

"I won't tell anybody. But I want to help her look for the lady."

Pete put his daughter down and knelt beside her. "You've been a good helper already today. Mallory was so glad to have you here."

"And you, too?" Polly's forehead wrinkled as if she were remembering the kiss she'd witnessed and still wasn't sure what it had meant.

"Yes, I think she was happy to see me, too."

He relived the awakening he'd had as he'd stood there and watched Mallory laugh and celebrate Polly's miraculous progress. He'd felt a bit more of Emma come back to him, just as he had in the break room. Had it been her approval, maybe? Her pleasure in him finding happiness again, just like their daughter? He was coming back to life, the same as Polly was. And he couldn't bear the thought of Mallory suffering in the midst of their triumph.

"Should we look for her mommy until she can come back outside?" Polly asked.

They could, he supposed, but he'd just agreed to butt out. Mallory needed to know that she could trust him to keep his word.

She'd said she'd stop by tonight. He was going to hold her to that. Until then he had some tricky explaining of his own to do. He was going to talk with his daughter about what she'd seen, and not allow her confusion to fester and become something even more difficult for them to deal with.

"I think we should let Mallory do what she needs to here, while we go home and talk a little."

Polly scowled, shuffling a step away. "About you giving her a mommy kiss?"

A mommy kiss. A kiss he'd have given Emma if she'd been there with him in that moment—a moment of connection so intimate, no matter how public, that even his seven-year-old hadn't missed the significance of it.

His daughter's eyes were sleepy. The joyous exuberance that had charmed him and Mallory was gone. But she didn't shy away when he reached for her hand. She was wanting him to explain what had happened instead of wanting him to go away.

Be honest, had been Mallory's wise advice—a woman who hadn't felt safe enough to be honest about who she really was with anyone in their community, no matter how much she clearly wanted to belong in their world.

Safety, he'd learned from both his job and the last six months as a single father, wasn't something you waited to come to you. You had to make your own safety happen. Each and every day you had to wrestle what you needed most to the ground. He'd forgotten that for too long dealing with Polly.

Mallory had helped him get a grip on what he'd let slip away after losing Emma—the solid relationship with his child he and Polly both needed to heal. While all along Mallory had been struggling with her own private battles as she hid behind her windows and unlocked doors and over-the-top Christmas tree.

"I like Mallory very much," he said out loud, getting the words out there where they needed to be instead of holding them inside where they wouldn't do anyone a damn bit of good.

Polly nodded slowly.

"I'll never stop loving your mommy." Pete cupped Polly's heart-shaped face, its delicate contours so much like Emma's. "You know that, right?"

Another nod, her bottom lip beginning to tremble in that way he couldn't stand. He pulled her into a fierce hug, not certain exactly what he was trying to say, but knowing for sure he'd do anything to keep his daughter's love.

"Would Mommy be mad?" she asked, holding on tight the way she once had every day.

"That I like Mallory?"

Polly nodded her head and sighed. She yawned so long and loud, the release seemed to come from her toes. "And that I like her, too, the way I liked playing with Mommy and going wherever she went? That I'm giving Mallory Mommy's treasures? That she's helping me forget?"

Magic, he thought, was feeling his daughter come back to him, one hug, one sweet question at a time.

He carried Polly to the Jeep and settled her into her booster seat, then stood beside her in the shade that began to fall so quickly, so early in the day this time of year. It was only one or two o'clock in the afternoon, but to look at the deepening blues and grays of the sky and the world around them, it might have been dusk.

He didn't rush to answer Polly's question, but he also didn't hurry to the driver's side of the car and hustle them back onto the interstate. And Polly seemed content to wait, watching him, giving him time to make sense out of the crazy disarray of his thoughts.

"Are you really forgetting Mommy?" he asked first, because it was the most important question he hadn't yet allowed himself to face. "With all the things you won't let me or Mallory really see, all the treasures that you've taken over to her place after school this week...Is any of it making you forget Mommy?"

Polly's fingers clenched around the straps of her booster seat. She shook her head no.

"Has having a good time here today helping Mallory and playing with the other kids made you forget Mommy?"

Another no.

"What did Mallory say about all of your memories, the ones she's keeping safe for you?"

Polly looked down at her lap, her chin trembling the way Emma's always had when she was trying to keep from crying. "That I could have them back anytime I wanted to stop. But I don't, Daddy. I don't want to stop…"

"Stop having fun and being with Mallory? Stop taking her Mommy's things?"

She nodded.

"Me neither." He smiled when Polly's head came back up. "I don't think she meant that she'd stop wanting you to come by when you stopped needing to bring her Mommy's pins. Or that you couldn't come help here or wherever else she works on the weekend, or that you'd have to stop visiting her clinic at school once you feel better. I don't think that's what she meant at all. About either of us still being in her life."

At least, he hoped Mallory didn't really feel that way.

Polly's head tilted to the side as she weighed what he'd said against whatever she'd been thinking.

"Maybe," he said, "what she meant was that you can remember Mommy and have all the other things you want now, too. Friends and fun and being with people who make you feel as good as Mallory does. Maybe she can help you not have to stop any of it—remembering or moving on from feeling so bad."

Polly hesitated, clearly still troubled, then she nodded again.

"Sweet pea, I don't want you to forget Mommy. Neither does Mallory. No one does. But sometimes we have to let go a little and trust someone else to help us, so remembering doesn't hurt so much. I think that's what Mallory is doing—for both of us."

It was exactly what she was doing for Pete—giving him a glimpse of the future Emma had said she'd wanted for him and their daughter, where they could live free of the pain of losing her.

"I think about her stories a lot." Polly reached into her pocket and produced a tiny bit of gold metal and glass, a tarnished, delicately crafted fawn that Emma had tied to one of Polly's Christmas presents only a year ago. The little deer's body was a crystal oval. Its legs and neck and head and tail were made from a sparkly metal. Even in its neglected condition, it was a beautiful reminder. "Every time I look at Mommy's animals and flowers and bees and things, I remember the stories she told me, and it feels like she's..."

"Here," he finished.

I'll be here...

Polly was staring down at the fawn she'd clearly meant to give to Mallory that morning. She'd forgotten or she hadn't had time. Pete had no idea. All he knew was that it was the first one of Emma's pins she'd shared with him. She wasn't giving it to him or telling him whatever story her mommy had told her. But she was letting him see exactly what the tiny trinket was making her feel.

A single tear trickled down her cheek, and she sighed, looking up at Pete while he brushed at her cheek with his thumb.

"Is Mallory keeping Mommy safe for you, too?" she asked.

He felt his own eyes grow wet. He heard his sigh, and then Polly's hand was wiping at his cheek.

"I think maybe she is, darlin'."

PART TWO

Staying

Chapter Twelve

If I can stop one heart from breaking,
I shall not live in vain...

Mallory stood outside the Lombards' front door for the first and likely the last time.

She wished she could see through its dark-stained wood into the lives that were being lived inside. The darkness of an early winter evening pressed close behind her. The darkest places in her mind that she normally kept closed off, like she did the empty bedrooms in her house that made her lonely each time she peeked into them, were inching even closer.

She wasn't good company tonight, not even for herself. But she'd promised to come by. Polly might be expecting her right along with her daddy. After what the little girl had seen happening between Pete and Mallory at the shelter, Mallory at least owed her an explanation. That didn't mean she was obliged to ring the bell, though. Maybe Pete was upstairs with Polly and wouldn't hear her tentative rap. So she knocked, prepared to slink away when—

The door swung open almost immediately.

Pete wore loose jeans and the same yummy UGA sweat-shirt he'd had on when they'd first met. His feet were bare. His long, powerful body called to her like a warm, restful dream she wanted to lose herself in. He looked clean and welcoming and worried and relieved, making her feel grimy and grumpy and flat-out confused, and more aware than ever of the chasm of fundamental differences separating them.

He also looked half-asleep already, even though it was only a little past eight.

"How's Polly doing?" she asked. "Is she still upset?"

He silently stepped back for Mallory to come inside. She'd been determined as she'd gotten out of her car at her house and walked along the street to his driveway, to go no farther than his front porch. The Lombards had the kind of perfect porch you saw on cable TV shows about perfect families. There were three rockers and a swing, hanging baskets for spring flowers, and even a mat in front of the door that read, *Welcome.*

She felt an invisible cord tighten and pull her over Pete's threshold into a cozy foyer with walls painted in a buttery yellow. There was a standing coat rack and an entry table with an arrangement of seasonless silk flowers on top of it. A low bench with an upholstered seat invited visitors to sit and rest, the space beneath doubling as storage—several pairs of Polly's shoes were lined up there.

The Lombard world, at least the entrance to it, smelled like a flower shop, or flower sachets, or maybe it smelled like Emma, because her touch was everywhere from the beautifully deco-rated dining room to their right to the casual comfort of the soft, inviting, slightly oversize couch and love seat in the living room down the hall. Pete stepped closer as Mallory turned from looking around, effectively blocking her from seeing anything but him.

Every drool-worthy, solid, even-more-inviting-than-ever inch of him.

She let her gaze look its fill, too tired and wired from her afternoon to care how obvious she was being at relishing the body of a man she'd practically been crawling all over at the shelter. Her attention finally locked onto his face to find him doing the same kind of careful sizing up, as if he, too, were falling back into those stolen moments when everything had stopped mattering except for being in each other's arms.

Then he cocked an eyebrow and shot her a devilish *So...* grin, and she almost smiled back. Instead, she snapped back to her decision to bring her relationship with him and his daughter to a healthy, if abrupt, end. She jammed both hands on her hips.

"Polly?" she asked, cutting to the chase.

"She seems better about me giving you mommy kisses," he said, his word choice opening Malloy up and laying claim to the heart she'd sworn had nothing to do with why she'd shown up here tonight. "But she's also exhausted. She's sound asleep already, in her room tonight of all places. I guess we're going to have to wait until tomorrow to see if there's any fallout on your end."

Mallory swallowed. Tomorrows, she'd schooled herself on the ride back from the city, weren't in the cards for her and this family.

"Did you find your mother?" he asked, cutting to the crux of things himself.

She cleared her throat and shoved at her hair, the sleeves of her own oversize sweatshirt bunching at her elbows. She wiped the top of one of her Converse sneakers against the back of her jeans, sweeping away nonexistent dirt. She felt even grubbier than before and out of her league and longing for the trappings of her Glinda getup to at least give her a part to play here, someone other than herself.

"She's gone," she said, "whoever she was. No one got a very good look at her."

"So you're not sure?"

She was sure.

The shopping bags had still been outside the Kid Zone, and the ziplock bag of news clippings had been where she'd last seen it in the lobby. Touching them, opening them, hiding them away in first the clinic and then her car so no one else would see them, had been like being sucked into a time warp. Or a black hole.

She'd wanted to tear up the bags and everything inside them, inside her, and toss it all away before it became too real. Instead she'd sat outside the shelter and then in her driveway, poring over every bit of it, remembering and wanting to forget and feeling more lost by the second.

"Come sit down," Pete said, his voice tight and his touch gentle as he attempted to steer her toward the living room. "I know you—"

"No, you don't." She eased out of his grip. "You really don't. You have to realize by now just how little about of my life you do know."

He just had to.

Because she wanted to sit with him and tell him everything she'd never told another soul. And she really, really had to go before she started to blubber all over him like the twelve-year-old who'd cried all over her grams—who also hadn't known her, not anymore—the day she'd arrived to take Mallory and her mama home.

"I know *you*." Pete looked a little angry now, and more than a little determined. Like he'd grab her if she bolted for the door the way she longed to. "I know enough. I know you'll never ask me for help with your own problems, but that you need it more than anyone I've ever met. Maybe even more than Polly and I do."

"I've been helping myself for a long time, damn it!" The rage coursing through her, the fiercely defiant anger, was familiar and misplaced. But it was her, more than her smiling clothes and pretend costumes and cheery clinic and sparkly Christmas tree. "It might not look like much to you, but my life is a hell of a lot more than most anyone would have thought I'd have once upon a time, including me. So find someone else to feel sorry for, someone who hasn't dug in and fought for every damn thing she has. Someone like…"

"Like your mother?"

Mallory trained her gaze on a patch of lemon-yellow wall just beyond his right shoulder. She bit the inside corner of her bottom lip, an old habit that hurt just a little but kept her focused. He wasn't going to stop pushing, and she'd promised herself she'd keep her cool with this special man for the short time it should take to disengage herself from his life. Feeling her control unraveling the same as it had the first night they'd talked at her place, she turned toward the door.

His arms slipped around her from behind, faster than she'd counted on. No hesitation. No second thoughts.

Pete curled her body into his, her back fitting perfectly against his middle, her head beneath his chin. Warmth and solid strength and belonging welcomed her as if she fit and mattered and would never be released, no matter how much she tensed up at his touch and struggled to be free.

"Don't go," he whispered into her hair. He brushed a kiss across her temple. "Don't walk out of here thinking you're done with us."

It was exactly what she'd been thinking the entire drive back from the city. Because saying she was done with them was so much easier than thinking of them eventually turning her away because she wasn't going to handle this well, the way she'd never handled losing her mother well. Which meant she'd no longer be the smiling, helpful neighbor they'd gotten to know and maybe even admire. She'd once more become the messed-up product of a difficult childhood—a woman who'd as recently as last spring lived a life eclipsed by the shadow of someone she hadn't seen for over fifteen years before today.

"It's getting too hard." Her hands came up to hold on when she should be pushing away. Her heartbeat roared in her ears, not in anger, but at the panicked thought of him letting go. "It's going to get harder, and you two don't need that."

"We don't need you spending time with us?"

"Us…" she said out loud, because they'd been so close to making that fantasy a reality. She'd felt it in his kiss. But it had never been right, her wanting this moment. She'd felt that, too.

The dreams she'd been having, the morning's creepy déjà vu, the ease she'd felt with Pete as they'd watched Polly blossom into a happy, playing child, their kiss, the very real possibility that her mother might actually be in Atlanta somewhere that Mallory could track her down…Each new thing she'd experienced today had been contradicted by the last. It was like being on the streets all over again. After everything she'd done to build a solid, unshakable base for her life, she understood now more than ever just how much she was still wandering.

It was a maddening place to find herself, but it was familiar. She could handle this. She could handle anything as long as she stopped feeling so damned weak and confused because she wanted something she didn't understand how to make hers.

"Talk to me," Pete said. "Tell me what's happening. You're the one who told me that talking is the way to heal the things inside you that no one else sees. I've been trying all week to get there with Polly. Today, in the parking lot before heading home, I think we succeeded a little. She let me try, at least. And that was all because of you. She knows that, too. I think she's ready to talk with you about Emma—probably more than she ever will to me."

Polly.

Polly was getting better, and she wanted to talk with Mallory about her mommy. How did Mallory walk away from that, even when her instincts were screaming for her not to care any more deeply for the child or her father?

"She can come over and talk with me anytime she needs to."

"And you?" Pete turned Mallory in his arms. His strong hands and long fingers framed her face as he gazed down at her. "Who are you going to talk to about what's happening?"

No one, her mother's long-ago voice reminded her. *Don't talk to no one. Don't tell no one. We're on our own, or they'll take you away from me.*

The memories rushed at Mallory, along with the helplessness of that last Christmas when she'd done the unthinkable and told—because her mother had been so sick with the flu Mallory had been sure she was dying.

"No one," she said out loud, her voice too soft and sounding too young. "I don't talk to anyone about it. It would only make things worse."

"Then what are you doing now"—he tipped her chin up with a single finger, his other arm dropping to his side—"if you aren't trusting me enough to talk about it just a little."

She was holding on to him still. Her arms had wound themselves around Pete's hips. Their lower bodies were merging, solidly connected, the contact comforting and thrilling. And she was doing it all herself.

"This is a very bad idea," she said. "I can't give you and Polly enough of what you need." *Love*, she wanted to add but didn't dare. They needed so much of it, and she hadn't a clue how to love them the way they deserved. "I'm no good at making relationships with people work."

"Then stop working so hard at it." He kissed the top of her head. No pressure. No pushing for more. He brushed his cheek against the same spot. "Rest your magic wand-of-all-knowing, Glinda, and let me listen for a while. Just talk to me. It'll feel good. You'll see."

You'll see...

She wanted to believe him so badly.

They were rocking back and forth, swaying, their unhurried rhythm a perfect slow dance. It was hypnotic, the security of his easy acceptance. It was a magnet for the words and memories bubbling up inside her, the identity she'd never buried deeply enough to make it disappear forever. Not even in a perfect place like Chandlerville.

It was all there now. It was all coming back, coming for her, on the tip of her tongue and spilling out of her into the beauty of Emma Lombard's fancy foyer, and into the reality of a man she'd promised to help who was now making promises of his own. Mallory couldn't refuse him or herself. She couldn't stop the words from becoming reality as she shared them.

And so they danced, her cheek against his chest as he listened and she remembered her last two dreams out loud, bringing more of what she'd left behind into his world. She told him about that first Christmas, and then the one six years later when she'd tried to make herself believe she could save her mama. She skipped the worst parts and how it had all ended, but she let herself remember what she thought he could hear—and what she thought she could bear him knowing.

She'd been right, she realized. Admitting the truth didn't make anything better. But being held while she faced it did. And Pete had been right, too. She *was* exhausted. She was practically asleep as they stood there, barely moving, and she talked until midnight with Pete catching each memory she released, never once letting her go until she begged him to.

***

Mallory wasn't asleep this time when the sliding sound of her patio door reached her. And she wasn't at all surprised by the late-night interruption.

She was wrung out from emotionally dumping all over Pete, taking in his comfort and letting his understanding wash through her. Then with only the briefest of kisses he let her go with a promise that he'd be over to check on her in the morning—sounding for all the world as if he couldn't wait.

Thank God she'd had the presence of mind to park her car at her place when she'd returned from the shelter. Or her very conspicuous Beetle would still be in the Lombards' drive for the entire neighborhood to speculate about once the sun was up. She'd been too brain-dead by the time she'd left to even navigate the thing next door. But for yet another night, she hadn't been able to sleep.

Sitting on her bed, facing her beautiful window overlooking her moonlit backyard, she'd seen the almost ghostly figure sneak through her fence's door. She'd called Pete immediately, waking him and telling him that Polly would be staying over but that he should keep away until morning, for Mallory's sake as well as his daughter's.

Because even more than she and Polly needed to cover some tough ground that the kid clearly couldn't wait to deal with, Mallory needed a few more hours to sort things out without Pete being so close, so open, and so available.

She'd told him everything she'd dared, but there was so much more she didn't know if she could share. He'd promised to help her any way he could if she wanted to keep looking for the barely there woman who'd slipped away from them at the shelter, but she wasn't sure she could handle that either. She'd looked so many times, and searching for her mother, thinking it would fix anything if she found her, was a mistake Mallory had promised herself she'd stopped making for good. Then just before she'd left his house, Pete had invited her to come to the Mimosa Lane Christmas party with him and Polly.

They'd just see about that, too, she cautioned herself, slipping out of bed and into her slippers. She walked down her hallway, more worried than ever that she was beyond the point of being able to turn away from the Lombards, even to save them all from the ugly way experience told her this would end.

The sight of Polly standing in front of her tree made Mallory's knees weak. Because she was remembering earlier that day at the shelter, yes. But also because she wanted so badly for this moment to be the breakthrough that it promised to be for the child. *Please,* she silently prayed, *please let me make at least this much right.*

Pete had said Polly was okay now, after catching him kissing Mallory. But if the kid was okay, what was she doing out of bed again so late at night?

Polly was sniffling a little as Mallory walked to her side, both of them staring silently at the tree. The little girl was holding another of the pins she'd brought over every day that week after school. She hadn't let Mallory get a good look at any of them since Whiskers, and as promised Mallory hadn't peeked inside the cookie jar.

"This is Bambi," Polly said, looking down at the piece of metal and glass sparkling beneath Mallory's Christmas lights. "He reminded my mommy of how much she wanted a baby of her own, until she and Daddy got me. Then he reminded her of how small I'd once been, after I started getting big."

Mallory knelt, taking a closer look. The artistry of the pin was quite good, just like Whiskers. She'd bet they were from the same designer, and both very old. Which fit Pete's story that they'd either come from Polly's great-grandmother or from vintage booths at flea markets. Either way, they'd both clearly been chosen with a discerning eye for elegance and beauty.

"I love that his body's made out of crystal." Mallory marveled at the delicacy of its construction.

"You can see right through him." Polly held the little trinket up to the tree, light twinkling through the glass. "Mommy liked to wear it with her pretty scarf—the one Daddy bought her—'cause everyone could see the flowers on the scarf through Bambi's tummy. Mommy loved flowers almost as much as she loved Bambi."

Polly looked so wistful as she remembered.

"Your mommy must have loved you very much," Mallory said, "to give you something so special."

Polly nodded fiercely. "She said"—her tiny fists clenched around Bambi, making Mallory wince at the thought of her accidentally breaking something that was so special to her—"she said nothing would ever matter more to her than me and Daddy. That's what she wanted me to remember, every time…"

She shoved the pin at Mallory, the motion stiff and jerky.

"Every time you looked at her pins?" Mallory cupped the little fawn in the palm of one hand. "That's what she wanted you to remember?" When Polly nodded again, Mallory was more confused than ever. "Then why give Whiskers and Bambi and the rest away? What did you come here tonight to tell me?"

Polly glared down at Bambi. "Were you little when your mommy went away?"

So she had processed at least something of what Mallory had said at the shelter.

"I was twelve," Mallory answered. "Twice your age now, but still way too young. It was very hard."

"Were you mad?"

She'd been furious for a long time—at everyone and everything, especially herself. "At my mommy, you mean?"

Polly nodded. "'Cause she went away and never came back."

"It's hard not to be mad when we're the ones left behind. Even when the person leaving can't help it."

"Your mommy couldn't help it, either?"

Mallory shook her head. She glanced under the tree at the doll she'd brought home with her and hadn't been able to take any farther than her living room. It was the only thing lying on the tree skirt, all alone, propped up against where the tree trunk came out of its stand, a reminder that there'd be no other presents for Mallory to enjoy—and that she'd been telling herself for years she didn't mind.

Mad didn't begin to describe what it felt like to know her mother had dragged a doll around with her all this time, but she'd never once come looking for Mallory.

"She was sick, too?" Polly's eyes scrunched up as she tried to understand. She followed Mallory's gaze to the doll, then looked to where Bambi still lay in Mallory's open palm.

"Not like yours," Mallory said. "She was sick in the way she thought about things and people and places."

"You mean like she left you again today, without even saying hello? That wasn't right, you know. She should have stayed with you. Daddy and I won't tell anyone about it, so don't worry. I won't tell anybody about your mommy and what she did. But I guess if she was sick, maybe she couldn't help it."

Mallory nodded, conflicting emotions warring for control. Amazement that Polly felt the need to protect her from anyone knowing about her own mother. Annoyance at how desperately Mallory still wanted to believe that it *hadn't* been her mother today. That her mama wouldn't have just disappeared again as if she hadn't recognized Mallory at all.

So then why had she brought the doll home? And why weren't the street lady's shopping bags and news clippings in the trash instead of the trunk of Mallory's car? Why was a part of her desperate for this to be some kind of storybook second chance she knew wasn't going to happen?

"My mommy's never coming back." Polly pointed at Bambi, her finger shaking, her voice sharply accusing as if it were somehow the little deer's fault. "That's why she gave me all her pins, so I'd remember her. But remembering is ruining everything. She's ruining everything because everybody's so sad still, and it's Christmas, and…Is that why Daddy kissed you?"

Mallory blinked at the unexpected shift in Polly's reasoning. *A mommy kiss*, Pete had called it. She looked down at the costume jewelry in her palm—it was a transcendent link between mother and daughter, no matter how bittersweet having it might be to Polly right now.

"I'm not trying to take the place of your mommy," Mallory insisted.

"But you were making Daddy happy, weren't you?"

"I…" Dancing with him in this child's foyer, kissing him earlier, both had been the closest Mallory could remember to feeling like she belonged anywhere.

"It's okay," Polly said with as much conviction as she'd said she wasn't mad anymore back at the shelter, and just now when she'd said she'd have Mallory's back with their Mimosa Lane neighbors. "I want Daddy to be happy. That's why…"

"That's why you wanted to forget your mommy?" Mallory remembered her saying that. "But all these special memories… Letting them go forever would make you sad, Polly. And I don't think your daddy can be happy knowing that you're making yourself sad."

Polly looked at the closed door to the kitchen, the room where she'd left so many other treasures that week. She turned back to the shabby doll beneath the tree.

"Do you have any memories of your mommy?" she asked.

Mallory rubbed a gentle hand over Bambi. "Not like yours, sweetie. I didn't have that kind of mommy."

"Because yours didn't die? Because she left you, like today?"

This kid was going to be the death of her.

But when Polly threw her arms around Mallory's neck, giving her a tight hug, Mallory suspected all over again that Polly and Pete might just be her salvation instead. If only she could let herself reach for that kind of dream and really hold on.

She hugged Polly's sweet little body. Behind them, outside her patio doors, stars twinkled in a cloudless, freezing sky like tiny jewels, each a perfect promise that the world was a beautiful place—promises Mallory normally sat up on sleepless nights staring at alone.

"It's okay if you're not ready to remember yet." She let Polly go and handed Bambi back. The design on the little girl's fluffy bathrobe was of a mermaid princess who was willing to sacrifice everything she valued most for love. "But I would give anything for the memories you made with your mommy. Don't give up on them, Polly. They're beautiful things, just like every minute you have with your daddy now."

"And with you? Like today, being the good witch for the kids and letting me help you keep them from getting sick? That's beautiful, too, right?"

So much of the day *had* been beautiful. They'd made the best memories together. Then she'd had Pete and his cozy house to come home to instead of her empty one. And now her sleepless night and cheap, store-bought tree were beautiful, too, because she was sharing them with Polly.

"If every day could be like today"—she wiped at the tears in Polly's eyes, then at her own—"I would be a happy woman. You and your daddy made today very special for me, because you were there to share it."

Polly wiped her tiny hand across Mallory's cheek. Then she grabbed Mallory's hand and led her toward the kitchen. They pushed against the door together and stepped inside, Mallory hanging slightly back and letting her young friend lead the way.

***

Polly laid Bambi on the kitchen table after asking Mallory to bring the cookie jar over.

"Are you sure, sweetie?" her friend asked.

That's what Mallory was.

A friend.

Even if she had kissed Daddy the way mommies did, Mallory was still a friend. 'Cause they were the same, her and Polly. They were. Even though their mommies were different, they'd lost them just the same. Maybe that's why Polly had always known she could talk to Mallory. That's why Mallory had always seemed to understand the way nobody else did.

"It's so late, and you're already upset…" Mallory put Mickey Mouse on the table, then sat beside Polly.

She didn't rub Polly's hair or try to pull her into her lap or hug her again or try to talk her out of it. Mallory just waited, like no matter how long it took she'd still be sitting there. The same way she hadn't sent Polly home when she'd found her in the living room again after bedtime.

"I called your daddy when I saw you coming through the back gate," Mallory said.

She did that a lot, too—she always seemed to know what Polly was thinking, which made it easier, because then Polly didn't have to explain so much. Mallory always understood. Like how Polly could still be sad after having such a fun day and talking with Daddy the way she had on the way home and feeling better with him, the way he was feeling better with her.

It was probably wrong to still be so upset, because Daddy feeling better was what she'd wanted, and Christmas would be okay now that he was. So why was it still so hard?

"He said it was okay for you to sleep over," Mallory said. "He's going to stop by in the morning for breakfast. You don't have to do this now, sweetie. There's no rush."

They could have a sleepover, because Mallory wanted her to stay even though Polly had been mad for a while at the shelter and Mallory was still sad about her own mommy. Polly could tell that her friend was kinda lonely, too. And that having Polly there was making it feel better, just like it was for Polly.

She reached for Mickey's ear and pulled his head off. She reached inside his tummy and pulled out her own mommy's favorite things. They were so shiny and sparkly, like she was holding a bunch of tiny Christmas ornaments that had lights inside them, shining out. They were pretty and perfect and everything she hadn't wanted to feel when she'd put them away. Because how did she feel that way and not miss Mommy so much she couldn't think about anything else?

But Mallory was there with her now, and friends could feel sad things together and maybe even talk about them, so maybe it wouldn't feel so lonely anymore. Polly had been sitting in her room tonight thinking of Mallory's mommy leaving and her mommy leaving and all the pretty things Polly had left in Mallory's house as if she didn't care about them anymore. Only she really, really did care, even if she hadn't wanted to talk about them yet.

"They're beautiful," Mallory said. "How many do you have?"

"A whole box. And there are more in Mommy's room. The whole bottom drawer of her dresser is full of her nana's jewelry, like a treasure chest."

"Is that a pony?" Mallory touched each pin as Polly laid them out, picking up the first one and smiling as she looked at it.

"It's a horse," Polly said, "from a car…a cara…"

"A carousel?"

"Like at the fair. The horses that go round and round. Mommy met my Daddy on a merry-go-round when they were really young. After they got married, her nana gave her this horse…and the swan."

The horse had lots of colors on it, and tiny, shiny stones. The swan Mallory picked up next was all gold. *Real gold*, Polly had kept saying whenever Mommy tried to say it was fake. Its beak and eyes were painted black. It was so much prettier than even the sparkly horse, because it looked like a real golden bird that was getting ready to fly away.

"You can see every feather." She touched the pin, her fingers touching Mallory's hand, too.

She didn't pull away, and neither did Mallory. So she left her hand there, holding on to her friend and the pin she could remember Mommy smiling at every time she showed it to Polly, all happy and lit up, just like Mallory was smiling now.

"It's like it'll always be floating on the water," Polly said. "I saw a real swan once, and she had babies. They went everywhere together, all over this lake that's not too far from here. Mommy said that swans never leave their families. Even once they're grown, they stay together. That's why her nana made this a wedding present. Because Mommy and Daddy were going to be together forever."

There was a boy pin and a girl pin made out of red glass and sparkles, the boy in long pants and a long shirt and a hat, the girl in a skirt with some kind of crown on her head. Polly moved the rest away until the boy and girl were side by side on Mallory's table.

"Mommy said Daddy got these for her their first Christmas after they got married. She wore them every year after that, to every party. She never told anybody where they came from, not till people noticed and asked where they could get them, too. Then she let me tell the story. How she and Daddy had danced in front of their tree that Christmas. How she'd dreamed of having a baby like me."

Mallory nodded. She picked Polly's favorite pin out of the ones she'd pushed aside. A Christmas tree, all lit up like Mallory's. She put it beside the dancing man and woman, then smiled and wiped her eyes. She didn't like to cry, Polly had figured out. Not in front of anybody, just like Polly didn't want people to see when she did. Even now, even Mallory, even though her nose and eyes were stinging.

"Do you miss your mommy at Christmas?" Polly asked, because maybe Mallory needed to talk some, too.

"I think I've been missing her a lot this year." Mallory touched the tree again, then the man and woman and all the rest of the pins, one by one. "Even though I don't have the same memories as you do, I've always wanted a magical Christmas with my mama. It never seemed to work out that way."

"Never? But you have the best tree on the whole lane."

Mallory laughed, giving her quick hug. "Thanks, sweetie. I think so, too."

But she didn't sound like she thought so.

"Was it hard?" Polly asked. "Seeing that lady today?"

Mallory nodded, picking up several more of the pins and looking at them for a long time. "These are beautiful, too."

Polly thought of all the times Mallory hadn't made her talk about anything she didn't want to. That's what Mallory needed now, about the lady she thought was her mommy and the Christmases she never had and how she'd said she'd grown up without a home.

Polly looked around her friend's fun kitchen and thought of the pink cereal they'd eat in the morning and of the tree she wanted to sleep next to on Mallory's big couch. She wanted to make her friend see all the amazing things Polly saw about her life and the Christmas they were going to have together now, but she didn't want to make Mallory sad talking about herself when she wasn't ready.

"Those are all the kinds of flowers my mommy used to grow with her nana," Polly said instead. "She said she couldn't remember whether they'd find the pins first and then go find flowers to plant to match 'em. Or if her nana would give her a pin each time my mommy grew a new kind of flower she liked. But it's like a garden every time I look at all them together. See?"

Polly laid the flower pins out. Not side by side, but spread around each other like a real garden, like she used to at night after she was supposed to go to bed, but Mommy would catch her and tell her more stories while they played with the flowers together. Next to them Polly put the puppy she'd brought over and Bambi and Whiskers and a frog and a silly-looking bee.

"Now they have a place to play," she said, "like the bunny I saw in mommy's garden last year, before she stopped planting flowers…"

"You were growing flowers with her, the way she did with her nana?"

Polly nodded, but she didn't want to talk about it anymore. The flower pins were pretty, but she missed the real ones, like she'd missed having a real Thanksgiving and wanted a real Christmas, only how could any holiday be real when you kept feeling so sad no matter how good a day you'd had?

"How are you doing, sweetie?" Mallory asked when it had been quiet for a long time.

How was she doing?

Polly wanted to break every pin and Christmas and the entire world into a million pieces until it all stopped hurting. She grabbed the pins up in her fists and shoved them back into

Mallory's jar, then she picked up Mickey's head and slammed it on top with a clank that sounded bad. When she looked closer at what she'd done, she saw that it *was* bad. Really bad.

A crack ran up Mickey's head now. She'd broken it, the special cookie jar Mallory had said she'd never even used yet. She'd let Polly put her mommy's things in it, and now it was broken. She started crying when she'd told herself she wouldn't. But she couldn't stop, like she couldn't stop shaking, either. She'd messed everything up, after Mallory had said she could stay all night, and she was so—

"Sorry..." she said, not able to catch her breath so she could beg to stay anyway. "Sorry..."

"Oh, sweetie." Mallory pulled her into her lap and hugged her hard and soft at the same time. "Don't worry about it. It's just an old thing I picked up somewhere. And I bet we can glue it together. It's no big deal."

But Polly couldn't stop crying no matter what her friend said. She couldn't stop seeing the broken cookie jar, and the pins inside that she wanted to throw away again, and the flowers she and Mommy had planted last spring, and the bunny and the bee and the bird that she'd imagined coming to play the next time she and her mommy grew something.

She cried, hating the sound of it and the feel of it, and hating her pins and Mommy and the stupid garden that was all grown over and dead now, where nothing would want to play ever again. She didn't know how long she'd cried while Mallory held her and rocked her and never said Polly had to stop. So she didn't. The memories her mommy's pins always brought back kept coming, and they were making her sad when they used to make her happier than almost anything, so she kept crying.

Then as each memory passed, it got easier somehow to hold on to her friend more and the memories less. Just like with each pin she'd brought over from home, it had been easier to bring over more, because doing that really had been okay the way Mallory had promised. Like remembering now was okay, too, even though it had made her so angry she'd broken Mickey Mouse. Because Mallory was picking her up and walking into the living room. She sat on her couch with Polly in her lap and curled her feet under her. And she still wasn't saying anything or wiping Polly's face or trying to make her tears stop.

Polly looked up at her friend, then at the glittery Christmas tree Mallory was staring at. Mallory had said she'd rather have Polly's pins and her mommy memories than her tree. Polly didn't understand that. It was the best tree in the whole world. It made Polly feel better just looking at it. It had from the start.

And now that they were looking together, it felt even better. She snuggled deeper into her friend's lap, thinking about what Mallory had said about things being better when you had someone to share them with. Mallory laid her cheek on Polly's head the way Daddy used to when he read her stories in the big rocker in his and Mommy's room, and the way he did now when they watched videos on the couch most nights. And it didn't feel sad anymore, or angry, or scared. It felt really, really good, making Polly want to stay right there forever and wish Daddy was there, too.

It was getting harder to keep her eyes open, she was so sleepy. She gave up trying when she felt Mallory sigh and snuggle closer, too, like they could stay just like this all night.

The tree was still there, after Polly closed her eyes, and so were her mommy's pins. All of them sparkly and bright and beautiful in her mind. A perfect Christmas dream was waiting for her, with bunnies and birds and bees dancing all around her and Mallory, while they and their mommies snuggled on the couch watching...

Chapter Thirteen

Unable are the Loved to die
For Love is Immortality...

"Y ou're a very brave girl," the nurse said, after Mal had been rushed away from the ER cubicle where they'd taken her mama.

She slid into a cracked, creaky chair. She was so tired. It had been so long since she hadn't been forcin' herself to stay awake, listening to Mama's breathin' get worse. She wanted to curl up on the cold, hard seat and close her eyes forever.

She wasn't brave.

She was scared, more scared than she'd ever been.

She'd told. First to the people at the shelter, because she didn't think her mama was breathin' at all. Then to the nurses and doctors at the hospital, because they said they couldn't help if they didn't know more.

How long had they been on the street? How many times had she and Mama been sick? Had any medicine ever made Mama feel bad? How old was Mal, anyway, and was there someone else they could call? Because they needed to know even more if they were gonna keep Mama alive. They hadn't seen a case of the flu this bad in a long time.

"I wanna stay with my mama." Mal was about to cry. Mama couldn't stand it when she cried, or when she told. But Mama wasn't with her now. Mal was all alone and she'd already told and she could feel the cryin' coming like if she started, she might never stop.

She'd messed it all up. She hadn't gotten her mama better. She hadn't known enough about what to do. She hadn't kept them goin'. It was all gonna be over now. That's what Mama would say. And it was gonna be bad, and it was Christmas, and Mal didn't think she could take it, and she just wanted to see her mama and make sure she was okay. She wanted to hear Mama say again that they could keep goin'.

"Don't worry." The nurse crouched down in front of her chair. "Your mommy's going to be fine. Until we can get her settled, why don't you tell me who we can call to take care of you? Do you know a number we can call, sweetie?"

Her mommy?

Mal had never had a mommy. And she hadn't been a sweetie since a long time ago, since the last time her grams had called her that—the day Mal had gone to school, slipped out the bathroom window like Mama had said, and met her mama in a nearby park so they could go away together. That was the day she'd promised to stay with Mama always. To never go back. To never tell.

But she hadn't been able to wake her mama up at the shelter—no one had. Which meant she might not wake up at all, even now. And even if she did, nothin' was ever going to be fine again. Mama was bad sick. And people weren't just gonna let Mal stay there and wait for her to get better. Someone was gonna come for her now. Someone was gonna take her away, like Mama said.

Another person in scrubs, a man, rushed up to the nurse and said something. Then the nurse said something back. Mal listened but couldn't hear all they were whispering. Their faces were turned from her as if that would make her not be there. But she heard a lot of the words, some that she kinda understood. All of them sounded bad.

Like indigent *and* vagrant *and* bronchial pneumonia *and* weeks of recovery *and* ICU. *She didn't know what* septic *was, but that sounded the worst of all, the way the man whispered it even louder.*

"She's lucky the shelter called us when they did," the man said in a more normal voice, which meant he wanted Mal to hear. "That kid let her pulse ox get down to under sixty. The woman must have been half dead for a day or so. Her lungs are full of fluid. She still might not make it."

"Shhh..." The nurse looked back at Mal. "She's just a little girl."

"Sorry." The guy shrugged. "But I don't know what gives with these people. Someone's going to have to pay for their health care, regardless. Why not come in off the street in the middle of flu season as soon as they get sick. That way it won't cost a fortune at least, before we get them well enough to turn 'em back out. Tell the kid her mother's stabilized and in and out of consciousness, but she's being moved to ICU. No underage visitors. Doctor's orders. And call Defax. She's going to need someplace else besides here to stay. From the looks of them both, someplace that'll find a permanent home for her. I doubt the state'll let that woman have her back."

The nasty man left then. Now all Mal had to do was make the nurse go away, too, at least for a little while. But her heart was pounding too hard to think straight. They wouldn't let Mama have her back, he'd said. *They were gonna take Mal away forever. Give her to strangers.*

The woman knelt again. Mal just sat there not looking at her, with all that she and her mama owned clutched in her lap. She'd insisted on taking Mama's shopping bags with her when one of the shelter ladies drove her to the hospital behind the ambulance.

The lady hadn't really wanted Mal in her car. She hadn't really wanted the pile of bags Mal had refused to leave behind, either. Mal knew how dirty and smelly she and all their stuff was. You didn't notice it so much till you were with clean people in a clean place like this. But once you were and you saw how they looked at you and tried to hold their breath, it made you want to crawl into the bathroom, into the sink, and scrub until people didn't treat you like they might catch somethin' if they got too close.

"Do you have people?" the nurse asked. Her nose wrinkling, she put her hand on the sleeve of Mal's nasty-smelling coat. It was actually her mama's nasty-smelling orange coat that Mal was wearing over her own things, so she didn't have to leave anything behind at the shelter. "Where did you say you were from?"

Mal just stared at her. She hadn't said. She wouldn't say, not to the shelter people or the ambulance people or hospital people once they got here. She didn't want to tell them anything more until she talked with her mama, which they weren't letting her do.

She dug her hand under the coats and her sweater and the two shirts she always wore. "'Cause you can never be sure," Mama always said, "when you'll have to leave where you are. And it's always better to have on more clothes than you need, in case you have to start over." Mal curled her hand into her jeans pocket and then around her quarter.

She didn't want to start over. She wanted to wait for Mama to get better enough. She wanted to keep goin'. She hadn't wanted to give her mama up, she really hadn't, no matter how bad this winter had been. She looked at the nurse, wanting her to say that the man had been wrong. That it wouldn't be weeks. That Mal wouldn't have to go.

"I know you love your mommy," the nurse said. "But she wouldn't want you out here scared like this. Look at you. You're shivering even in all those clothes. I can get you something clean to wear, and we have a shower in our break room. We can get you cleaned up and something to eat. But we've got to find you someplace to sleep, honey, and I know your mommy would rather that be with someone you know than with strangers. It's the middle of the night. There has to be someone you can call."

Clean. The word felt dirty, because it wasn't where Mama would be. Sleeping. Mal wouldn't be able to. All she knew how to do when Mama was sick was to stay awake, on watch. Hungry. That was just the way it was. Mal didn't mind so much, not as long as she and Mama were hungry together.

"It's Christmas," the nurse said. "Don't you want to be with your family for Christmas?"

The tears were there before Mal could stop them. They were running down her cheeks and under her chin and into the corner of her mouth. It had been so long since she'd let herself believe she could have a Christmas, she didn't know how to feel what the nurse was wanting her to feel, not without crying. Because Mama would hate her. She'd hate her forever if Mal wanted Christmas and clean and sleep and not being hungry more than she wanted to stay with her.

Mal could have her grandparents and all the other things she dreamed of when she did sleep—Christmas most of all—or she could have her mama.

And suddenly she was six again and standing in the bathroom of her school staring out the window, making the same decision.

Which did she want more: the life she could have if she stayed where she was, or the one waiting for her if she left? She was as scared of goin' now as she had been then.

But she was scared of staying, too. She was scared for Mama. No matter what Mal did, nothin' made her better. She'd been getting worse all along. And sicker the last few years, because she wouldn't eat the food Mallory got for them or take the medicine she stole or get out of the rain and the cold, even when they had a shelter to go to with people who cared and didn't want to turn them in and would take them to the hospital in their own cars if they had to, no matter how bad they smelled or looked. And most of all, Mama wouldn't stop drinkin' and making herself even sicker.

The man was right. They coulda gotten help sooner, only Mama wouldn't. Just like she wouldn't get better, even if it meant keepin' Mal. She never had, not in six years, just like Grams and Papa had said Mama never would without doctors to help her.

Mal was so scared. And cold and cryin' and dirty and tired. And she couldn't stop. She couldn't stop cryin' or wanting her grams and papa now as bad as she wanted her mama. And she wanted the rest of what she never let herself dream of anymore. Especially a real Christmas. After all these years, Mal had wanted a real Christmas most of all.

"I'm going to get you something to eat and drink," the nurse said, lookin' like she wanted to hug Mallory but couldn't make herself do it. "You wait right here. You'll feel better once you eat something. You'll see."

She left, and Mal was finally alone. She could run now. No one would be able to find her, and she could take care of herself as long as she needed to for Mama to get better. It's what she should do. What Mama would say to do. Instead she wiped her face and snuck across the big room with all the plastic chairs and pushed through the doors to the area inside where they took care of people. She snuck all the way down the hall while nurses and doctors were too busy to even know she was there.

She slipped through the curtain to the corner place where her mama was alone now, hooked up to machines and tubes and a bag of something clear that hung on a pole near her head. She looked at her mama and back at the last six years, at never getting better and never making it and every winter getting worse than the last.

Mama didn't want to get better. She didn't want sleep or food or Christmas…or Mal. Not as much as she wanted to keep goin'. And Mal couldn't do it anymore.

She put their bags down so she could open the knots that kept one of them closed, carefully undoing everything without tearin' the handles so she could tie them back up and Mama would never know she'd been inside. If the hospital let Mama keep them at all when she went to wherever ICU was. Mal pulled out what she'd been looking for.

After tying the bags back up she took off her mama's coat and laid it on top of them. Then she walked the rest of the way to the bed and placed the shabby doll beside her mama, swallowing at how dirty it looked next to the clean sheets. The tears were back. Because it was all Mal had to give, and her mama wouldn't want it or keep it or want Mal once she woke up and found out what Mal was about to do. But Mal had to try. One more time, she had to try to make her mama want her enough to get better.

Mal could barely even picture Grams and Papa now. She wanted to stay with her mama. She really did. But too many things had gone wrong. She couldn't fix all them on her own. Mama had almost died, Mal was so bad at fixing things.

"We've gotta let the people who can help her, help her," she remembered her grams saying. "Your Papa and I done done all we can. We're making her sicker now by letting her keep goin' like she is. And we can't do that. You can't do that, Mallory Jane. We don't know enough how to help her. We've gotta let the doctors take over."

They'd been planning to call the hospital where people who were sick like Mama went. The next day. The day Mama snuck out of her bedroom window and Mal snuck out of school and they'd gone away together. 'Cause Mal had told then, too, when she'd promised Grams she wouldn't. They'd be back before that Christmas, Mallory had thought when she'd told Mama Grams and Papa's secret. Then everything would be better. Fixed. Sparkly and bright. Perfect.

"Merry Christmas, Mama," she said, stepping away from her doll and the bed, from Mama and the family they should have been but never were. "I love you so much. Please don't go away... No matter what I have to do next, please don't go away forever."

She dug her hand into her pocket for her quarter. Tears choking her, she backed away, trippin' over their bags on the floor. She fell, then pushed herself to her feet and ran through the curtain, right into someone who was standin' there.

"Hey!" It was the nasty man from before. "How did you get back in here?"

Mal ran. She ran through the doors to the room with the chairs, then out of the hospital and down the street, for street after street, shiverin' now that she was outside and it was snowing still and she didn't have two coats on. She ran till she was sure no one was following, then she ran some more, hunting for a phone booth even though it was hard to see. And all the time she was cryin'.

"You're a brave little girl," the nurse had said.

Mal crashed into a phone booth and shoved the door closed behind her to keep the wind out.

A sick green light flickered on, making it not so dark. She reached for the phone and pulled out her quarter, but she didn't put it in the slot. She clenched her arm to her side wishing she had her doll back to make her feel braver somehow, like a big girl one more time.

Would Grams and Papa even want her back? Would they still come for her after all this time?

She put the quarter in and punched the numbers. Almost right away a voice said she needed more money, or to press zero to talk to someone. The lady who answered after zero said that if Mal had no more money she'd have to make a different kinda call. Collect, the lady said.

"What's your name, darlin'? Who you callin' at this time of night on Christmas Eve? You in some kinda trouble?"

A golden kind of light from across the street made her look closer, through the dark and the snow. It was a Christmas tree like the one she remembered from home, better than she did the faces she'd left behind. It was all lit up and magical. It was the kind of tree that families had, the kind happy people sat around all the time and looked at because it made them happier. The kind of tree she'd thought she and Mama would have by now, somewhere together where it was better and safer and happier than Mal had ever dreamed of.

"My..." Mallory scrubbed her tears away and told herself that dreaming of perfect Christmases was for stupid babies. She wasn't a baby anymore, and she'd never be that stupid again. "My name's Mallory Jane Phillips...And I need to call my grandparents. I... We need to go home."

Chapter Fourteen

Where Thou art, that is Home…

Pete knocked on Mallory's patio door, feeling a bit like a spectator, one who had no idea what was going to happen next in the movie of his life. The past twenty-four hours had been that mind-bending.

He'd kissed Mallory at the shelter. He'd danced with her in his house, even though she'd never gone farther than the foyer he'd painted with Emma. She'd talked—really talked—about her past and herself. Then they'd held each other until she was either going to leave or he was going to lead her upstairs to the bedroom he'd shared with his wife and make the sweetest, deepest love to her he knew how.

He'd promised to visit today, needing her to let him when she'd felt so close to letting go when she'd first arrived last night. She'd agreed that they should talk more, sounding a little like she was swallowing some particularly nasty medicine rather than looking forward to it. Then he'd gotten another midnight call about his child that had helped him relax a little about whether she'd honor her commitment.

This time Mallory had asked him to let his daughter stay, at least until morning.

As he waited for her to answer his knock, he remembered how freaked he'd been the first time he'd visited, dreading dealing with the stranger inside. Anticipation hummed through him now. He needed to know more. She had to tell him more. And he had to find some way to convince her that regardless of her secrets they still had a shot.

Mallory had survived so much more than the little that she'd shared with him so far—and what she'd revealed had been heartbreaking enough. She seemed to be fighting the emotional connection she clearly still felt to her mother, as much as she distrusted the efforts folks on Mimosa Lane had made to become part of her life. Yet her heart kept making room for his child. And what about him? Was she willing to make a bigger place for him, too?

He wasn't altogether comfortable with how much he wanted that answer to be yes. But being comfortable wasn't what drew him to Mallory, he'd accepted. Feeling alive was. Every time they were together she challenged him to grab for life again with the same fearless, relentless determination she did. Her grit and faith and hope, after everything she'd fought her way back from, were awe inspiring.

After Mallory's call he'd stared across their backyards from Polly's room, at Mallory's tree and the solitary world she'd built for herself on the other side of her sturdy fence. He'd resolved almost nothing about whatever they were becoming to each other, except that he wished he had half her strength. And that he wanted to help Mallory believe in the love and belonging she so clearly wanted, as successfully as she was helping him be the father Polly needed.

There was no answer to his knock, just like the last time. He squinted through the wall of glass that the morning sun had turned into a reflective mirror. In the shadows beyond he saw a nearly empty living room the same as before, with one poignant exception.

They were curled up together on her nondescript couch, like kids snuggled before the Christmas tree waiting for Santa. They were both in their pajamas, their hair wild and covering much of their beautiful faces. They looked so peaceful with Polly's body sprawled half on top of Mallory's, both of their heads resting against the cushions.

He slowly rolled the patio door open, expecting Mallory to wake at any moment. She was a light sleeper, she'd said. Considering everything he'd learned about her, the wonder was that she'd mastered the art of sleeping at all. Her formative years had been spent guarding her mother and their belongings through endlessly long nights, often in places where they had to have been in very real danger.

She sighed as he stepped around the sheers that as far as he knew had never been released from their wall-mounted ties. But instead of waking she curled Polly closer, her cheek pressed to the top of his child's head. Watching them, Pete felt his life click into sharper focus.

Waking without Polly to get up to begin living their day together had been difficult after a week of focusing on nothing but rebuilding his connection with her. He hadn't known what to do with himself and hadn't been able to wait for Mallory's call. Only it hadn't just been Polly he'd come searching for. He knelt in front of the beauty before him. He'd rushed over in his sweats and bare feet without having even his first cup of morning coffee, needing to be near both of these mysterious, mesmerizing creatures.

You'll find me again, in someone else...someone who'll show you the way...That will be me, Pete...

He ran gentle fingers down the flannel sleeves of Mallory's red nightgown, until they tangled with her own. He squeezed, wanting to believe she'd give them a chance. He lifted her hand to his lips. Smiling, he watched her eyes drift open as if he'd awoken a princess in a fairy tale.

She smiled back, an instinctive response so free of self-preservation it grabbed at his heart. Then her eyes closed again, and she nestled deeper into the cushions. Polly's head lolled against her breast.

"I haven't seen her sleep this soundly in a long time," he said.

Mallory yawned, her eyes still closed. "She was up late last night. I doubt she'll wake before lunchtime."

"You planning on being lazy, too?" He kissed the corner of her mouth. *That* got her eyes open again. "Or can I tempt you with some coffee?"

She straightened, caution creeping into her expression. But something of last night's dance still remained. Enough that she squeezed his fingers back before letting go.

"Come with me to the Christmas party next weekend," he asked again, needing her to say yes so he'd know she wasn't already planning her escape from what had deepened between them. "It's no big deal. There will be so many neighbors there you won't have to spend any more time with any of them than you want to. It would mean a lot to Polly—and me. Let me show you the best parts of Mimosa Lane. Let me show you that there's a place for you here."

"Coffee," she said in a hushed voice, the last of sleep's softness evaporating. She scooted out from under Polly and resettled her gently on the pillows. She rose to stand beside Pete, revealing a screen print of Grumpy scowling back from the flannel that fell in soft folds all the way to the bright-blue polish on her toenails. "I can't deal with neighbor talk without at least one cup of caffeine in my system."

She led the way to the kitchen that perfectly matched her nightclothes. The playful ways she managed to celebrate life in her own unique way, while other parts of her world seemed so barren, made him smile. Was she making up for some of the things she'd missed as a child? Was she refusing to see her world as anything but a bright celebration now that she'd come so far? She was a puzzle he wanted to take his time figuring out.

She pulled a container of coffee from the sky-blue refrigerator and tossed it to him. Before he'd even caught the thing, she'd slumped into a chair beside the table, her elbows propped up, her head dropping into her hands.

"Is this what a hangover feels like?" she mumbled.

Chuckling, he crossed to the coffeemaker, found a fresh filter in the cabinet above, fed grounds into the thing, and filled the reservoir with water.

"You've never been drunk?" After turning the appliance on he took a seat beside Mallory, his hand reclaiming hers.

"I've never had a drink." She yawned and reached for the Mickey Mouse cookie jar that stood watch in the center of the table. Its lid came apart in her hands, two chunky pieces falling in opposite directions.

"Not once? Not even in college?" He peered inside Mickey. The sight of Emma's beautiful jewelry jolted him. But he reminded himself that his wife would have been glad that Mallory had come into his and Polly's lives the way she had.

Mallory looked from him to Emma's trove of vintage Trifari pins, then back. "I worked my way through college. A lot of nights. When I wasn't working, I doubled up with extra classes, trying to minimize my expenses and get out as quickly as I could. There wasn't time for partying. Even if there had been, my mother was bipolar and self-medicated with booze since she was a teenager. Losing control isn't high on my list of fun things to try for myself."

"Were you worried it was hereditary?" he asked, not surprised by her mother's diagnosis but hurting for Mallory even more now that he knew it.

She pieced the two parts of the cartoon mouse's head back together. "I think this'll be fine with a little glue." She looked up at him, as if it were the most important thing in her world that he agreed. "Do you have any superglue?"

"Yeah." He took the broken lid and studied it carefully. "I have exactly what you need to fix it."

She nodded. She reached into the cookie jar and pulled out several of the pins, different types of flowers, blue and yellow and white.

"I knew before I went to college that I probably wasn't going to be like her." Her thumb traced the delicate curves of Emma's jewelry. "My mom had been sick since she was a little girl. She got pregnant with me in the middle of a hypermanic episode and never remembered who my father was. She was only sixteen when I was born, and was in and out of the hospital for treatment until she ran with me. You usually present symptoms in early adolescence. I was probably out of the woods by the time

I'd caught up on my studies in high school and was ready for college. But…"

"You weren't taking any chances." Her home life must have been a cautionary tale to never lose control or take chances, even before she'd run with her mother. "So you decided to focus on school and work and your family and everything else that was important to you?"

She sighed, tilting her head to the side, her expression both sad and serene—her gaze unflinching. "I never got my family, Pete. It was already messed up when I was born, and we did the best we could, especially my grams. But there was too much wrong from the start, too many daily battles and disappointments—including me. Can you imagine what it must have been like for my grams and papa to raise me because my mother couldn't? Then to have her snatch me away, thinking they'd never see me again? And when I came back home, I couldn't…I just couldn't be there and be happy the way my grams needed me to. She wanted a granddaughter, someone to love and spoil. And all I ever wanted was my mother…"

"Your grandfather was gone by then?" Pete tried to picture a disconnected home life like the one she was describing. His own parents were gone now, but before he'd lost them to a freak car accident, he'd always known he could depend on the people who'd nurtured him for anything he needed.

"Papa died while I was wandering around with my mother. When I decided to go with her, when I told her my grandparents were going to have her committed to a long-term facility and ran when Mama asked me to, I gave up my chance of ever seeing him again."

When *she* decided.

She gave up.

"You were only six," he pointed out, in awe of her courage and capacity to love deeply, despite every obstacle. "And you left them to take care of your mother."

She shook her head. "You need to stop thinking that my life has been anything like any of the people around here who you're sure I'll fit in with at that party. If you're looking for me to have any clue what makes real families happy and healthy and whole, you and everyone else are going to be disappointed."

She had a beautiful kitchen, a fantastical tree, a whimsical wardrobe, and it was all wrapped up in an empty house full of curtainless windows through which she could see the picture-perfect world going on around her, outside of her, just beyond her reach…

No, he didn't have any trouble picturing Mallory not being able to trust in what a nurturing, thriving family could be like.

"Your grandmother took you back?" he asked, unable to stop the questions from coming now that he had her talking. "You said you were homeless until you were twelve."

"Since I was six, yeah. Until my mom was so sick I had to call my grams to come get us. And, yeah, she always did whatever she could for me and my mother, no matter what we put her through. But by then something was just broken that no one could fix."

"Between you and your grandmother?"

"Inside of me, I think. I couldn't be happy with her with my mother gone, wondering where Mama was and needing her to come back for me."

"You were twelve and hardly knew your grandmother anymore. And I can't imagine what it must have been like trying to take care of your mentally ill mother under such extreme circumstances. Of course that changed you."

"I tried. I really thought I could. I tried for six years, and then I had to be the one to turn my mother in. I didn't have a choice. I called my grams and told here where we were, and within a week my mother was in a hospital near her house and I was back in my old room like none of it had ever happened. Except it had. I started volunteering at my first shelter for a high school project, and *that* felt like coming home again. Before long, I was spending every free minute in the assistance community instead of with Grams."

Pete tried to match the end of her story to the snippets that she'd shared last night. He wanted to understand what she was trying to tell him. "Helping people like your mother is why you became a social worker?" he asked. "Then a nurse?"

Mallory shrugged.

"I absolutely think," he pressed, "what you've been through is why you understood how alone Polly was feeling. Like no one was really listening to her or understanding how much her world had changed forever after losing Emma. It's not hard to understand how your wandering life with your mother made you gifted at helping other people find their way. Charlie and the other kids at the shelter, and Polly, and me. You know better than any of us what hurting that way is like, and you pulled yourself out of it at an age very few people could have."

"Don't make me out to be something I'm not." She tensed and dropped the pins back into the cookie jar.

Pete wasn't feeling exactly relaxed himself. The emotions storming through him were too close to the surface—desperation and panic that he wasn't used to having muddle his thoughts about things. Suppressing his reaction to stress was part of his job. But dissociating from his emotions at home had nearly cost him his daughter's love. He didn't want to make that mistake with Mallory, so he let the feelings fly free. He could deal with whatever he had to if it meant understanding better what she was going through.

He walked to the coffeemaker, poured two mugfuls and brought them back with him. He hadn't seen sugar on the counter or in the cabinet. He guessed that meant she liked hers strong and black like he did. She took a sip and sighed.

"So what *aren't* you?" he asked, wrapping his hands around his mug to keep himself from reaching for her.

Polly hadn't liked that, his wanting to hold her and make her better at times when she simply couldn't *be* better. Now that he looked back, there'd been times when Emma had pulled away, too, from his insistence that she was going to make it. Even at the very end when the doctors had said there was no hope, he'd wanted her to believe she could beat her cancer. He'd let his need to believe it, his fear, become a burden to her for too long.

"I'm not some tragic heroine," Mallory said, "in a story about how everything works out beautifully in the end, and all you have to do to make your dreams come true is love hard enough. You do have to believe, and you do have to love, and you have to hope and keep hoping or you'll lose your mind and give up. But none of that makes the worst of what's happening to you go away. It just helps you keep going and doing the best you can, no matter how bad it gets."

Pete drank his coffee. She sounded so matter-of-fact talking about devastating emotional scars and her growing acceptance that she was too deeply tied to her past still to ever heal completely—at least not enough for her to share more than a few passing moments with a family like his or the Perrys or the Davises. As if she weren't freaking amazing for becoming what she was now—a survivor and a warrior who everyone on Mimosa Lane would feel privileged to know if she could relax enough to give them the opportunity. Somehow he had to find a way to convince her that she could. For Mallory's sake, and not just because he was more desperate by the minute to keep her in his life.

"How did your mother end up back on the street if your grandmother put her in the hospital once you came home?" She'd gone out of her way not to explain that one obvious piece of her story.

She raised her mug in a toast. "There you have it. The key to me and her that's not going to change even if I do find her wanderin' around Atlanta somewhere. No matter what I did, she stayed sick. She was too sick from the start for me to help, and too sick to see what that was doing to me and my grandparents. And in her eyes I betrayed her when I called my grams. When Mama woke up in the hospital she'd been transferred to, she refused to talk to us. When she was well enough, before anyone knew she was strong enough or thought to move her to a secure room in the psychiatric wing, she ran again. Alone."

"She left you." He'd already guessed, and he hated the defeat in Mallory's tone, her empty acceptance.

"She was never *with* me," said the woman who'd bumbled every attempt her neighbors had made to draw her into their community. "Mama was so young when she had me, and so sick, and so in denial, from the start she was never with anyone but herself. Of course that didn't stop me from trying to be whatever I thought she needed me to be, to get her to choose me over getting away from her parents. I tried so hard she nearly died before I stopped."

"But your grandmother was there for you. She took you back home, right?"

"It doesn't really work that way, you know. Just being near someone doesn't mean you're with them. Grams tried. I tried. It shouldn't have been so hard, having the simple things I'd always wanted that other families had. But I couldn't...attach again. I couldn't be with Grams the way she needed me to. Just like my mother never could be with me. It took me a long time to accept it. I looked for her for years, all over Atlanta and the rest of the southeast, making calls and asking around. As recently as last year I was still putting feelers out every once in a while. I knew I'd never find her if she didn't want to be found, but I couldn't accept it. When I left social work and moved to Chandlerville I told myself I was finally done. My mother was gone for good, and I was happy it was over. That's what family turned out to mean to me."

"You're being awfully hard on yourself." She sounded like she was going to be physically ill.

He thought of Charlie and of the shelter volunteers talking about how much of herself and her time and her own money Mallory poured into Atlanta's assistance and homeless community—for the benefit of people she hardly knew and might never see again. He considered her short-lived career as a social worker and the way she'd become instantly attached to Polly.

Mallory's problem wasn't that she didn't allow people into her life and her heart. It was that she couldn't handle trusting them once they were on the inside. Yet she was a woman who needed to be loved, to love, so desperately she'd made a life out of caring for people who could have her for only a moment before she moved on to the next crisis.

"Being honest is important to me," she said. "It's what's gotten me as far as I have."

He looked around her kitchen—the Lancers' kitchen, in a modest but not insubstantial house in an upper–middle class suburb.

"Honesty got you here," he pointed out. "Honesty and your grandmother. Don't tell me you could afford this place on a social worker's salary, after you worked your way through college. Don't tell me your grams didn't love you, if she helped make coming to Chandlerville possible for you."

Mallory flashed him a brave smile. "She wanted me to have my dream one day. She knew her heart wasn't strong, and she knew I wouldn't want to keep the house I'd grown up in in Decatur once she was gone. She made me promise not to spend the money from selling it."

"Spend it, or give it away?" It wasn't hard to imagine Mallory blowing every scrap of her inheritance on other people and having it feel better than buying something she wanted desperately for herself.

"Grams left the money in a trust for me to buy a house with when I was ready." Mallory gestured at their candy-colored surroundings. "She said one day I'd be strong enough to let everything I wanted in life want me back. She always believed I'd make it to a place like Mimosa Lane. This was my do-over. I convinced myself I could belong here the same as I did in the city. That without the daily reminders of where I came from, I'd finally have the life and the Christmas I'd always told Grams I wanted."

"Your grandparents sound like they were wonderful people." Pete heard the loneliness she'd glossed over and the clear love in her voice for the family she insisted she'd never bonded with. "They did everything they could to make your life and your future the very best it could be."

"They were good people."

"Come to the Perrys' party with me," he pressed. "Come get to know some more good people who want to make your life better."

She drank her coffee without breaking eye contact. "The Perrys?"

"Your neighbors two doors down, across the cul-de-sac from my place. They have two rowdy boys and do Christmas like a SWAT team of elves. It's really something to see. You shouldn't miss it."

Mallory giggled.

He laughed, too, grateful he could bring some lightness into her life, even if it was only for a moment. "Sam and Emma were friends. Brian's a good man, a great dad, and one of the coaches of some of the community ball teams. Sam's quiet and shy, but she's a sweetheart. I know they'd love to meet you, to really get to know you. A lot of people on the lane would."

Mallory shook her head. "I don't think I'm up for that. Not now."

"I don't think I'm up for it, either," he admitted. "But they're Polly's family, too. These are the people she's seen her mom and me enjoy being with, more than she's seen us with her grandparents who live in Boston. Her whole life, these people have been there at school, on playdates, and at the bus stop and picnics and block parties. They were a big part of her world, and I've been keeping them from her, using her unhappiness as an excuse. I don't want Polly to end up thinking that being alone is better than being part of other people's lives. That's no way for anyone to live. For her or for you."

Even Mallory's tears were inspiring, because although she was fighting not to cry her lips were softening into that smile that spoke of hope eclipsing sadness.

"You make it sound so amazing," she said. "So easy. Just show up and they'll want to get to know me the way they do the both of you. The way I'm sure they did the first time they met you and Emma."

"Like I did the first time I met you."

"Oh, yeah." Her snort would have done the real Grumpy proud. "I was a delight that night, pontificating to you about doing what was right for your daughter because what you'd been through didn't mean jack when a little girl was hurting."

He leaned forward, desperate to hold her because she was talking about so much more than him and Polly. The bitterness, the impatience, the anger, the almost hatred in her voice…It was directed at herself.

"Mallory," he said as he curled her close, "what did you and Polly talk about last night?"

She held herself so rigid in his arms he should have let her go, but he couldn't. Eventually she relaxed and leaned in, her head resting on his shoulder, her lips brushing the side of his neck.

Except for him and Polly, how long had it been? How long had this woman gone since she'd held on to someone just for her? Had she let her grams comfort her? Had her mother even tried? And all the patients and even the men in her life since… Had any of them simply held her because she'd needed to know what it felt like to be the center of someone else's world?

Pete had taken so much for granted when Emma was alive. And when she was gone, he'd let himself stay blinded for too long to all the things that remained in his life that he should be grateful for. His child, his friends, even his in-laws who'd smothered him and Polly so completely at Thanksgiving.

"What did you two talk about last night?" he asked again.

"Mothers." Mallory trembled as she said the word.

"Did it help?"

"I think she's doing better."

"Did it help *you*?" His hand slid through her hair, his fingers brushing against her cheek and tipping up her chin. He kissed her, softly, when all night he'd dreamed of devouring her lips with his own, taking and giving.

She laughed sadly and kissed him back. "Don't I sound better?"

His touch grew firmer. "You sound like you expect to be alone for the rest of your life. That that will be all you can ever handle, no matter what your grandmother or I or anyone else thinks. And you're telling yourself you don't really mind. Don't help my daughter love her mother and me again, don't hold Polly in front of your Christmas tree, don't kiss me like you do…Don't reach for us the way you are and tell yourself you can't handle it, Mallory. Don't give up the way you seem to be okay letting everything else go before it can hurt you like your mother did."

"What do you want from me?" She jerked away from him. No more self-deprecating laughter. No trace of tears in her level, emotionless gaze. "At the shelter. Last night in your foyer. Just now. Kissing me and dancing with me and holding me. Inviting me to be your plus-one to go meet your neighbors—"

"*Our* neighbors."

"Whatever you want, whenever you're ready to go there again, you could have it a hundred times easier with another woman. Someone just like your wife and your friends and everyone else you know. Someone who doesn't hate her mama for abandoning her. Someone who didn't make her grams pay for the childhood she'll never get back, no matter how hard she's searched for it everywhere she went *except* at home. Someone who doesn't want to run every time she turns a corner and finds something from her past making everything in the here and now impossible to feel real."

"I want someone who never quits when she's needed, no matter how hard the next choice is or how afraid she is of making it. She's brutally honest and doesn't let the people she loves quit, either, even though she thinks she'll fail at helping them and might never be able to make them love her back. Even when the one woman she wanted to help most never let her, and she's been trying to make up for that her entire life. I want someone who knows how badly love can hurt, real love—not the fairy-tale thing movies and books tell us caring about someone should look like. But no matter how hard she tries to protect herself, she can't seem to stop caring about people."

"Pete...I..." She shook her head, as if the words she wanted to say simply weren't there.

"Come to the holiday party with us next weekend. In the meantime, let me help you look for your mother. Because I know you're going to even though you're talking like you're through with her. You can't help yourself. You'll volunteer wherever you're supposed to be tomorrow and do whatever you can for as many people as you can. You'll be at school next week, beating back the flu before Christmas break starts and making sure Polly keeps getting better. But the whole time you'll be using every contact you know to look for your mother—even when you don't think she'll want to be found. Won't you?"

She nodded, looking impossibly young as she smiled ruefully. "She's my mama. What else am I gonna do?"

"You're going to let me help you search for what's left of your family, Mallory. Whatever you think about her, whatever happens once you find her, you need to see this through. And you don't have to go through it alone. Not this time. Then come to the Perrys' party so Polly and I won't have to go *there* alone. Doesn't that sound fair?"

"What"—she shook her head, her voice a little girl's whisper—"what are we doing, Pete? I don't understand what we're doing. What any of it means. And I…"

"I don't understand, either. Not fully." He pulled her into his arms and began rocking them both, like last night. Like he rocked Polly when nothing else seemed to get through. "But I'm strong enough to find out, mostly thanks to you. And I think you are, too, just like your grams said all along. Being alone is a choice. It's how we protect ourselves, and it's how we give up when it feels too hard to keep fighting to belong. But if you still wanted that, you wouldn't have moved to Mimosa Lane. Don't give up, not this week. Let's give this a shot."

Chapter Fifteen

I dwell in possibility...

"She wore this one all year long," Polly said Tuesday afternoon. She'd come over after Mallory had gotten home from work—just as she had on Monday. She'd brought more of her mother's pins and more of Emma Lombard's stories, wanting to share them with Mallory now before putting the pins in the cookie jar Pete had expertly repaired on Sunday.

Then she'd reached inside to pluck out one of the treasures she'd shown Mallory Saturday night.

"It's a beautiful Christmas tree," Mallory responded. And it was. Vintage and nostalgic looking, it was like a miniature of something you'd see in a Currier and Ives print, or Norman Rockwell, or some movie on the Hallmark Channel. "She wore it all year long?"

"She loved Christmas. It made her happy even when it was hot outside. She'd sing Christmas carols whenever she wore it, one time at a Forth of July barbecue. Everyone started singing with her. It was crazy, but everybody loved it. We had so much fun that day."

Mallory smiled and sipped the coffee she'd poured for herself after making hot chocolate for her guest. They were munching on celery and peanut butter, with raisins sprinkled on top—one of the few snacks she remembered from when she was very little. Polly had come a long way from Franken Berry.

Not that she and Mallory hadn't dived into bowls of that, too, once the kid had woken up on Sunday. Her daddy had already headed home, leaving them to their girl time. He hadn't pressured Mallory to talk about their kisses and the dance they'd shared, more of her memories or the raw truths she'd told him that she'd never discussed with anyone but her grams. And he hadn't insisted on an answer for whether or not she'd join him and Polly at the neighborhood Christmas party. At least not beyond saying and doing all the right things to tempt her beyond bearing.

"'Rudolph the Red-Nosed Reindeer' in July, huh?" she asked. It sounded amazing, being that easy and free about life, having fun and not worrying about whether anyone would accept you, because everyone always did. "I bet she hoped one day you'd want to wear all of these, too."

Polly had also brought over an owl that her mother had made a habit of wearing to school events, because owls were so smart and never forgot what was important. And yesterday she'd shown up with a family of butterflies—two big ones and lots of baby ones, some gold, some silver, others with painted wings. Because butterfly families were free, her mom had said every time Emma and Polly saw the beautiful creatures at the park or at home in their garden.

Polly's hands slid to her lap while she finished chewing her latest crunch of celery.

"Would wearing your mom's pins be too weird?" Mallory asked, broaching the question the little girl's stories seemed to be leading them toward.

"Wasn't it weird, bringing your mom's doll back with you Saturday?" Polly asked. "And keeping it under your Christmas tree?"

Mallory nodded.

Touché.

"It's really weird," she said. What had Pete said about allowing herself to see what love really looked like? "But actually"—there was more than peanut butter clogging Mallory's throat now—"it's not my mom's doll. It's mine. At least, I think it is. I couldn't leave it there at the shelter…alone, for someone else to find and throw away. Because it was mine, and…"

"And your mommy kept it for you since you were little?"

"Yeah, I think so. Like your mom kept all of these for you."

Though the realization didn't warm Mallory's heart the way she was hoping, Emma's pins were starting to become sweet memories for Polly. Emma had fought to the very end to stay with her daughter, which made all the difference in the world. Mallory couldn't wait for the day when Polly really got that. It would be like every Christmas fantasy of Mallory's all rolled up into one perfect present.

The little girl sniffled. She was crying just a little after letting even fewer things get to her this week at school than last. She seemed less emotionally fragile by the day—bravely looking for her answers while Pete gave Mallory the breathing room she needed to do the same.

"I know everything reminds you of your mommy, sweetie," Mallory said. "I know how that is, and I know how hard that can be. But eventually you won't want to hide all these beautiful things away." Mallory collected the Christmas tree and the owl and put them inside Mickey's tummy along with the butterfly family and the rest. "One day you'll realize you want to wear one of them. Then you'll want to set them all free to be memories again by sharing them with other people besides just me. You'll sing your own Christmas carols. And everything will be right here waiting for you. Take all the time you need. Whatever it takes, just so you don't throw them out of your life for good. That's our deal, right?"

Polly nodded. She pushed her plate away after eating almost as much of their snack as Mallory had. She reached for her hot chocolate, mirroring Mallory's motions as she drank.

"You haven't found your mommy yet, have you?" Polly asked. "And you haven't decided if you're coming with us to the party on Saturday?"

Mallory's hands clenched around her mug.

Pete had told his daughter about his invitation, which shouldn't have been a big deal. Except Mallory smelled a rat in the overbright smile suddenly spreading across her little friend's face. So much for Mallory's breathing room.

"I'll hold your hand the whole time," Polly rushed to say. "You'll see, it'll be fun. You won't have to go alone. We'll do it together, and that will make it easy, really. Give it a shot."

Let's give it a shot...

The phrasing was too spot-on to be a coincidence.

The man who seemed so certain he understood Mallory enough to know what she could and couldn't handle on Mimosa Lane hadn't learned jack about when to stop pushing his luck.

"I'm sure we'd have a great time, sweetie." She took their empty mugs and plates to the sink and rinsed them. "And if I decide to go, I can't think of anyone I'd want to go with more than you." She turned toward the table and smiled when she saw Polly slipping the Christmas tree from the cookie jar and pinning it to the front of her pink corduroy jumper. "Why don't we go find your daddy? He's probably getting ready to call you home anyway for bath time and dinner."

Pete had made a point of sticking to an afternoon schedule so Polly had a new routine to immerse herself in. Which meant Mallory would likely find him in the Lombard kitchen when she confronted him about using his daughter as a guided missile aimed straight at Mallory's heart.

She and Polly threw on their lightweight jackets. The weather had warmed since the weekend to hover most of the day in the low sixties. Polly insisted on heading out the front door instead of using the patio. She rushed down Mallory's driveway and across the cul-de-sac to the house two doors down from Mallory's and across the street from her own. The Perry house.

Mallory followed at a more leisurely pace, shivering a little in the deepening twilight. Pete was there, talking with a petite redhead who seemed to have been digging in the flower bed beneath her mailbox. She wore jeans and an oversize men's rugby shirt, probably her husband's. There wasn't a hint of makeup on her face. Not that her features needed a single artificial thing to enhance their natural beauty. She was exactly the type of woman Mallory envisioned a man like Pete falling head over heels for.

Beneath the brim of her straw hat, the woman smiled shyly at whatever Pete had last said. Her soft hair fell in loose curls to her shoulders, reflecting the last rays of the setting sun and the indirect light of the gas lamppost that stood sentinel on the edge of her property. Behind Mrs. Perry, lush, overflowing beds of plants and still-blooming flowers hinted at the hours and hours she dedicated to their well-being.

"I hope you and Polly can make it," she was saying as Mallory stopped beside Pete. "And this must be the amazing Mallory

Phillips, the best school nurse and the best friend any little girl has ever had. I'm Sam Perry." She smiled at Mallory, then at the way Polly hugged Pete's leg and laid her head on her daddy's waist. She knelt down until she and Polly were eye to eye. "It's great having you back at the bus stop this week, even if you have your own personal chauffeur again back and forth to school. Who could pass up a choice deal like that?"

With that, Sam stood, smiled Mallory's way a final time, and headed toward her house.

Pete had been studying Mallory's face since she'd arrived. "Would you mind if Polly hung inside with Cade and Joshua for a few minutes?" he called after his neighbor. "Mallory and I need to talk."

Sam turned with a flash of alarm on her face.

"That...It's okay," Mallory rushed to say. She might be irritated, but she wasn't confronting Pete in the middle of the cul-de-sac for God and everybody to speculate about. "I just wanted to make sure Polly found her dad, and when she took off down the driveway—"

"Please, Sam." Pete grabbed Mallory's hand, holding tight. He glanced down at his daughter, his gaze snagging on the pin Polly had attached to her sweater. "It'll only be a few minutes. Then I'll take her home for dinner."

Sam looked as if she were mentally bracing herself.

"Come on, Polly," she said in a forced tone she clearly wanted to sound welcoming. "I baked the boys Toll House cookies after school. I bet your daddy won't mind if you have one as long as we find you some milk to drink along with it."

Sam held out her hand. With a kiss from Pete to the top of her head, Polly followed without complaint. She looked over her shoulder at Mallory, who nodded in encouragement. Why make this any harder for either the kid or Sam, just because Mallory was boiling by now, feeling manipulated twice in one night?

Once the pair had headed up through the decorative door that sported lead glass insets, Mallory rounded on Pete.

"Polly got around to inviting you to come to the party on Saturday?" he guessed before she could say a word.

"*Give it a shot*?" Mallory mocked.

Pete winced. "For the record, she asked me if you could come when she decided yesterday that she wanted to go herself. I didn't want to speak for you since you hadn't made a decision yet. And I didn't know how to explain why I wasn't sure you'd want to go to a neighborhood get-together when simply walking across the street and meeting Sam Perry is enough to spike your blood pressure."

"I…"

Mallory could hear her heartbeat in her ears. She knew if she held her hand in front of her face she'd see it shaking. Yes, she was angry. But Pete was right. Her physical symptoms were about much more.

"Anytime I'm close to you," she said, owning it, "you and Polly and Sam or any of you people…Yes, I want to turn tail and run."

He laughed softly as if it were no big deal, her phobia of being around people she had nothing in common with. Why couldn't he just get it already—that she was too messed up for this to ever work—and put them both out of their misery? Instead, she was in his arms suddenly, and she didn't remember who'd moved first.

There had simply been the feeling of her reaching and being reached for, blindly searching and being sought after, her anger giving way to the honesty that seemed so easy, so disturbingly easy, with him.

"It's not hard at school," she said. "That's work and I deal mostly with the kids. It gets more difficult when parents and volunteers show up as often as they have the last week or so. The shelters are no problem—no one has time for anything but work there. And that's helping people, too."

"And helping more kids." Pete's hands rubbed away the chills coursing through her body. "I heard from Dennis Cooper. He asked if he could use me as a reference for the cleaning job. It sounds like he's a lock for the position. So chalk up one more family you've made life better for."

She beamed up at Pete. "That was all you."

"Hardly."

"You save people every day."

"So do you. But it's not a tenth as hard for me to do what I do as it must be for you. Including living here and working at Chandler and taking Polly on as a cause. She's wearing Emma's holiday pin. You know how much of a milestone that is. Working with her rips you up inside sometimes, but here you are still fighting for my daughter—and for yourself. A part of you belongs here, Mallory, no matter how much we scare you."

"All of me." He'd gotten Charlie's dad a job that would change that family's life if Dennis pulled himself together and stopped drinking and made the most of it. Just like that, Pete had created a miracle, because that was how the Lombards' world worked. That's how lives on Mimosa Lane were lived. "All of me wants…" She gestured around them instead of saying that ever since Sunday night it was Pete she'd found herself wanting most of all. "All of me will want all of this forever."

She looked up at the clear, nearly night sky already bright with icy, white stars. Her breath misted in the air, frosting everything with a hint of unbelievability. There was no window now between her and the sky. She was part of it, drinking in its beauty. She felt herself opening up to the view, to the man sharing it with her, craving the normality of standing with him on a beautiful cul-de-sac after spending an afternoon with his child.

He cuddled her closer. His gaze dropped to her mouth. She lifted onto her tiptoes, wanting his lips again, banishing the last of the space between them.

Their mouths touched, their breath mingled, misty and warm and feeding her need to believe that this fairy tale was exactly where she should be. That sharing Saturday's invitation with him would work the way she longed for it to.

She broke away, far enough to end the kiss.

"I couldn't be with you and Polly at the shelter," she reminded him, "once I saw someone who might be my mother. I'd take that screwed-up moment and a million more like it with me to the party. Eventually, probably not long after we arrive, I won't be able to be there with you, either. Crowds do that to me. People do that to me. I…do better when I have something else to focus on. When I don't, I panic. I just…can't."

"But you stayed with Polly Saturday. The same night that you saw your mom and you went home from my place because it was too much for you to stay with me, you were with Polly all night. And don't tell me that was about work. You're here with me now, and there's nothing to distract you from how good and bad this feels. And as upset as you were, you were very kind to Sam just now. You can handle people, especially when you realize you're not alone."

"She…" Mallory's mind blurred past everything he'd said to the memory of Sam Perry's too-bright, too-quick smile and the way she'd practically cringed at the thought of having even sweet little Polly into her home. "Sam feels alone, too, doesn't she? At least I'm betting she needs to be a lot of the time. The holiday party isn't going to be much fun for her, either."

"I'm sure Julia pulled out all the stops to convince Brian to host it. Julia's purpose in life, like yours and Sam's, seems to be helping other people. Sam's lost her way. A lot like you have, though for totally different reasons. And Julia's technique for helping lost souls can resemble plowing folks over with a bulldozer. Sam and Brian have lived here since before their boys were born, and Sam's been struggling from the start. It's hard for all of us to watch and not be able to help. Looks like Julia's taking matters into her own hands with the Perrys, since she couldn't make any headway with me and Polly."

"Is that what everyone's going to be doing Saturday? Watching? Sam. Me. Polly. You."

"They're going to be spending time together, and the whole neighborhood's hoping you'll join them now that the word's out about your volunteer work. You have Polly to thank for that. Before I drive her to school every morning now, she stops and tells everyone at the bus stop more stories about what you do and who you help and how amazing you were pretending to be a good witch to convince the kids at the shelter to get their flu shots. Everyone's already in love with you."

"I…"

"Don't want them to be?"

Mallory shook her head—not sure herself whether she was agreeing with him or denying his ridiculous statement.

"You're wanted here," he said, "just the way you are. But that's not what's worrying you. You don't care if people are watching or how you look to them. You live your life your way, to hell with what anyone expects from you. You can't help yourself. It's one of the first maddening things I admired about you. What you're afraid of is that you'll be all the things you think folks won't understand, and you'll find out you're welcome anyway. And I'm convinced a part of you still doesn't believe *you* can deal with that."

"I…" She wasn't her mother, wandering from one town to the next, one set of nameless people to avoid after another, shameless and ashamed and never really being anyone to anybody. "Just because I can't make myself like parties and hordes of people doesn't mean I don't want to be here."

"You don't have to make yourself do anything." Pete kissed her firmly, longer and longer until her latest flash of irritation bled away and there was only him in her mind, making her feel priceless and special because he was overwhelming her senses with how much he wanted her in his arms. "Let this Saturday be whatever it's going to be. Stop expecting it to be anything. Stop feeling different because that's more comfortable than the possibility that you might actually belong. Be who you were that first night you ranted at me and dragged me over to your place to find you spoiling my child until she couldn't help but fall in love with you."

"Who?" His kiss, his words were impossible to resist. "Who was I that night?"

"A woman falling in love herself." He had tears in his eyes. "You opened your heart to Polly. You were ready to rip me a new one if I didn't wake up and start taking care of her the way I should have been all along. When are you going to give the rest of us a chance to mean that much to you?"

Sunday, he'd asked her for a week.

Only two days later, it felt as if he was wanting so much more.

"What…What if I can't do this?" she whispered, clinging to him because she wanted to be wrong. "Even with Grams, I've never been able to make normal work."

"You already are," he promised. "Stick this out, Mallory. Fight for something new, something beyond helping people and then watching them move on. No more sitting alone, staring at your beautiful tree with no presents under it, thinking that's all the holiday you need. No more telling yourself that the rest of us aren't just as messed up as you've convinced yourself you are. Come see the three-ring circus we like to call a Mimosa Lane Christmas party. You're already head and shoulders beyond the rest of our half-baked attempts to look pulled together. You just don't realize it yet. Give us a chance."

You're a brave little girl, the nurse had said when Mallory had been a wandering no one, a nobody with only a quarter to her name, terrified of making the only choice she had left to make. A choice she'd secretly wanted to make for six years. A choice that had probably saved her mother's life even if it had meant losing her forever.

The happy, fulfilled life Mallory had been grasping for since age twelve still wasn't hers. Not really. Not if she let what she'd lost with her mother keep her from believing in people and trusting the ones she cared for to always be there for her in return, no matter what. That was the world, the home, Pete wanted her to see on Saturday.

"There's nothing I've ever wanted more." She grabbed Pete in a crushing hug. "My entire life, I've wanted to believe in something like you and Polly and this beautiful place."

"We're right here," he said, holding her. "We've been right here waiting for you to find us. Tell me you can believe that."

***

Pete heard himself begging the way Polly used to when she didn't want to go to school. Him. Begging. Emma used to tease that he'd welcome a lump of coal in his Christmas stocking before he'd admit that he needed or wanted anything more than what he already had.

Well, he needed this chance with Mallory.

He felt his heart soar when she nodded yes against his shoulder. Then she held on even tighter.

"I've put the word out within the rescue community," he said. She'd agreed to let him help, and he'd been planning on calling to share his update later that night. "At fire departments and police precincts and even city hospitals—wherever I have contacts. Everyone I know in the city is searching for the woman we saw at the shelter, on top of everyone from your network. We'll find her. I know how hard seeing her will be, but we'll get you there. Then we'll get you through that, too."

And they'd all make it through the holiday party when a part of him knew he'd want to run the same as Mallory as soon as they arrived. Polly probably would, too. But together the three of them would find just a little bit of Christmas to enjoy.

"You can do this," he said, kissing her softly. "You'll see. We all can."

PART THREE

Healing

Chapter Sixteen

I'm nobody. Who are you?

Julia Davis smiled from behind her living room curtains, charmed by the sweet scene unfolding across the lane. Pete Lombard and Mallory Phillips were wrapped around each other like long-lost lovers.

She wasn't all that surprised. The way Pete had bragged to the families at the bus stop about just how fabulous Chandler Elementary's school nurse was and where Mallory spent all the free time everyone had been so curious about…Clearly, he was already half-smitten.

Julia had admired Mallory herself, that day at the school clinic when Polly had gotten so upset. Mallory had handled Julia's nosy bossiness with the grace and tact of a seasoned politician. Then she'd faced down Julia like a dragon while her supposedly shy, introverted, hands-off neighbor had held a crying Polly as if she'd never let her go. Julia had wanted to applaud.

She felt the same way about the embrace and the kisses Mallory and Pete were sharing now beneath golden lamplight and a crisp December sky. It was a beautiful moment. She should look away. But she couldn't, like she couldn't stop trying to remember the last time she'd felt so connected with another human being, so in the moment that everything else faded away.

She was watching people connect in a way she hadn't experienced in her own world, in her family, for years. Possibly in forever. Mallory had made an impact on Sam just now, too. Something that had taken years for some of the other women in the neighborhood to achieve. Sam had hesitated, but for Pete and Mallory's sake she'd escorted Polly inside, an offer to come closer that she never would have made on her own. And an offer Julia was certain Polly wouldn't have accepted before a couple of weeks ago.

There was something about Mallory that seemed to transform everyone she came into contact with. Yet she appeared to be more than a little lost herself, unable or unwilling to take part in the community thriving around her. Her defenses were coming down, though, at least where the Lombards were concerned. And hopefully now the Perrys, too. Polly had mentioned just that morning that Pete was trying to convince Mallory to attend the holiday party with them. Something told Julia he'd just succeeded.

A twinge of jealousy made it harder than normal to smile as she walked into the den to find her husband and boys glued to whatever ball game was playing on the TV. She headed into the kitchen to prep for dinner, shaking off her melancholy. This was their nightly routine. It was comfortable and welcoming and peaceful, knowing her way around a life that floated along as it had for as long as she could recall.

Then again, not being able to remember when she'd last clung to her husband or looked into his eyes and felt both lost and found, safe and consumed, left her heart aching a little. The thought of Pete finding love again so soon after losing Emma brought tears to Julia's eyes.

The younger couples in the neighborhood kept Julia young, she'd always told herself. Even watching Brian and Sam Perry, as difficult as Sam's condition made their relationship, was often like watching a romance novel come to life. The way they gazed at each other in unspoken devotion over the heads of their boys, or when Brian left for work each morning and Sam watched him go as if her day wouldn't be completely right again until he returned. Touching tableaus like that used to remind Julia to count her blessings and the bounty of her own happy life.

Lately, though, signs of the intimacy others shared made her feel old. Given the challenges the Perrys, the Lombards, and Mallory Phillips were facing in their hectic lives, why was it starting to feel as if Julia would have to be extra cautious at the Christmas party to hide just how envious she was of the lot of them?

***

Mallory couldn't help but stare Saturday night, her mouth practically hanging open as she and Pete and Polly walked into the Perrys' house and the Mimosa Lane Christmas party.

Sam's decor was a surprise. It wasn't nearly as formal or close to suburban perfection as Mallory had expected. Like the woman's gardens, there was a casual, laid-back elegance to what she had accomplished indoors with her mix of contemporary and antique pieces. Dark woods, glass-and-metal accents, ornate fixtures, and rough-hewn, distressed-looking picture frames and moldings. The natural colors of outdoors filled each room, mixed with the vibrant reds and more subdued jewel tones that

covered the furniture and softened the windows. And all of it
worked together somehow, along with the frenzy of holiday
decorations strewn pretty much everywhere.

Mallory smiled as Pete introduced her to Brian, Sam's husband. She held tightly to Polly's hand amid the bustle of adults
and kids of all ages milling around the spacious first floor of the
house. Polly had been so excited about the party when she and
Pete had shown up at Mallory's place. Now she appeared to be
as rattled as Mallory was by the mayhem they'd walked into.

Did this many people actually live along the twisting turns
of Mimosa Lane?

Pete swept them into more introductions. Mallory shook
with her free hand and smiled, ever aware of the clinging weight
of the little girl who was sticking to her like glue. Polly's hold on
Mallory grew tighter and tighter by the moment. And through
it all, the half hour it took them to complete the entire circuit
of the party, Mallory felt her own anxiety deepen as she tried to
relax into everyone's exuberance for the holiday season.

There were snowmen and Santas and elves adorning every
flat surface. Each room had its own Christmas tree, some more
than one, in all shapes and sizes and styles. Some were live trees,
while others ran the gamut of what was available on the artificial end of the spectrum. And each tree had been designated
its own theme.

Victorian, animals, snowflakes, modern, fishing, baked
goods, pets, and the list went on. One even sported miniature
garden implements and flowers and so forth, and Mallory was
guessing that one was Sam's favorite. And in the media room,
which also seemed to function as the Perry boys' playroom, was
the tree that was Mallory's favorite above all the rest.

Cade and Joshua, the adorable yet already wanting-to-be-grown Perry boys who were playing foosball with some of their buddies, had made a typical mess of most of the Christmas art they'd done over the years at school—the kinds of projects teachers had students create as presents for their parents. But Sam and Brian had clearly treasured each Popsicle stick, construction paper, and macaroni creation as if it were cast from gold.

A floor-to-ceiling artificial white tree boasted the collection of mostly red-and-green ornaments. There were some turkeys, created for Thanksgiving but nonetheless included in the mix. The rest of the decorations consisted of every possible Christmas-themed project that could be made from snapshots and handprints and footprints and poems, garlands and popcorn and dried berries and nuts. All hastily crafted and colored the way most boys attacked artwork, as if they were speeding to be finished first and competing to see who could act as if they cared the least about the quality of the result. But each and every lovingly hung ornament was breathtakingly beautiful to Mallory.

"They do this every year," Polly said beside her, speaking for the first time since they'd arrived. She let go of Mallory's hand to step closer and finger several of the ornaments hung low enough on the tree for her to reach. "The boys get their own tree, and they mostly act like it's a pain to have one in their game room. But last year Mrs. Perry said they wouldn't put it up if that's what Cade and Joshua really wanted, and Cade went and dug the tree out of their storage room in the garage and pulled it out himself. He's the oldest," she said in awe, as if the older boy who looked to be around twelve were closer to twenty-one. "He said he didn't want to make his mom sad, since she'd miss having it. But I think he secretly likes it as much as she does."

Pete had stepped a few feet away to talk with Brian and another man—Julia Davis's husband, Walter. Mallory knelt beside Polly and reached out to touch a red-and-green-painted, glitter-adorned paper plate that had been hacked up to resemble a snowflake. Turning it over, she read the inscription on the back. It had been written in a teacher's steady hand.

Love you always, Joshua. Christmas 2009.

She smiled, watching Polly until the little girl looked over at her and smiled, too.

"You guys have no idea how much the littlest things mean to your parents," Mallory said.

Polly nodded, gazing at the years and years of Christmas that had been draped over every inch of the tree. "My mommy kept a whole box of mine. She kept everything. Daddy would tease her about it, but she said she found him looking through the box some nights when he couldn't sleep and he didn't think she would see. Maybe I could…"

She brushed her hand over the tree as if it were infinitely precious and fragile.

"Maybe you could what?" Mallory asked.

Polly looked around at the crowd of people filling the one room. Most of the dads were there, watching sports on the flat-panel television behind the bar. Cade and Joshua's friends seemed to be playing every game the boys owned—pool and air hockey in addition to foosball, board games, and there was another group slouched on the sectional sofa playing the video gaming system attached to a smaller TV, loudly cheering one another on.

"Maybe next year," Polly said, cringing closer to Mallory as the noise level in the room rose and rose with no limit in sight. "Maybe I could ask Daddy if a tree like this would be okay in my room."

Her own tree. One that her parents had never put up or decorated themselves. Something for the holiday that would be Polly's alone, her very own private perspective of what Christmas meant.

Mallory hugged her close, thinking that sounded like a wonderful idea. "You keep believing that you can have Christmas exactly the way you want it, however you want it. I've gone for too long thinking the holidays were for other people, and that I'd never have a real one." She once more took in the rowdy, comfortable, friendship-filled room. "I've never let myself have one that felt as real as this."

"Because you didn't have a mommy?" Polly's eyes teared up. It was hard to tell if her emotion was for herself or for Mallory.

Mallory nodded. "The way I lost her..."

"Made it hard to want Christmas anymore?"

Mallory nodded again, facing her own truth the way she'd tried to help Polly face hers. "It was hard to want holidays and birthdays and family and, well, people in general, thinking about how much wanting them could hurt if..."

"They all went away, too?" Polly nodded. "I want...But I just can't..."

"You can't want everything you had before?" Mallory finished for her this time. "Not this year? That's okay, sweetheart. You just lost your mommy. It's okay not to want anything right now but your Daddy and the things you and he need to do with each other to get better. But dream about what your Christmas will be like next year. Let your daddy and people like Mrs. Perry and even Mrs. Davis help you make that happen when the time's right."

"And you? You'll help me, too? You have the best tree on Mimosa Lane. You'll help me when I'm ready, won't you?"

"Oh, sweetie. That's my I-don't-have-a-clue-what-I'm-doing tree. I'd give anything to be able to have a Christmas like the Perrys. One like the ones I thought I'd have when I was a little girl, once everything was better or I was old enough to do what I wanted. Somehow I've never figured out how to do that."

"So you'll let people help you do what you want next year, too. Maybe Mrs. Perry would help you. And me and Daddy, too."

"Maybe." Mallory hugged the child, wanting that dream of a magical holiday to come no matter how many Christmases past she'd failed to make special. "I hope so, sweetie."

She looked around a little desperately for something to distract them from their impromptu heart-to-heart. It suddenly dawned on her that she hadn't seen Sam, and they'd been there for close to an hour.

"Where is Mrs. Perry?" She eased away and gave Polly a watery smile the kid eyed suspiciously.

"Upstairs. She's like you and me. She doesn't like so many people anymore. Not as many as come to a Christmas party."

Mallory took in the playroom again and the clamor of nonstop Christmas cheer filtering in from the rest of the party. "But she's done such a beautiful job. It must have taken her days to get all of this ready."

"All week. I helped some. Tuesday night, she let me decorate some of the Christmas cookies."

"Then…Why wouldn't she want to enjoy her own party?" Sam had created this amazing, perfect thing that Mallory would love to be able to pull off on her own. And the whole world seemed to have shown up to help her celebrate. Yet the beautiful mother of two wasn't there in the middle of her triumph, laughing and enjoying herself along with her heartthrob-handsome husband.

She's like you and me.

"I think it scares her a little." Polly fussed with the red bows on the front of her emerald-green dress, revealing nothing more. Maybe she didn't know any more about where Sam's fears had actually come from. And maybe—no, definitely—it didn't really matter. "But I think it makes her sad. Not being able to be like everyone else and feel happy like normal people do."

Mallory took the little girl's hand, stopping Polly from picking one of the bows undone completely. "Do you think she's upstairs where it's quiet because it's easier for her not to be down here?" When Polly nodded with a touch of longing, Mallory squeezed her fingers. "Do you think she'd mind if you took her up a Christmas cookie so she wouldn't miss out on all the fun? I bet she had a great time having you over for a while on Tuesday. I bet you guys had a blast decorating, cooking, and being quiet and just enjoying being with each other."

Polly nodded, slowly at first. Then she smiled. The ribbons holding her hair in ponytails flew. She grabbed Mallory's hand and dragged her toward the door. "Come on. The cookies will be in the kitchen."

Mallory glanced over her shoulder to make sure Pete knew they were heading out. He was tracking their escape. He nodded that it was okay while a worried sort of smile curled at his lips. She tamped down on the impulse to join him for another of the soft kisses he'd given her at her front door. Torn, sharing Polly's enthusiasm to run, she gave him a wave and consoled herself that they'd have more time together later. And that it, like coming to the party, would be worth the risk she was taking in getting closer.

She'd worked in the city all that morning at a shelter closer to Piedmont Park, distracted and agitated because there was still no news about her mother. She'd missed having the Lombards with her, she and Pete agreeing that a day downtown would have been too much for Polly on top of the Perrys' party. Now she had them close again—Pete and his smile and the promise of his touch and his kisses, and Polly, whose hand held Mallory's trustingly as they wound their way around happy groups of their neighbors.

They ignored the curious glances cast their way and the polite attempts to say hello. Polly was on a mission, heading straight for the cake stand on the rustic kitchen table. There were multiple layers of tiny brownies and chocolate-covered strawberries and hand-decorated cookies.

Polly dove in, picking out the most garish creations of the bunch, no doubt the cookies she'd adorned herself with red and green and white icing, plus sprinkles and sparkly sugar crystals and tiny silver balls. Her youthful enthusiasm for the holiday seemed to have exploded all over the snowmen and reindeer and Christmas bells and Santas she selected.

Mallory grabbed a cut-glass plate and an embroidered napkin, charmed by her young friend's selection. "I think that's good for now," she said when Polly would have dived back in for more. "We don't want to send Mrs. Perry into sugar shock."

Polly giggled. She glanced around Mallory at Julia Davis and a pair of other women Mallory recognized as some of the moms on the lane. They were headed their way from the living room. Polly grabbed Mallory's hand and giggled again as they made their grand escape, darting up the staircase at the back of the kitchen. They tiptoed like thieves across the second floor's plush beige carpet.

Christmas was everywhere up there, too. Mallory glanced into each bedroom they passed. The decorations were more charmingly done, more subdued. But this was clearly a holiday the Perry family reveled in, milking the weeks between Thanksgiving and New Year's for all the goodness they could charm out of them.

"Wow," was all she could say.

"Mrs. Perry says it takes weeks to put everything away," Polly said. "She keeps it all organized so Mr. Perry can find stuff again next year and put it all back out again after Thanksgiving. He doesn't mind, he says. Anything that makes Mrs. Perry smile makes him and Cade and Joshua happy, too. She doesn't smile so much, you know?"

Polly checked to see if Mallory did in fact know. And while she didn't exactly, Mallory nodded mutely, because they'd stopped at the end of the hallway, and the woman sitting on the pillow-covered couch in the office to their right was staring at them. Sam had heard every word Polly had said. With little girl innocence, Polly grabbed the plate Mallory was carrying and rushed toward their stunned neighbor, thrusting the treats at her.

"We brought you some of the party," she said with a proud grin. "Because we understand why you don't want to be around people even though you love Christmas as much as we do."

"There are too many people for us down there." Mallory approached more cautiously, trying to gauge whether the silent, composed, casually dressed woman wanted them to turn tail and scamper back down the stairs to rejoin the rest of her guests. "Polly and I needed a break, and she wanted you to have the best of the cookies before they're all gone."

Sam swallowed. Her pulse pounded away at the base of her neck. Mallory could only imagine the tantrum Sam's heartbeat was making beneath a navy-blue sweatshirt that boasted an embroidered over-jolly, rosy-cheeked Frosty the Snowman. Her ensemble made Mallory feel better about the gaudy Rudolph sweater she'd chosen to wear herself, having no idea what would blend in at her first neighborhood party.

Sam looked at Polly, and it was as if she fell in love with the child all over again. She took the plate, then opened her arms to receive Polly's smothering hug.

"Thank you, sweetie," she said. "You know I think each of your creations is an absolute masterpiece. I was hoping there'd be one left later when I headed down." She cast Mallory a welcoming grin. "Have a seat. Only the very brave venture this far upstairs. You'll be safe here until things quiet down a bit."

Mallory crossed to the couch. Picking up a book that sat open on the cushion, she sank gratefully into the rose-emblazoned upholstery that staked the other woman's definitive claim on the room. Looking down, she saw that she was holding a yearbook—from Booker Primary, the cover said, the 1999–2000 school year. LEARNING LARGE IN THE BIG CITY, the tagline read. The words floated over one of the world's most recognizable skylines. She flipped back to the pages the book had been lying open to, a retrospective of the preschool holiday program.

"How cute." She handed it to Sam while Polly crawled onto the couch to sit between them. Mallory's thoughts ran toward her own preschool experience—it had been the year just before her mother had taken her away from her grandparents. "Did you—"

"She used to teach school in New York," Polly said, which went a long way toward explaining the uniqueness of Sam and Brian's accents.

And now she hid herself away in her house, and apparently couldn't tolerate the bustle of a sedate place like Mimosa Lane?

Sam studied Mallory's silent reaction. Then she sighed, closing the book and rubbing her hands over the raised image on its cover.

"I was right out of college," she said. "This was my first class of students all my own. Pre-K. I taught in a private elementary school. At the time, it was located across from the Twin Towers. Of course they've moved now, several blocks away from the reconstruction."

1999–2000.

Learning Large in the Big City.

Sam's second year of teaching would have started in the fall of 2001, right across from the World Trade Center.

Mallory suddenly couldn't breathe.

The reality of what her neighbor had just shared sank in like an anvil landing on her heart. A school of young boys and girls, little more than babies, learning in the shadow of one of New York City's largest business complexes. Mallory thought of the kids she'd gotten to know in just the few months she'd worked at Chandler Elementary, then of the threat of anything happening to them.

"We got all the children out just fine," Sam explained, keeping the details cryptic enough for them not to affect Polly, who sat happily between them munching on one of her cookies. "The city was shut down that day, of course, once it happened. No cars or public transportation in or out. We had to walk them off the island and wait in one of the boroughs for family to come for them. But all along, we knew...Most of their parents worked in the towers. And it was only a matter of time before we began to hear..."

"You were there?" Mallory wanted to pull Polly into her lap. She wanted to sit closer to Sam, maybe take her hand. As if that could dissipate the trauma of what the other woman had been through, the effects of which Sam was clearly still dealing with more than a decade later. "You saw it all happen?"

"We heard them hit." Sam flinched as if reliving the shock of hearing planes tear through buildings and lives and futures. "We kept the kids inside…until it was over, but we heard the buildings come down. Then when they told us to evacuate, we had to…walk through all of the debris, even though our school wasn't right at Ground Zero. And all my kids…"

Mallory couldn't imagine. She was startled when Polly chose that moment to crawl into her lap. She hugged the little girl's sweet, healthy body close.

"You were their hero that day," Mallory said, thinking of the fire and rescue warriors, like Pete, who'd given so much—some of them had given their lives—to keep so many safe. Hadn't Sam and her fellow teachers, little more than young girls themselves, done the same thing for their students?

"It wasn't enough," Sam said. "Their parents…Most of them didn't make it. It took us all day to get to Brooklyn. Brian met me there, but I couldn't leave. Not until everyone had family to go home with, my kids that year and the ones I'd had the year before." The story was tumbling out now, flowing from Sam's memory in a jerky rush as she clung to the yearbook. "It took forever, but…"

"You loved them." Mallory fought to keep her voice even. That degree of devotion and dedication and unrelenting love was mesmerizing. No matter how terrified and devastated Sam and the other adults in her school must have been or how many of the parents who'd died had been personal friends, she and her colleagues had stayed for their kids.

"I couldn't..." Sam put the book on the small table to the right of the couch. "After that day, I couldn't see them again. Any of them. Not even my coworkers. I couldn't..." She watched Mallory hug a sleepy Polly. "I miss it sometimes. Especially around the holidays."

Mallory's mind spun with Sam's story and what little she'd learned about the Perry family. Sam's obvious desire to stay connected with people despite her trauma, through things like living where she did and hosting the party rocking away downstairs without her, might just be the bravest testament to resilience Mallory had ever encountered. Her neighbor looked like a fragile Christmas ornament—huddled in her corner of the couch about to break from the strain and confusion of getting through everyday things everyone else took for granted.

"I haven't been able to feel the holidays since I was a little girl Polly's age," Mallory blurted out, wanting to say something in that moment to let the other woman know she wasn't alone. "I want to. I keep trying to. I've always tried to. But it just doesn't work for me. I've never had a Christmas since..."

Sam sat a bit straighter and stared at Mallory as if she hadn't heard her right. "Ever?" She looked beyond the office toward the jolly sound of revelry reaching them from below. "You've never..."

"Been able to enjoy this time of the year? No, not that I can remember. I grew up on the streets, wanting nothing more than a magical tree and a Christmas morning full of presents and a happy family and dinner at a beautifully set table. If I could make that perfect moment happen, everything else would be okay, you know? My grandmother tried after I returned home. But I could never...snap back from what I'd been through. I guess I still haven't, or I wouldn't be up here with you tonight, would I?"

"You were—"

"Homeless." Mallory raised an eyebrow, stunned more than her neighbor by how easily the admission had rolled from her lips. *You're wanted here, just the way you are...* "For six years, until I was twelve."

"Like your mommy?" Polly peered up from Mallory's lap. "Like the lady we saw downtown last weekend?"

"Your mother's still on the streets?" Sam was absolutely riveted, focused on Mallory now instead of her own demons.

"I don't know. She left me with my grams when I was twelve, and she never came back."

Mallory's throat closed up with the conflicting waves of rage and guilt and longing that came with her memories, and now everyone on Mimosa Lane and at Chandler Elementary would know. She hugged Polly a little tighter, grateful to her soul when she felt the little girl cuddle up, her soft hair tickling Mallory's neck and chin. Sam's features had softened with an encouraging smile.

Give us a chance...

"I..." Mallory said. Her voice snagged on the fear of being seen so clearly for who and what she was. She cleared her throat. "I looked for her when I was younger. At some point I had to stop, or I'd always be looking back. But that woman I saw in midtown last week...She could have been in Atlanta for heaven knows how long, and if I'd only been trying to find her—"

"You couldn't." Sam's voice was fierce, overflowing with conviction. "Not and save yourself. You had to save yourself and get away from what you needed to, to survive, even if that meant not looking for a mother who clearly didn't want to be found. You did what you had to do, Mallory. You survived."

Mallory felt Polly nodding her head. She realized she was silently doing the same as Sam's understanding beat away at the guilt of seeing her mother in such deplorable shape, still wandering the streets. No matter how furious Mallory still was with her mama's choices and refusal to accept the help she needed, she still felt responsible for the woman. And that destructive compulsion to fix problems she was never going to be able to fix was what she'd moved to Chandlerville to distance herself from.

"Sometimes," Sam said, "when there's nothing anyone else can do, you have to be your own hero." Her voice was fragile again. Shaking. "Don't you think?"

Time stood still around them. Holiday noises and ghosts from the past and unfulfilled expectations for the future couldn't touch any of them in that moment. An unspoken connection grew, tying Mallory to this brave woman and the remarkable child between them.

Heroes could look like Pete at work as an EMT or like the parent volunteers swooping into the school to help with a flu outbreak or even like Mallory dressed in her Glinda finery entertaining kids so they wouldn't be scared of getting their shots. But sometimes, for some people, when the decision that had to be made was so terrible no one else could make it better, the only hero who could save you was yourself.

It had been an unspoken, unconscious mantra for Mallory for so long. And for Sam, too, evidently. So much so, being alone and protected and separate had become a lifestyle for them both.

"How's girl talk?" a feminine voice asked from the doorway.

Julia Davis stood there, smiling gently at whatever she'd heard.

"Are you escaping, too?" Sam's fondness for the other woman was clear as she waved Julia in to join them. "Have things really gotten that crazy downstairs?"

"They're perfect, as always." Julia relaxed into a nearby club chair with an ease that hinted that this was a regular pattern between them—Mimosa Lane's outgoing, bubbly social maven settling in for an intimate chat with her introverted friend. "I missed you, and I was jealous. You always have the best time up here, and I didn't want to be left out of the fun."

Polly, preening that she was evidently at the best place in the party, offered Julia the plate of cookies. "I brought all the good ones up for Mrs. Perry."

"Of course you did, angel," Julia said. "Because the hostess of such a fabulous extravaganza deserves no less than the very best of everything, right?"

Polly nodded enthusiastically. Her happy grin grew even wider, and then she looked up at Mallory. "Help Daddy and me do a New Year's party for everyone. Then you and me could be the hostesses, and everyone could bring us things!"

Mallory gave a startled laugh at the thought of her and Pete and Polly hosting anything together. Or that the people she'd just met downstairs would converge on this hypothetical event bearing gifts, because she'd of course execute things as flawlessly and beautifully as Sam.

"Um…" she hedged.

"That sounds like a wonderful idea," Julia replied.

"I'm in," a deep voice said from the doorway.

Pete, leaning against the doorjamb with his arms crossed, smiled at the sight of them sitting there talking as if they were lifelong friends.

"Daddy!" Polly shoved her plate at Mallory and bounded off the couch into her father's outstretched arms. "Can we have a New Year's party for everyone? Really?"

***

"Do you want a party at our house?" Pete smiled down at his child, basking in Polly's excitement.

He'd been intrigued but oddly not surprised to find Mallory so at ease with Emma's two closest friends. It shocked him all over again how completely he'd misjudged his extended family on Mimosa Lane. Being with them again tonight had felt as easy as coming home after a particularly grueling day at work.

Seeing Mallory in these ladies' midst, listening to her caring response to learning about Sam's situation and witnessing her willingness to give Julia a second chance and finding his child curled up beside her, relaxed and part of the group the way Polly had always joined in when it had been Emma sitting on Sam's couch talking, keeping her friend company during a party...

He felt Mallory Phillips claim an even bigger piece of his heart.

"A party," he told Polly, "will mean kids crawling all over your room and the basement playroom, and the house swarming with everybody who's here tonight and maybe some of my friends from the station and your mommy's from school."

The best part of a party, Emma had always said, was mixing people from all parts of their lives, not just those they knew on the lane. Before she'd gotten sick they'd entertained at least once a month, opening their home to music and movies and games and as many people as it could hold, the fun often spilling out into the backyard or the cul-de-sac until it became more of a block party.

Once Emma became too fragile to handle that kind of exuberant craziness, their home had gone quiet, visitors arriving to see them in ones and twos, voices hushed and careful, no more music or games or out-of-control laughter. For the sake of his daughter's fraying nerves since her mommy's death, he'd expected to keep things that way indefinitely, never dreaming Polly would want anything different.

She nodded enthusiastically now. "Can we have pizza and an ice cream cake and bake cookies that everyone can decorate themselves and do sparklers outside and let the kids draw all over the driveway with chalk?" She was rattling off her year-round party favorites, no matter that it was finally freezing outside and the weatherman was warning that they could see snow by Christmas.

"You got it." Pete would set up their water slide on the front lawn if she asked for it. "It'll be the best party we've ever had."

He grinned at the ladies who were listening to them. There were some suspiciously teary eyes to go along with their enjoyment of Polly's enthusiasm. His daughter yawned and nestled her head against his shoulder, reminding him of his original excuse for sneaking upstairs and spying on whatever was going on in the office.

"I'd better get her to bed," he said, "so she can dream up even bigger New Year's plans."

Everyone else pushed to their feet, Julia and Sam hanging back as Mallory stepped to Pete's side and took the hand he offered her. He drew her fingers to his lips and kissed them. He couldn't help himself. She smiled and took an instinctive step closer.

He didn't actually remember walking down the hallway and stairs. They were simply at the front door suddenly, him realizing that in just a few short minutes they'd be back at his house and tucking Polly into bed, where she'd started to sleep again a few nights ago—real sleep, instead of merely dozing with him on the couch. Then he and Mallory would have the remainder of the night to themselves.

Julia had disappeared, mingling once more among their neighbors. But Sam was there to see them off. Brian had joined her, his arm protectively encircling his wife's waist.

"It was great to have you here." He shook hands with Pete. His smile widened as Mallory hesitated, then she let go of Pete's hand to shake as well. "I'm glad we finally had the chance to meet you. Everyone's blown away by Pete and Polly's tales about your selfless, costume-wearing volunteer work. It sounds like we have a real-life fairy godmother in our midst."

Mallory ducked her head, her cheeks turning pink. "Thank you," she said. Her attention shifted to Sam. "I...I bet you'd be great with some of my midtown kids, if you'd like to come for an hour or two one weekend. It might be a fun way to get back some of what you've been missing so much. You know, working with kids who'll adore any time you can give them without having to commit to an entire class of them. And you wouldn't be connecting with any of them long-term. It might feel...safer somehow, you know?"

Pete saw Sam tense and Brian's embrace tighten, as if they were both bracing for one of the debilitating panic attacks she still suffered, often with little or no warning. Then Sam's head tilted to the side as if she were suddenly considering the world in a way she never had before—a state of awareness he was beginning to suspect was an everyday occurrence for whomever fell under Mallory's spell.

Sam nodded, slowly, looking up to her husband for reassurance. Brian's easy, hopeful grin must have been exactly what she'd needed to see.

"I'd like to try that," she said in a voice that was determined, if a bit unsure.

"Maybe sometime after the holidays," Brian added.

"Anytime," Mallory offered. "We'd be lucky to have you with us."

"Maybe…" Sam straightened from where she'd been leaning against Brian. She focused on Pete. "If you need any help planning your party…"

"Party?" Brian asked.

"I'm doing New Year's at my place," Pete said.

"Wow," Brian replied.

"And I'd like to help," Sam added. "Maybe I could come over the morning of and get the food sorted out."

"Wow," Brian repeated. "Maybe I could wave a magic wand and produce the genie who's magically pulled the two of you out of your shells all of a sudden." His confusion evaporated at the site of Mallory's hand tucked within Pete's grasp and the relaxed way Polly was sleeping in Pete's arms. Brian gazed at Mallory with admiration. "Then again, maybe you're a genie, too, when you take time off from your fairy godmother duties."

Brian winked as his wife elbowed him in the ribs. He opened the front door so Pete and Mallory could escape into the frigid quiet outside. Mallory laughed at Brian's statement, warming up even more to the neighbors she'd been so nervous to meet.

"Night," Pete said to them, steering Mallory down the lighted walkway and across the street to his place.

They stepped inside, into the warmth of the foyer. The front door closed behind them, and he was home. But he could sense Mallory giving in to the nerves she must have been feeling from the very start of the party. She stayed by the door as he walked toward the front stairs.

Would she still be there after he came back down from tucking Polly in? Or would she have disappeared behind her fence and her windows and expect him to leave her alone to rationalize away the ever-tightening connection growing between them? The pull of it had him shaking. It must be scaring her to death. But if he didn't feel Mallory in his arms again soon, he was going to lose his mind.

"Help me put Polly to bed?" he asked, knowing his heart was in his eyes. His pulse stumbled at the thought of her refusing.

Her hands were behind her, wrapped around the doorknob. "I'm not very good at this," she said.

"Looking terrified of reaching for what you want?"

"Playing at being part of a family."

Regret pulsed through him for how long she'd deprived herself of consciously needing and depending on anything beyond herself.

"Then stop pretending," he said. "Let yourself feel something good, Mallory. Just because it's good. You deserve to feel every good thing in this world. Don't overthink this. Stop protecting yourself from me. From us." He jostled Polly's head higher on his shoulder. "We're not going to hurt you."

He reached out his hand, desperate for her to believe how much he cared, the same as he was certain her grandmother had longed to make a bigger place for herself in Mallory's heart.

Mallory stared at the floor, torturing them both as she hesitated. Then she raised her head, her bottomless need to love and to be loved shining freely in her gaze. She let go of the door and walked across the foyer. Her hand gripped his, and she let him lead her upstairs.

Chapter Seventeen

❦

That till I loved
I never lived Enough...

"Daddy, we need to give Mallory her Christmas," Mallory heard Polly mumble as Pete tucked his daughter into bed. He'd already pulled off the little girl's clothes and stuffed her into her nightgown. Forgoing bath time and brushing teeth for the sake of letting sleeping princesses lie, he'd simply settled her under her covers and kissed her forehead.

"She wants one so bad." Polly rolled onto her side, her sleepy eyes opening to stare into her daddy's. She clearly didn't realize that Mallory was standing only a few feet away. "Let's give her her Christmas, Daddy. Better than she ever dreamed of, with a real tree and presents and everything. Okay?"

From the doorway Mallory looked around the princess-perfect room full of every material possession a happy little girl could want. Draped across a puffy white chair was the second-hand Tinker Bell robe Mallory had given the child the first night Polly drifted over to her place. It warmed Mallory now to think that a part of her had been there comforting Polly all this time.

She drank in the site of the brave if floundering father kneeling beside his daughter's bed. He'd been amazing the last two weeks, helping Polly learn to feel good things again—because he'd been strong enough to feel all of his little girl's bad things right along with her.

"Okay," Pete said. "We'll make it the best Christmas of her life."

He turned to look at Mallory. Polly's eyes were closed again. She'd drifted back to sleep. It was only him and Mallory now. He'd been speaking to her—directly to her heart and to every dream she'd ever had. Mallory shook her head, fighting the urge to run.

Everything inside her that still believed in the same kind of storybook magic as his daughter craved what he was promising. A life where second chances, or third or fourth chances, really did work out and new starts weren't wasted time and tomorrow really could be all that you wanted it to be, if you'd only let yourself believe long enough to get there. Wanting all of that as badly as she still did terrified Mallory.

Pete was standing in front of her now. His strong hands cupped her face in that way she loved. His lips were feathering over hers, silently asking her to let him touch her more deeply, then demanding it as his kiss hardened, sweeping away her doubts until there remained nothing but an answering ache. She kissed him, her mouth making demands of her own. She wanted to know this man, all of him. She wanted to know what it was like for him to want her and keep wanting her, no matter how different they both were from everything they were used to.

Together they were lightness to balance shadow, courage to champion vulnerability, hope to overcome loss and grief. He was real and damaged yet somehow the perfect prince she'd once longed for when, as a lost child, she'd thought of another life—any other life but her own. He was clutching her closer, as fiercely as she was clinging to him, and he was promising to never let go.

"Pete…" Her fingers dug into his shoulders. Her arms slid around his back and down to his waist, holding him, pressing her body to his. "Pete…"

She couldn't tell him how empty she felt or how much the last few hours had filled her up, only to hollow her out as she left the Perry house with him and Polly, so unsure of whether she'd be able to deal with the awareness shining in Pete's eyes and his touch and his smile. Now here they were, losing control together, trembling together, wanting together. He was right there with her, lost with her, needing her.

"Would you…?" He scooped her up, cradling her in his arms. His breathing deepened as he carried her into the hallway. He hesitated. "My room…I want to take you there, but—"

She placed a finger over his lips, charmed by his insecurity. She kissed him, trying to tell him it wouldn't matter to her—making love with this amazing man in the same room, the same bed, that he'd shared with his beloved wife. It would be one of the sweetest memories of her life to know she'd been that important to him, that special.

"Is it too soon?" she asked. "We can wait. I'll still—"

He kissed her instead of allowing her to say that she'd still want him in the morning or a dozen, a hundred mornings from now, even if he needed to stop this tonight.

"I'm not letting you get away from me," he said. "It's just—"

"Emma. Would she mind?"

"I think she's cheering somewhere right now." He headed toward the closed double doors at the other end of the hall.

"You've brought so much back into our lives, Mallory, mine and Polly's. Emma would want to thank you."

Transferring her weight to one arm, the impressive muscles in his forearm bulging while not even straining, he opened the doors and carried her into the master suite. The walls around them were a serene blue. There were dashes of sunny yellow and hints of red everywhere, in the comfortably upholstered chairs and bedspread and pictures. Portraits of Polly covered every available surface, from birth to the age she was now, smiling and loving life in solo shots and grouped ones with Pete and the beautiful brunette who'd helped him create and raise such a wonderful little girl.

It felt as if Mallory were looking straight into the heart of the man who was setting her on her feet. She was seeing all over again what a parent could truly be when he made his world about loving his family. She turned in his arms and caught him staring at a picture of Polly and Emma blowing bubbles through daisy-shaped wands.

His sadness was palpable, but when he looked down at Mallory and hugged her closer, his arms linking around her, he was smiling again. Some of the worry tying knots in her diaphragm began to untangle itself.

"Second thoughts?" she asked.

He shook his head and let her go long enough to close the doors behind them. Then, his hands on her waist, he began backing her toward the bed, a mischievous light glinting in his eyes. "Finally having you here is the best Christmas present I could have gotten. Do I get to open my present early?"

Finally...

He'd wanted this as long as she had. She was something special to him, a present he'd been hoping for. He watched her, unblinking, as the back of her knees met the mattress and he gently lowered her, his hand cupping her head before it touched the bedding, as if she were *his* dream come true.

"Well, that depends." She reached for his sweater, preparing to pull it over his head in a race to see who got to unwrap their present first.

"On what?" The hem of her own Rudolph-emblazoned sweater was in his grip. He gazed down at it and chuckled, waiting for her answer.

"Have you been a good boy, Pete Lombard?" She raised an eyebrow, trying desperately to keep herself grounded to them and only this moment instead of letting her thoughts stray to all the things that might go wrong tomorrow. "Are you planning to be a good boy tonight, so Santa will keep you on his list?

Pete grinned. He pulled her top off and pinned her arms with it, raising them over her head so he could stare his fill at the way her breasts were spilling over the edges of the silk-and-lace bra she'd worn tonight, just in case this fantasy became a reality.

"Absolutely not." He kissed her chin, her neck, then down her chest. "This is the only list I care about—all the parts of you I've been dying to love. You're mine tonight, Mallory. All mine."

***

Mine...

Hours later, curled up against Pete's warm, sleeping form, her head on his chest and her lower body sprawled across his, Mallory couldn't keep his words from echoing through her mind.

All the parts of you I've been dying to love...

Her hand smoothed up and down his arm. None of what had happened that night felt real yet. But this moment of peaceful perfection was all her fantasies come true. Compared to this, *real*, whatever that turned out to be, was highly overrated.

Her gaze traveled about the room. This was Pete's life, not hers. Yet at that moment she couldn't get her head around belonging anywhere else but there, with his arms wrapped around her and Polly sleeping peacefully down the hall.

"Don't stop," he murmured.

A quick glance told her that his eyes were still closed. But a contented smile was creeping across his face.

"Rubbing my arm," he explained. "It feels good. Don't stop."

It did feel good. Mallory relished the tactile sensation of brushing her fingertips across his skin. His hand came up to tangle in her hair, his fingers massaging the pressure points at the base of her skull.

"You doing okay?" he asked. "You're awfully quiet. A man learns that a quiet woman is usually up to no good."

She tugged at the patch of hair curling on his chest.

"Ouch!" His eyes jerked open to find her smiling as she propped her chin on his arm. "I rest my case."

"A woman learns never to back down from a challenge," she warned. "Not if she's going to keep a man on his toes."

He drew her closer until their faces were inches apart. "Something tells me that running circles around men has never been your problem."

"No." She kissed him, then snuggled back down, her lips brushing across his neck. "My problem has been hightailing it in the opposite direction just when I have a man exactly where I want him."

Pete lay quietly instead of launching into the fresh batch of questions she was certain her admission had inspired.

"It's amazing, what you did tonight for Sam and Brian," he finally said. "I haven't seen her extend herself that much since Emma and I first moved here. Sam loves her boys and her husband, and you can see her wanting to get her life back on track. But she's been so—"

"Broken…" Mallory trailed her fingers down his chest, then back up, the motion soothing her. "But she's a fighter. It's amazing she's managed as well as she has. Has she been formally evaluated and diagnosed with anything she can have treated?"

"PTSD. Brian and I talked about it once when she was having a particularly hard time one Labor Day. She's not seeing a doctor anymore. She refuses to take her meds more often than she's on them. The panic and anxiety aren't as bad when she's at home with her family and can spend most of her time working in her gardens. But the depression flares up pretty often, and then everything goes off the rails. It's starting to take a toll on the boys, how isolated she keeps herself. It really took a lot for her to invite Polly inside the other night so you and I could talk, then to host the party and to sit there talking with you and Julia. You're making quite an impact on her life."

"Your daughter's doing most of the work." Mallory kissed his chest, shrugging off his praise. "I think she understands."

"About what happened to Sam?"

"About how it feels to be so lost and afraid that you don't think you'll ever find your way back again. She wanted to take the party up to Sam tonight so she could enjoy it and still be alone. What seven-year-old understands human nature that well? She's amazing."

His heart began beating faster beneath her ear. "You mean like Polly understands you?"

Mallory shrugged.

"Like she wants you to have the same magical Christmas you're helping make come true for her?" he pressed.

"You don't have to—"

He sat up, bringing Mallory along with an unrelenting grip until she was straddling his lap, the covers falling away, leaving them skin to skin. She was instantly swept into the perfect feel of it, unable to look away from the awareness spreading across Pete's face as his hands brushed up her back and then around to cup breasts. She shivered at the depth of sensation he was igniting in both of them.

She was reminded all over again that the powerful man in her arms didn't know how to lose once he'd set his mind to something.

"I know I don't have to do anything," he said. "And if it were anything but a privilege and an honor to help my daughter make one of your dreams come true, I assure you, you wouldn't be here right now. But you are. And I am. And it'll make Polly and me happy to make you happy. So relax about your Christmas." He kissed her, his tongue swirling with hers in just the right way to numb her through and through, then set a fire along the same path of nerves until her hips were rocking against his. "We've got you covered."

Smiling, twisting her lower body against him until he groaned, she pushed at his shoulders. They fell back into the pillows. Her hands went searching and found him.

"Who's covering whom?" she asked, loving how he seemed to enjoy it each time she challenged him.

Smiling, he rolled them over, settling between her raised thighs.

"You tell me."

"Like I said." She laughed softly. She groaned as he sank into her. "Right where I want you."

He drew her nipple into his mouth. "There's no running now, Mallory Phillips. I'll catch you if you try. I'll always catch you."

"Promise?" she said on a hiccupping breath, tears flooding her eyes. She turned her head, not wanting him to see.

"I'm one of Chandlerville's finest, ma'am." His hands slid beneath her hips and tilted her closer. "I live to serve."

Laughing again, the desperate weight that had been dragging at her releasing, she was nearly lost in his rhythm when the phone rang.

Only it wasn't his phone, she realized. It was her cell.

"Oh my God." Pushing against Pete until he eased away, she scrambled naked across the bed, shivering already from losing the warmth they'd created. "I have to get that."

No one who had her mobile number would be calling this time of night on a Saturday if it weren't an emergency. And the only emergency she could imagine would be happening was—

"You think it's your mother?" Pete asked, aware of her growing desperation for news that someone might have spotted the woman from last weekend.

Mallory pushed out of bed, snatched up her jeans, and dug in her pockets for the phone that thankfully hadn't yet gone to voice mail.

"I don't know," she said as he wrapped her in the quilt from the foot of the bed. "Finally!" She thumbed the button on the phone to answer it. Her hands shaking, she brought it to her ear. "Hello?"

Chapter Eighteen

That it will never come again
Is what makes life so sweet...

Pete caught his daughter's reflection in his Jeep's rearview mirror. Polly had barely woken when he'd scooped her from bed and bundled her into her coat, Disney nightgown and slippers and all. At the last minute he'd draped her in Mallory's purple-plaid bathrobe from the other night.

He glanced at the woman sitting tense beside him in the passenger seat as he drove them down the deserted stretch of I-85 South that was the quickest way into midtown at three in the morning. There wasn't another car in sight traveling in either direction. Not that Mallory would have noticed if they'd been stuck in rush-hour gridlock.

He'd expected pushback when he'd offered to take her to midtown's Open Arms Shelter after someone there had called about her mother. Instead, she'd merely nodded, sitting huddled in a quilt at the foot of his bed, her expressive features suddenly blank. He'd thought for a moment that he'd have to help her dress as well, but she'd rallied after he'd thrown back on his clothes from the party and was heading down the hall to take care of Polly.

When he'd returned, his daughter in his arms, Mallory was sitting in the same place, her clothes on, her cell phone still in her hand.

"They'd said they'd call if it looked as if she was going to leave. But it's so cold outside…The weatherman said it might snow." Panicked, she'd flipped her phone from one hand to the other and gotten to her feet. "You don't think she'd really head back outside on a night like this, do you?"

Not knowing without agitating her more how to say that he had no idea, he'd pulled her to his side with his free hand and steered her downstairs and out to the Jeep, carefully strapping her in the same as he had Polly.

"We'll be there in ten minutes," he said now, wishing he were still holding her.

It hurt, not being able to feel her next to him. They seemed a million miles away now from the intimacy they'd forged earlier.

"Is this a good thing for you?" he asked, worried. "If you're not ready to talk with her, I could…"

"I can do this," she insisted, her tone clipped and impatient and simmering with an anger he knew wasn't directed at him. So much was pressing down on her, and she was still trying to shoulder most of it on her own.

"Of course you can. But you don't have to do it tonight if you're not ready. And you don't have to do it alone."

Only by the second she was morphing back into the stranger who'd moved onto Mimosa Lane. Mallory's complicated feelings about her mother were full of rage and need and love and betrayal and the most desperate kind of hope. Pete knew a lot about that kind of confusion—he'd been going through it himself since losing Emma. But Mallory had been dealing with her loss alone her entire life. Even after her grandmother took her back. She clearly expected this night to be no different.

What they'd shared over the last few weeks and at the Perrys' party and then in Pete's bed should be making all the difference in the world. But would she let it? Would she let him in, all of him, and open up whatever parts of herself she was still holding too closely for him to know? Those dark places were taking over again—the ones feeding her need for unlocked doors and unobstructed windows and megawatt Christmas lights and a tree just for herself, all while she couldn't abide the personal relationships that would have enriched her life even more.

As his Jeep ate up the remaining miles between them and what he expected would be a heartbreaking reunion, he could feel Mallory's past stealing her away from him and Polly all over again.

"I'm proud of you." He squeezed her hand. "I can't imagine how hard this is going to be. Whatever happens, I'll be right beside you the entire time."

She didn't glare at him the way he'd half expected her to, or tell him to mind his own business. Instead, all the energy seemed to drain from her body. She slumped in the bucket seat, still staring out the window. She squeezed his fingers back. She seemed absolutely crushed, this woman who'd fought so tirelessly for his daughter and his family and everyone else she'd made it her job to help.

He'd seen it before. He'd seen that same giving up consume his wife's spirit once Emma had accepted that she was beaten and there was no use wasting another moment resisting the inevitable.

"I'll be right here," he insisted, the same as he'd promised Emma on that awful night when they'd faced reality and the end that was coming. A lump rose in his throat, so big he was choking on the rage and denial he'd be damned if he'd throw at Mallory when she needed him to be strong for her the way no one else in her life ever had been. "I won't leave you for a second."

***

She was there in front of the shabby tree where the shelter volunteer who'd called Mallory had said he'd spotted the old woman.

She was sitting on a worn-out couch, her filthy orange coat still on, her gray hair dirty and matted around her face, plastic shopping bags clutched in her lap and around her diminutive body. She'd lost weight, and the years of drinking and living on the street hadn't been kind to her skin—wrinkles had formed trenches and crevices, branding the delicate areas around her eyes and nose and mouth. She looked as if she were in her sixties instead of her early thirties. But there was no doubt about it this time.

Mallory was certain she was looking at her mother.

She'd stood motionless on the other side of the room watching the woman for what seemed like an eternity. It felt like a dream as well as a nightmare. Everything she'd imagined for more than fifteen years might happen in this moment seemed to be drowning her, and she couldn't pull back. She couldn't step forward. She couldn't think.

She'd had a week to imagine how she'd handle this—how she'd bring back the doll and the bags of flotsam that her mother had left behind, how she'd use them to hopefully create a connection of some kind. How she'd try to reach her mama on a personal level, getting her to recognize Mallory enough, and want her enough, to not disappear again.

But Mallory couldn't move or make any of those things happen. She hadn't gone back to her place for her mother's things. She'd barely been aware of anything going on around her as Pete had helped her into his Jeep and driven her here.

The place inside her that had been numb ever since she'd called her grams and given up on her life with this woman felt as empty as it ever had. There were no feelings to battle back. Every emotion she'd once had toward her mother had been shoved aside years ago so Mallory could get on with her life. And they still felt hidden away, despite the anxiety of the last week and the fact that she'd rushed here to stand in this desolate place and stare at the shell of the woman who'd given birth to her.

"She likes the tree," Polly said in a hushed voice. She was standing next to Mallory, wearing Tinker Bell and clinging tightly to Pete's hand.

They'd stayed by Mallory's side, no matter the ungodly hour or the gloom of the shelter's poorly lit lobby. They seemed impervious to the wave of hopelessness that clung to this night. The same holiday decorations that Mallory had helped put out, mostly for the staff's benefit so people didn't spiral into a depression every time they showed up for work, seemed like a cruel joke now—a taunting reminder of what had never been Mallory's, thanks to her mama's problems.

"It's almost like she's come back to wait for you," Pete said, an eyebrow rising when Mallory turned to him. "It's the same shelter as before. The same tree. She disappeared last Saturday. Now she's right back where you surprised her, like she knew you'd come if she showed up again."

"I doubt she recognized me before." Mallory heard and tasted the bitterness of her words. "I doubt she has a clue where she is."

"Something must have registered." Pete hadn't tried to touch her again, not after helping her out of the Jeep and then doing the same for Polly—who'd woken up finally, excited by the adventure of finding Mallory's mommy in time for Christmas. "Otherwise, why would she return to the very same spot that she last saw you?"

Because she's screwed up, Mallory wanted to scream at him, *just like me. Because we'll both always be in this same spot, no matter how far away we try to wander...*

"I don't think she ever saw me, really," she said instead. "I don't know what I'm doing here. All these years, she could have come home. If she'd heard I was in Atlanta, she could have asked someone on staff about me anywhere, and they'd have gotten in touch with me. She's..."

"Broken," Pete said, using the word Mallory had earlier to describe Sam Perry.

Mallory nodded. "She'll never want to be fixed."

"Then don't make this about fixing her." He sounded sad, on her behalf. He sounded scared. "Do whatever you have to tonight for yourself, Mallory, so you can move past this, healthy and whole."

So they could be together, he left unsaid.

She could see it in his eyes, though. She'd felt it in every touch they'd shared while they made love. She heard it in every fresh, hopeful, excited thing that came out of his daughter's mouth. These two wanted to give Mallory a better Christmas, a better life, and they wanted that better place to be with them. The only real question that remained was whether or not Mallory could believe in that kind of second chance after walking away from so many others before them.

She looked back at the lonely, lost old woman staring at the dilapidated tree. And for a crazy moment what she saw was herself. Always looking, always watching, but never belonging or having. Once more, she could keep the half-life she'd been living, or she could grab hold of the one waiting for her if she'd only fight for it one last time.

The premonition of where she might end up if she didn't once and for all confront this moment drew her toward her mother. A tiny hand curled around her fingers, and she found Polly there beside her, taking the lead and helping her step closer still, until they were in front of the couch. Polly pulled her down until they were sitting, the little girl putting herself between Mallory and the old woman who didn't acknowledge them.

"Mama?" Mallory said, hating her desperation for the word to mean something to the other woman.

Of course it didn't. Her mother didn't so much as blink.

There had been times when Mallory was a child when she'd watched her mother go for what seemed like hours without blinking or reacting to the world in any way. Mallory knew she wouldn't be able to bear it that long now. She was already flying apart, deep inside where she wished she were still feeling nothing. Instead, screams and tears and hatred were building, because she hadn't been able to stay away and spare herself this last reminder of how completely her mother had abandoned her.

"Did you come back for your doll?" Polly asked.

The woman dropped her head. She began fidgeting with a broken button on her coat. It was the only button left—the rest had fallen off. It wasn't until a tear splashed onto dirty, weather-roughened hands that Mallory noticed her mother was crying.

"I left her," her mother said in a raspy, unhealthy voice that was too familiar to be anyone else's. Her words were slurred. A faint whiff of alcohol accompanied them. "I didn't mean to. I forget where I am, and then where I've been. I waked up, and she'd been gone I don't know how long or where. Then I remembered this tree…"

"She was here." Polly turned to Mallory, clearly thinking they were talking about the doll and not aware of the undercurrent of meaning beneath the older woman's words. "We're taking good care of her. If you still want her, we could—"

"No, she's better off with them people who took her. She needs them more than me. She needs somethin' better, and that never was me…"

Polly's hand grabbed Mallory's again. Mallory, her head down, too, could see tears splashing on Polly's tiny fingers. *Her* tears.

"But she needs you," Mallory said, not daring to look up. She knew what was coming, and hearing it was going to be bad enough. Seeing the emotional nothingness in her mother's expression while she said it would destroy her.

"She needs…more." Her mama stood, her bags bunching on her arms where she'd hooked them at each elbow. She didn't move away. Not yet. "She's better off with them other people."

With the grandmother Mallory had never connected to. Living a better life that would never feel real. Growing into a woman herself, but always feeling like a homeless little girl.

Mallory stood, too. She couldn't stop herself from trying one last time.

Please don't go away…No matter what I have to do next, please don't go away forever…

She stared into her mother's almost unrecognizable face, willing her to snap out of the haze that had long ago taken over her senses. "She's alone everywhere she goes, Mama, just like you. She's never with people, just like you. She'll never have anything else, not even the Christmas she's always wanted, because you never tried to help yourself, let alone her."

She was shouting, her speech becoming a full-on tantrum. She was shaking, her legs impossibly weak. And she was leaning against Pete's strength, because he'd come up beside her. His arm curled around her waist and shifted her even closer. Her mother kept staring at the floor, at nothing, maybe at the past. Or maybe what she was seeing was whatever world existed in her mind that had always been so much more valuable to her than reality.

Mallory's mother reached out a filthy hand to cup Polly's cheek. "You take good care of her now. She's always wanted to be with you anyways."

Mallory swayed. If it weren't for Pete, she'd have hit the floor.

Those had been the last words she'd heard her mother speak, at the hospital when her mother was growing well enough to be transferred to the psych ward. Grams had brought Mallory to visit her mama one last time, because kids weren't allowed in the psychiatric wing.

They'd thought it would be weeks, maybe months, before Mallory would have another chance to see her mother. Her mama had said good-bye forever, though, just like she was now—to Grams, not to Mallory. She'd already planned on sneaking away. She'd known she wasn't ever coming back.

"I wanted you," Mallory said now, when she hadn't known to then. "I've always wanted you."

"We could invite her to our New Year's party." Polly rushed to Pete's side. "We could give her the dolly back then."

Mallory snorted at the image that must be playing through Polly's mind, of Mallory's mommy coming to Mimosa Lane's next neighbor-filled celebration, feeling welcomed and deciding she belonged there just like everyone thought Mallory should.

"She doesn't want her back," Mallory said. "Do you, Mama?"

She watched as the woman she'd rushed to see shuffled silently away, leaving behind Mallory and the life Mallory had scraped together without her—as if it were all as insignificant as the crap she carried around in her shopping bags.

"Wait!" Polly ran after Mallory's mama. She pulled something off Mallory's bathrobe. It was Emma's precious Christmas tree pin.

"Merry Christmas," Polly said, attaching it to the old woman's threadbare orange coat.

Mallory stood beside, stunned. Her breath rushed out when her mother's hand came up to feather a soft touch across the beautiful thing. She looked down at it in wonder, then at Polly, and smiled.

"You always were so beautiful," she said. "The most beautiful thing in the world."

Then she turned and walked out of Mallory's life all over again.

Polly ran back across the room. "You're not going to let her get away, are you?"

Mallory looked at Pete instead of his daughter. "Do you want Emma's pin back?"

"No," he said, gazing deeply into her eyes. His hand rubbed up and down the sleeve of her sweater. "Are you okay?"

"Why wouldn't I be?" Silent screams were building again. He must have heard them, because he pulled her into an embrace that she fought.

He refused to let her go. "Do you want to go after her?"

"Mallory?" Polly tugged at her sleeve. "She's getting away. You have to—"

"I don't have to do anything!" Mallory jerked away from them both, seeing in an instant Polly's wounded expression and her father's desperate need to pull Mallory back and somehow comfort her. "She doesn't want my help. She doesn't want me. I don't have to keep chasing after her and letting her do this to me. I came here to say good-bye for good. Nothing more."

"But…" Polly's lower lip trembled. She huddled against her father's leg. "She's your mommy. You still have a mommy, and—"

"And some mommies are better off gone, because they don't care about you. And it hurts too much to keep letting them throw you away. Some families are better off broken, and no amount of wishing or sparkly Christmas pins or being a big girl is ever going to change that. Sometimes you just have to grow up and stop believing in pretty pink fairy tales that mean nothing they're so ridiculously stupid!"

Mallory heard the cruel, unforgivable words come out and covered her mouth with a trembling hand. But the damage was already done.

Pete lifted a softly sobbing Polly into his arms. His stony expression mirrored his demeanor the first time he'd come to Mallory's house on another late night when he'd confronted her as if she were a threat to his child.

Clearly, he'd been right from the start, because *this* was who Mallory was beneath all the other things she'd hoped would make up for it. This shrewish, harried thing standing in the deserted lobby of an assistance shelter, railing at the world for the unfair hand she'd been dealt as a child yet refusing to let the past go—this was the woman Pete had slept with in his wife's bed, down the hall from his beautiful, impressionable, emotionally fragile daughter. Mallory never should have allowed him to become so attached to her. He and Polly shouldn't be there now, finally seeing the worst of her in all its ugly, uncontrollable glory.

But she'd allowed herself to awaken to the dream of a soft, sweet world where a good man wanted to make a good place for her in his life. She'd started to believe that amid not-so-perfect families like the Lombards and the Perrys she could make for herself a holiday and maybe even a future that was light-years away from the empty life she'd known.

But Mallory simply wasn't made that way. And she'd led them all to this place where she was the one destroying a little girl's belief in happy endings. The kindest thing she could do now was end this before she did any more damage.

"I'd like to go home," she said, turning away from them and heading outside to wait beside the Jeep.

***

Pete stood in his backyard, barely feeling the freezing night as he stared at the fence separating his house from Mallory's. The door was still ajar from Polly's last visit next door. His daughter was sound asleep upstairs, exhausted from the emotional roller coaster of their trip into town, and sad and worried and hurt by Mallory's reaction to seeing her mother. Pete was, too, as he stood there wondering if he would make things better or worse by barging through his neighbor's patio door in the middle of the night the way Polly did.

Mallory had made him let her off at the curb before he'd even pulled into his driveway. With Polly in the backseat wide awake and still making sniffling sounds, aware of everything that wasn't being said in the painfully quiet interior of the Jeep, he'd had no choice but to temporarily let their neighbor go. It had taken him nearly a half hour to tuck his daughter into bed and make certain she was once again sleeping. Especially after she'd been gazing out her window at Mallory's tree and they'd both seen their neighbor cut the lights on the thing.

"She's giving up on Christmas," Polly had whispered, tears rolling down her cheeks. "Just like her mommy gave up."

It hurts too much to let them keep throwing you away...

Pete couldn't stop Mallory's heartbreaking admission from replaying through his mind as he stared into the night that had begun with her in his bed, behaving as if she never wanted to be anywhere else but with him and Polly.

What did it do to a child to feel as if she were never going to be good enough to earn her mother's protection? To have to decide at age six to leave behind the only stability in her life in order to take care of that parent and then to believe at age twelve that she'd failed? Her mother had rejected her outright, choosing a mentally ill life on the streets rather than fighting to overcome whatever she had to, to keep her daughter with her.

He'd thought he'd understood something of what Mallory had been through. He'd thought he could make up somehow for her inability to believe that others, given the chance, would love her differently, fully, the way her mother never had. But tonight, watching Polly's innocent reaction to the broken interplay between mother and daughter had shown him just how vulnerable Mallory must have been at the same age. And how idealistically she must have gone into her homeless journey with her mother, believing she could save the woman if she loved her enough.

He couldn't stop picturing it.

Polly, living on the streets, filthy and wearing rags. Polly, dreaming of earning her Christmas back while she took care of her mother and hoped that one day the woman would be well enough to be a mommy again. Polly, learning in the hardest possible way that the only person she could ever really depend on was herself, and that she might never fit in with anyone who believed the world worked differently.

The real miracle was how Mallory had survived with even a rudimentary ability to enjoy life. Yet she was still trying to heal and fix people and make lives better, while she'd kept large parts of herself detached enough not to be hurt if things didn't work out. Then she'd met Pete and Polly, and it had all come roaring back, all the longing and hope still inside her for the things she'd never found in life. The magic Pete wanted so desperately to show her.

How did he convince her not to give up on the promises their bodies had just made to each other, commitments that must seem more terrifying to her now than ever?

A crash from next door sent him sprinting across the yard and through the opening in the fence, to find Mallory standing just outside her sliding glass door. She'd tossed her Christmas tree, lights and ornaments and all, onto the patio.

She's giving up, Polly had said.

Striding closer, suddenly furious, he grew even angrier when he found Mallory watching him without a hint of emotion on her face. He wanted to grab her, shake her, force her to deal with what had happened tonight without retreating into whatever place in her mind protected her from pain and disappointment. He stopped a few feet away, on the other side of her tree, his breath misting beneath the full moon that had peeked from behind a cloud bank. It shone down on them like a spotlight.

"You're not giving up," he said, the same as he had to his wife before it had become clear that him holding on would only cause Emma more pain. "What happened with your mother is tragic, and you have every reason to be upset and to need some time to deal with it. But you're not giving up on everything you've fought so hard to have here. You're not giving up on us."

Mallory inhaled, her features still a blank. "You need to keep your daughter away from me until I can get this place sold and move. If I price things right or luck out finding somewhere cheap to rent in the city, I should be gone by the time school starts back. Until then you're going to have to make Polly understand that she can't come over anymore. If you want to step inside now, you could get Emma's pins and take them back to her. That way Polly won't have to see me again after the awful things I said to her."

If he wanted to step inside?

"You're not moving away." Sheer terror rocketed through Pete, announcing just how completely he'd fallen for the second love of his life, and how unprepared he was for losing Mallory, too. "You wouldn't do that to yourself or Polly or me."

"I screamed at your kid tonight when she was just trying to be nice to me."

Mallory laughed. It sounded ugly and full of self-loathing and darker than the parts of herself she'd allowed him to see before now.

"I've let her get close to me and believe I was going to be part of her life," she went on, "when we both know that was never going to happen, not long-term. Wake up, Pete. I might look sparkly in a Glinda costume and put up one hell of a cheap-looking Christmas tree and be good in bed, but we both know you're better rid of me now than later. I'd hurt you more if I hung around until the next explosion or the next one, because I can't pretend every damn minute of the day that I'm not who

I am. Only then you'll feel like a shit because it'll be you having to call things off because—"

"Because you're too messed up for me and my child to handle? Because you're unlovable, and we're just too stupid to notice? Or should we toss you out because the only way you think you can feel safe is by helping everyone except yourself, and wouldn't it be easier if Polly and I bowed out peacefully instead of bothering you with untidy things like turning your back on love and commitment and someone's honest desire to help *you*?"

He was seething. Furious. Exploding. It had been forever, it seemed, since he'd accepted there was no hope, that he was powerless to help his wife. He'd had to suck down all that rage and get on with living—for Emma and Polly's sake. But not this time. He wasn't letting Mallory off the hook. Not this way.

"Okay," he said when she didn't respond. "Curl up in a corner and pretend you don't need the rest of us. *I'm* not giving up. I'm not doing it this time. I won't sit by and watch you piss all of this away and pretend it's not going to destroy you as much as it will us. I don't want to be alone. I don't want to be unhappy my entire life and forget that there's another way to live. You've taught me that, because you were the only one who knew how to show Polly how much more there was in the world for her. Now you can teach yourself, or you can let us do it for you. But I'm not going to help you give up, so you can just forget about tossing us aside the way you have your freaking tree. And if you want to throw Emma's jewelry back at Polly along with your promise to keep her memories of her mother safe, then you break her heart on your own. I won't be doing that for you, either."

He was close to hyperventilating. He couldn't see, even though there was plenty of light from the moon. A red haze had overcome his senses, dulling his vision and his hearing as he raged like he'd never let himself vent before. His loss. His despair. His fury and denial for what had happened to the happy life he'd thought he'd have forever. His life with Emma…

It was all still there, and now it was out, spewing between Mallory and him, when what she'd needed was for him to be there for her, listening to what she was feeling and fearing and accepting her for all that she was and wasn't. She needed to know she could break apart and he'd still be there for her when she came back to herself—the way she'd taught him to help Polly push through what she had to.

Only that wasn't what he'd just done at all.

This was Mallory, not Emma. He was falling in love with her, not recapturing what he'd lost with his wife. This was Mallory's decision—whether or not she wanted him and Polly enough to get better. His mistake was clear when he could finally focus on Mallory's expression and saw her devastation, her regret, her slipping even further away.

"I'm sorry," she said, no longer distant, but still no longer his. She was crying now. "I can't be the happy, hopeful, positive replacement you were wanting. I can't help you host your New Year's party or be there with Emma's best friends. Not even for Polly, when I wanted to help her have the best holiday she could possibly have this year. I really did, Pete. I used to tell myself I didn't get it, how you could all be so joyous about your lives. But now I know it's because you can choose to be that way, no matter how many bad things happen or might happen down the road. You can choose to be happy, and then you find a way to make it work. But I can't. I tried. I really did. But I'm not like Emma or Sam. I'm that woman I became at the shelter who could throw her mother away and feel nothing but anger. A part of me always will be, and that means none of me belongs in a place like Mimosa Lane. Because all I'll do is hurt you and Polly and everyone else who thinks they can change me, or change what happened to me."

"No one wants you to change." But a part of him had, or at least a part of him had assumed that she magically would change once she'd glimpsed the kind of world they could have together. "All I want is for you to let me help you. Give us a chance."

"I did." She looked down at her tree and winced. "I shouldn't have. Now it's all ruined, and I could have spared everyone this if I'd just stayed where I belonged in the first place."

"You don't have to be alone anymore to be safe. That's not the life you want, or you wouldn't have moved here."

"I hope you and Polly get your happiness back this Christmas," she said. "But Mimosa Lane was never my life, Pete. I'll always be wandering, just like my mama. I belong near people who can put up with that sort of craziness and not let it bring them down, too. I'll be fine. I…" She gestured to the tree with a sense of inevitability. "I'll just get this to the curb, call a real estate agent in the morning, pack up the few things I brought with me, and head on back to midtown where I belong. I'll be fine."

And she would be. She was a survivor. It was the one thing Mallory's mother had taught her well—how to endure whatever she had to and get on with life the best way she could.

"But when will you be happy?" he asked, thinking only about Mallory now and kicking himself for not doing it sooner.

She shook her head, crossing her arms over her wacky Rudolph sweater from the party, looking miserably out of place in it now.

He wanted to press her for an answer, a sign that she was hearing him. He wanted to know that there was a spark between them still, no matter how small, to build on going forward. Instead, he tried to respect her need to disconnect from everything she was terrified of losing. But every muscle in his body still strained to snatch her close and never let her go.

He looked down at her tree, its glorious sparkle gone, its cheap, mass-produced ornaments bent, some of them broken. He tried to picture what it must have been like for her to drag such a beautiful, exuberant thing out of her house and dump it into the cold.

"I'll take care of this for you," he said, "if getting rid of it is what you really need."

A moment of panic seemed to consume Mallory, flaming in her eyes. He held his breath, waiting for her to say she wanted more time, that maybe she'd made a mistake. Then her control returned, and she took an awkward step backward toward her darkened living room.

"Thank you." Her eyes were filling with tears. "Meeting you and Polly…Thank you for taking me into your world and letting me help just a little. I hope she gets over what I said tonight, that it didn't—"

"Polly will be fine. You've shown her exactly what she needs to do to make certain she's going to be just fine."

But when would Mallory herself stop hiding the way Polly had, so *she* could finally, truly, move on?

"Take care of yourself, Pete." She turned. Halfway inside, she pivoted back when he didn't respond.

He nodded, incapable of wishing her the same.

She needed time. She needed distance. He could give her both. But he'd be damned if he'd ever let her go.

Chapter Nineteen

Before the ice is in the pools,
Before the skaters go,
Or any cheek at nightfall
Is tarnished by the snow,

Before the fields have finished,
Before the Christmas tree,
Wonder upon wonder
Will arrive to me...

Mallory woke from a light doze, which seemed to be the only kind of sleep she managed anymore. It was early Christmas morning, so early the sun was hours away from rising. And it was her last day on Mimosa Lane.

In the week and a half since she'd lost her mother for good and run Pete and Polly Lombard away, she'd grown to accept why she couldn't stay in Chandlerville. Facing her neighbors every day and wanting to belong to something that she hadn't been built for wasn't going to end well for any of them. Her reboot here had been a mistake. From the start she'd been destined to leave. It was time to get back to the kind of life she could handle far better than Mimosa Lane.

She'd made the right decision, she'd kept reminding herself as her remaining time on the cul-de-sac passed in a blur of insomnia and cleaning and packing. A real estate agent had priced her house to move. Despite the economy and the slow holiday showing season, prospective buyers stopped by every day. She might have an offer as soon as the first of the year. In the meantime, she'd secured a midtown apartment to sublet.

She'd given notice at Chandler Elementary. Kristen had written her a generous recommendation and given her a lead on a clinic position at another school closer to the city. Mallory had put the word out in the assistance services community that she was available to fill in for any staffing needs that arose—part-time work that would tide her over financially and distract her from everything she was leaving behind tomorrow when she drove away from the magical world beyond her window.

Her packing was nearly complete. What little she owned was once more sorted, stowed, and labeled in cardboard. In the morning she'd load up her Beetle and a rented trailer and hit the road. She was all but gone already.

Which would make her a coward in the eyes of many, the way she was cutting ties so completely with people who'd never done anything but be kind to her. But she couldn't face Pete and Polly Lombard every day and not want them forever. And she'd already gotten too close and caused too much pain to let herself keep dreaming that she wouldn't hurt them even more in the future.

Look at how completely she'd fallen apart, how awful she'd been to them when they'd tried to help her deal with her mother at the shelter. The toxic confrontation that had followed—first with Polly and later with Pete—would be just the beginning if she stayed. They'd reached out to help her, and she'd slapped away their concern and support.

They'd been there for her when she'd needed someone the most, and she'd been the one to pull away in a frenzy of self-protection—the same as she had for years with her grams. She could over-attach to strangers who needed her. She could shape her whole world around the chance to help people like her mother, whom she'd never see again. But building her life with someone who genuinely wanted to be part of her forever...

The therapist Grams had taken her to for a while had said that accepting and trusting love would always be difficult. But there was *difficult*, and then there was *impossible*.

Mallory hadn't wanted to believe she was capable of turning on Pete and his beautiful child, panicked and angry and blaming them for not understanding how much they terrified her. But her behavior the night of the Perrys' party had permanently planted her in the *impossible* column for long-term relationships. The Lombards had enough problems of their own to work through. Mallory needed to make a clean break before she behaved even more appallingly and hurt even more people and still walked away in the end, because that's what she always did.

She'd practically exiled herself to her house. Meanwhile, she couldn't close her eyes without seeing Polly's beautiful face, Sam Perry's brave smile, or the love and hurt in Pete's expression as she'd turned away from him that last time. Facing any of them again, in the driveway or in the cul-de-sac or looking across their yards, would make it even more impossible for Mallory to do what she knew she had to do.

She'd find a place where her work, not dreams of community and family and friends, could once more consume every waking minute of her day. She'd make her reboot work somewhere else, where she could help people but still sleep through the night. She'd return to a world that didn't make her want the kind of happily-ever-after fairy tales she couldn't hold on to.

A rustle from the direction of the living room had her jack-knifing up until she was sitting, her bedding bunched around her, her heart pounding.

Polly?

No, she scolded herself. No one was there. She was only hearing things, projecting the sound of a sweet little girl coming back for one last hug and kiss. It had happened several times over the last week and a half, even though she kept the patio and the front doors locked now. She doubted she'd ever completely stop looking over her shoulder, hoping to find Pete and Polly there.

She'd pulled the drapes on all the windows, too, starting with those facing the backyard and the fence she shared with the Lombards. Pete had called and left messages on her machine, but she hadn't trusted herself to answer. Sam had tried to reach her once. And Christmas cards had arrived in her mailbox from several of the neighborhood families she'd met at the holiday party. She hadn't let herself reply to any of them, but she'd kept every single cheerful one. She'd replayed Pete's messages over and over, cherishing the way he'd asked if she was okay.

She stepped away from her bed now, shivering in the early morning chill. She reached for the sheers she'd pulled across her bedroom window. Before anyone else was up, she wanted one last glimpse of this world she'd tried to make her home. Pulling back the curtains, she gasped.

Snow.

It was finally snowing. Illuminated by her patio light, her backyard resembled a real-life snow globe. The sky was raining thousands of tiny, wispy drops of frozen white perfection. Her grass was covered with it, resembling a layer of the vanilla frosting Polly had smeared all over her Christmas cookies. Mimosa Lane would have its white Christmas, and Mallory had stayed long enough to see it happen.

Even though there was no tree in her living room and no one to open presents with, seeing the world beyond her window so sparkling and beautiful was a perfect parting gift.

Her gaze tracked to her fence. Her smile froze, then dissolved completely. Tracks marred the blanket of snow between the fence and her house. There were two sets of footprints, one much tinier than the other. And something had created a wider path off to the side of the larger marks, as if it had been dragged behind them.

The rustling came again, for certain this time from her family room. A part of Mallory wanted to hide, not that anything could have stopped her from heading slowly, tentatively, down the hallway. She didn't bother with her robe or slippers. She was shivering in only her flannel nightgown. Her heart was racing harder than it had the first night when she'd had no idea who she'd find lurking uninvited in her home. But she didn't stop.

She'd promised herself she didn't want this last chance— that keeping to herself was safer. But how could she not see the people she knew were waiting for her? How could they not be welcome wherever she was, no matter how far away she ran?

In that moment, she accepted the truth that her heart would never be free of them. Wherever she ended up, whatever her next "new" life turned out to be, it would never feel like a home. Not the way this empty place did even now—because the people she'd pushed away had barged back into her life, if only to say good-bye.

Lord, how was she going to say good-bye all over again?

In her family room she found a handsome hero of man and a beautiful child waiting for her in front of a Christmas tree. Their backs were turned to the hallway as they hung tiny decorations she couldn't quite see on an honest-to-God real fir tree.

The refreshing scent of pine pulled her closer. As did the beauty of whatever they were hanging and how it made the tree sparkle as if it were covered in diamonds, gemstones, and priceless gold and silver. The realization of exactly what they were using as ornaments hit her suddenly, misting her vision.

"What…?" She couldn't say another word.

She clung to the back of her couch rather than running into Pete's arms as he turned from lifting Polly so the little girl could place an ornament high up near the top of the tree. He smiled, stunning Mallory with how much she'd missed him, and how much she still wished he could be there like this every morning of her life.

"You caught us," he said. "We were hoping to finish before you woke. Maybe make you some breakfast. We…"

"We didn't want you to miss your Christmas again," Polly said, holding on to Pete so easily now, hugging his neck.

It hurt a little.

A lot.

Mallory had grown used to Polly rushing to hug her, and the little girl wanting to be next to her every time they were together. Polly was eyeing Mallory now as if she weren't sure of her welcome after Mallory had completely lost it the last time they were together. The child's hesitation hit home harder than all of Mallory's packing and planning for the move.

She wasn't just leaving another place that hadn't worked out or another job she never should have taken. She was leaving people who'd become the closest thing to having a family of her own she'd felt since losing her mother. Beautiful, hardworking, flawed, still-struggling people who'd needed her as much as she needed them.

"This…" She stared over Pete's shoulder at the tree, blinking back her tears. And even then she couldn't see the decorations clearly. They were so tiny, each one reflecting the white tree lights as if colored stars were bursting on every limb. "This won't make me change my mind. I appreciate it, but I meant what I said. I'm…"

"You're not ready." Pete gave a tight nod. His smile dimmed, but it didn't disappear. "I understand. We both do. Polly and I have talked about it a lot. About how friends don't try to force each other to do and feel things before they're ready. They accept difficult emotions for what they are without trying to make people change so that everyone else can feel better. You taught us that. That's how we're working through what we need to about Emma. You made quite an impact on Sam and Brian, too, spending time with Sam and listening to her while she hid from her own party. They both were sad to see your *For Sale* sign go up, but none of us would ask you to be less than honest about what you're going through, right, Polly?" He hugged his daughter. "All any of us want to do is help you."

"But"—they were supposed to be saying good-bye—"you shouldn't be here like this, talking like…Wait a minute. How *did* you and the tree get in here? I've kept the doors locked since—"

"Charlie Brown," Polly answered.

Mallory blinked, checking the child's winter coat for pictures of the cartoon character she'd named. She found nothing but sturdy down-filled pink nylon. "Who?"

"Mommy used to come over and feed the Lancers' puppy, Charlie Brown, when they were out of town."

"Oh." Not really following, Mallory drank in the sweet reality of Polly remembering her mother and sounding happy about it. She *had* done a lot of good here.

Pete dug beneath the hem of his faded UGA sweatshirt and pulled from his jeans pocket a keychain with a single key on one end, a brass basset hound on the other.

"I remembered Emma kept a spare key in her desk," he said. "It was sitting right there, where it's been since the Lancers moved out." He gave a short laugh, then another smile, this one making him look ten years younger as he, too, talked freely about his beloved wife. "I figured someone who usually never bothers to close her curtains or lock her doors wouldn't have gone to the trouble of having new keys made."

Mallory shook her head. "But...why? The tree, the ornaments...They're beautiful. But it—"

"You should have your real Christmas," Polly said, "before you sell your house. So we came over to help."

All any of us want to do is help you...

By giving her the Christmas she'd told Polly she'd never had.

Mallory stepped closer despite her determination to keep her distance. After every unkind thing she'd said, after she'd moved heaven and earth to get away from them as quickly as humanly possible, they'd done this for her.

It was Christmas morning, their family's first Christmas after losing Emma. And these two had traipsed across a dark, snowy morning to Mallory's packed-up, empty house, determined to make her holiday beautiful. She inhaled the scent of the most gorgeous tree in the world. It was as if a fairy tale of her very own had sprung to life in her living room.

"We didn't know how to re-create what you threw out," Pete explained. "Polly thought up this on her own. She wanted what we made for you to be special."

Special?

Mallory squinted, refocusing on the ornaments scattered about the tree limbs. "What...What did you do?"

Her gaze fell to the bottom of the tree, and there on the carpet sat Mickey Mouse, his head resting on the floor, his tubby belly open and empty. Beside him was the doll she'd left lying there when she'd thrown out her own tree. And there were the neighborhood Christmas cards she'd placed around the bare tree skirt, thinking they looked a little bit like presents.

"You used Emma's pins..." She stepped closer in wonder. "I was trying to find a way to get them back to you without...I was going to leave them with the Perrys tomorrow when I left. What...Why would you do this?"

"You need them more than I do now," Polly said. "'Cause your mommy left you, too. And you needed a tree for this morn-ing, like the real ones at the Perrys' house. And you needed stories of your own that you can remember, like the ones my mommy gave me. So now they're yours, too, so you can always remember us the way we'll always remember you."

Emma's stories. Her treasures. Her glittering, vintage ani-mals and flowers and bees and butterflies that she'd left her daughter to remember her by. Polly wanted Mallory to have them. The child was not only giving her the Christmas morn-ing of Mallory's dreams, but also the family mementos Mallory hadn't kept when she sold her grams's house.

Because Mallory needed them now more than Polly did.

It was as if the tree had come to life with whimsy. Across its soft limbs was every special memory Polly had at first wanted to hide, then had shared with Mallory. Now they were glittering with the exuberant holiday joy Mallory had longed for her whole life.

"I…" She didn't know what to do, what to say. "I can't… This is too much."

"It'll never be enough." Pete stepped closer, bringing Polly with him. "Even if we have to hunt you down every Christmas and fill your tree with even more special ornaments, it will never be enough. And we will, if you'll let us. We'll come for you wherever you are, Mallory. We'll make at least this one day of the year perfect for you. Let us love you on Christmas. Let us show you how special you are. That's what we came to tell you. Let us fight for you however you need us to. Just tell us what you need, and we'll be here whenever you'll let us."

She shook her head. "You can't…You can't keep doing this. You can't—"

"Love you?"

"Don't say that. You know—"

"That you're not ready to hear it?" His smile was still there, even as she was once more pushing him away. "I know. But I'm ready to say it. I should have said it last week, but it was too sudden, and I wasn't sure how you'd respond when you were so upset. But then I realized, after you'd closed yourself in here and away from everyone you thought you could walk away from so easily, that I can handle you being upset. Polly can handle it. All of us can. What we won't get through is you thinking the easiest solution to our situation is to walk away and—"

"Easy?"

He had to let her go. If he kept showing up doing crazy, amazing things like this for her—dear God, *every* Christmas?— she'd never be able to stay away from the love shining in his eyes.

"You think this is easy for me?" She stepped past them to the patio doors. "I don't want to hurt you two. I don't want to hurt anyone here. You have to stop thinking that I won't."

They'd tied the curtains back again. Beyond the wall of translucent glass was a snow globe world, Christmas showing off all its finery, turning Mimosa Lane into a winter wonderland.

"I'm thinking you're as terrified as we are of being hurt," he said. "Polly and I are dealing with that—how protecting ourselves ends up taking us away from the people we love. You showed us that. I can't imagine what you must be feeling after what happened with your mother, and no one blames you for being angry or upset or even acting out because of it, just like Polly and I went off the rails after Emma died. But don't go away completely, Mallory. We won't let you forget what happened here like we never existed. You're already in love with us and this house and"—he nodded behind him—"even this tree, or you wouldn't have opened your home and your world and your heart up to us the way you did, and you wouldn't still be standing here talking to us. Polly and I are going to find you wherever you go. We're going to keep fighting for you until you can believe in all of this and fight to keep it yourself."

We're going to keep fighting for you...

Mallory turned back to them, shivering. Every lost Christmas from her childhood was right there, waiting at the back of her mind, pushing forward, threatening to rip her away from the magic of this moment. The past would always be there, if she let it, covering everything with its shadows. No matter where she went, no matter that her mother was gone from her life for good, she'd never be rid of what had happened.

Give us a chance...You don't have to be alone anymore, to be safe...

Us.

Us was the present they wanted to give her for Christmas, as Emma Lombard's beautiful memories shined and sparkled and winked behind them from the Christmas tree. Pete and Polly Lombard wanted Mallory Jane Phillips with them. Even knowing the unbelievable mess going on inside of her, these two were brave enough to keep fighting for the beginning she'd dreamed of building with them, only she hadn't been strong enough to make what they should have had work.

Sometimes, Sam had said, *when there's nothing anyone else can do, you have to be your own hero...*

Polly pushed against her father's chest. Pete put her down. She walked over to Mallory, her hand digging into the pocket of her pink corduroy pants. She held something up in her palm—it was Emma's favorite pin.

"Whiskers?" Mallory whispered. She took the smiling little cat and remembered the very first story about Emma that Polly and Pete had shared. "Your mother always wore him so she'd remember how much her grandmother loved her."

"I saved him for you to put up yourself," Polly said. "So you wouldn't forget, the way you wouldn't let me forget."

Mallory picked the child up and gazed at Pete, her tears falling in earnest.

"Don't ever forget how much you're loved here," Pete said. "No matter where you go, just tell us what you want, and we'll move heaven and earth to make it happen."

"Don't forget us, Mallory." Polly wrapped her in the sweetest, fiercest hug of her life. "We don't care if you get angry or sad or need to cry. Just don't leave us. Please don't go away forever..."

What do you want? It was what Mallory had asked the first night Polly had visited, searching for her own Christmas miracle.

*Please don't go away forever…*she'd begged her mama as a little girl.

Mallory hugged Polly back and thought of *us* and felt herself stumbling into Pete's open arms. She lost herself once more in the dream of trusting a family to support her, even when she kept failing at making it happen for herself.

Love…

Pete and Polly were offering her everything. Community and friends that she didn't have to run from. Belonging that didn't mean she had to fit in any more than she could. Love that accepted all of her, even the messed-up and wandering parts. She didn't even have to stay. They'd come find her wherever she went. They'd never leave her to try to make her safe place happen alone.

They were even giving Mallory the Christmas of her dreams. A beginning. A promise of a life full of memories to come, picnics and barbecues and the sound of kids playing and adults laughing and people living and sharing. And she would have a real place in that world. No more wandering. No more watching from a distance.

The fantasy of it felt so close, as close as Pete's strong arms holding Mallory and his kiss brushing at her temple and the sound of Polly giggling because she'd been trapped between them and thought it was a silly game.

You're strong enough to make anything happen, her grams had said. *You just keep on bein' strong…*

Clasping the pin in her hand, Mallory allowed herself to say the words she hadn't said to anyone since she was twelve.

"I love you so much," she said, surrendering to her dream, trusting them with it. "I don't ever want to be anywhere else but right here with the two of you for the rest of my life. But I…I'm so scared. What if I can't? What if I do to you what I did to my grams, and all it does is hurt you even more and—"

"The only way you can hurt us is by quitting," Pete said. "And you never quit. You're a fighter, just like Sam. *My* fighter. All you have to do now is keep fighting for us, and we'll make it. I promise."

They were her words, her advice for how he could reach Polly, finding its way back to Mallory and begging her to never let them go.

"Merry Christmas!" Polly wrapped her arms around Mallory and gave her cheek a sloppy kiss.

"Merry Christmas, sweetie," Mallory said back, smiling at Pete as snow softly fell outside and Emma's treasures twinkled on the tree and Mallory held the family of her dreams in her arms. "You and your daddy are the best present I ever could have asked for. I can't think of anywhere I'd rather be but right here with you. I love you both so much."

Pete kissed her, the caress full of passion and the promise of a lifetime of healing, discovering what came next, and dreaming of every magical tomorrow they could grab. He rocked her as they stood there holding his daughter, the three of them dancing now.

"Merry Christmas, my love," he said. "Welcome home to Mimosa Lane."

Dear Reader,

I love talking with readers, and with each new release, I do as much work with book clubs as possible. Time doesn't always allow for as many appearances as I'd like, though. When my editor gave the green light for including a reader's guide with *Christmas on Mimosa Lane*, I was thrilled that I could reach out to even more of my fans.

I hope to one day have the chance to hear your thoughts in person or via Skype so I can share my own about the layers and themes of this story. In the meantime, here are some tidbits to get the conversation started with others who've enjoyed the book.

Happy discussing!

Anna

Questions for Discussion

1. In *Christmas on Mimosa Lane*, love comes in many forms, and some of our favorite characters aren't ready to trust it when their chance arrives. In the midst of the glitter of the holiday season, difficult realities and recoveries make the journey to and the joy of a satisfying ending so much more rewarding. Are there any darker themes that surprised you? What are the points of connection that lead Mallory, Polly, and Pete to the happily ever after they deserve?

2. Do you have a favorite scene in the story? What are the most emotional turning points for you?

3. There are so many themes and symbols to explore. How does the repeated imagery of things like the Trifari pins, make believe characters, the dazzle of pure white versus the starkness of midnight blacks or grays, and both perfect and less than ideal Christmas images affect your connection to the characters and their stories?

4. The novel is broken into three sections: wandering, staying, and healing. How do the characters change and grow throughout the book? Which parts of their stories speak most directly to you?

5. In what ways are Mallory and Polly a reflection of each other's lives? What are the key scenes for you, where a character became another's guardian, guide and voice?

6. How do the themes of mother-daughter relationships affect you as you read? Do you long to remember, forget, or reevaluate more of your own experiences with the mother figures who've influenced you?

7. Mallory, Polly, and Pete become a family, when the question of what it means to be a family, is what's troubling them all so deeply. How many different family "units" do you recognize as you read? Which seem familiar to you, which challenge you to perhaps see your own relationships a bit differently, and do any make you long to reach for more in your own life?

8. It's an interesting paradox—the interplay between what makes us feel safe and what challenges us to step outside our comfortable lives. What do you see pulling Mallory and the other characters out of their shells, compelling them to interact? How do their different lives and backgrounds merge to create an extended family that works by the end of the novel? Do you see elements of this interconnection working in your own life and community?

9. From the very first to the last scene in *Christmas on Mimosa Lane*, the past and present flow into and around and over each other. What memories from your past follow you into present day experiences? Do they enrich current experiences, or do they perhaps prevent you from appreciating moments as fully as you'd like?

10. Snippets of Emily Dickinson's poetry were carefully selected to reflect the tone and theme of the chapters they introduce, and the growth of the central characters at various stages in the story. What are your favorite excerpts, and can you identify experiences in your own life that make these words ring true for you?

Acknowledgments

Some books require research and learning new things so you can write outside your comfort zone with some degree of authenticity. Others follow you around for years, swelling up from endless experiences and relationships and conversations and interests, making it impossible to pinpoint where they began and on whom to shine a spotlight as your inspiration.

With Seasons of the Heart I bring you the Deep South as more than a cliché. Southern communities and small towns are magical places. Down here, a magnificently confusing network of friends and frenemies evolve from merging your life with others. And southern families are as complex and challenging as they are heartwarming and beguiling. Set aside your desperate housewives expectations, y'all, and prepare to fall in love.

This is the world of my childhood, youth, and adult life. I've watched and at times felt lucky enough to be a part of the types of connections that spring to life in these novels—and I've always craved more. My editor said not long after reading the first few chapters of Mallory's story that she wanted to live on Mimosa Lane. So do I, I assured her. So do I.

To all the flawed, fascinating, and surprising southern families, friends, and acquaintances who've from my first book fed my obsession to write and create—Thank you, and welcome home to Mimosa Lane.

DON'T MISS ANNA DESTEFANO'S NEXT
"SEASONS OF THE HEART" ROMANCE!

As winter gives way to spring and spring to summer, a
life-changing moment draws Samantha Perry deeper
into her Mimosa Lane community—a world she has
been hiding from for over a decade...

SWEET SUMMER SUNRISE

Coming Summer 2013 on Amazon.com

About the Author

Anna DeStefano is the award-winning, best-selling author of more than sixteen novels, including *Secret Legacy* and *To Save a Family.* Her background as a care provider and adult educator in the world of crisis and grief recovery lends itself to the deeper psychological themes of every story she writes. With a rich blend of realism and fantasy, DeStefano invites readers to see each of life's moments with emotional honesty and clarity. The past president of Georgia Romance Writers (GRW), she has garnered numerous awards for her writing, including winning the RT Reviewers' Choice Award, the Holt Medallion, the Golden Heart, and the Maggie Award for Excellence. She has also been a finalist for National Readers' Choice and Book Sellers' Best Awards. DeStefano lives in North Georgia.